An Unmarked Grave

An Unmarked Grave

Charles Todd

wm WILLIAM MORROW *An Imprint of* HarperCollins*Publishers*

HarperCollins books may be purchased for educational, business, or sales promotional use. For information please write: Special Markets Department, HarperCollins Publishers, 10 East 53rd Street, New York, NY 10022.

FIRST EDITION

Library of Congress Cataloging-in-Publication Data

Todd, Charles
   An unmarked grave: a Bess Crawford mystery / by Charles Todd. — First edition.
     p. cm.
   ISBN 978-0-06-201572-3
   1. Crawford, Bess (Fictitious character)—Fiction. 2. Nurses—Fiction.
3. World War, 1914–1918—Fiction. 4. Influenza Epidemic, 1918–1919—Fiction.
5. English—France—Fiction. 6. Great Britain. Army—Officers—Crimes
against—Fiction. 7. Murder—Investigation—Fiction. I. Title.
PS3570.O37U56   2012
813'.54—dc23

                                                         2011050979

12 13 14 15 16 OV/RRD 10 9 8 7 6 5 4 3 2 1

For the National World War I Museum in Kansas City—for gathering in one place the record of a war that changed a generation and even a century. In gratitude for asking us to speak there and for hours exploring a remarkable and moving collection.

An Unmarked Grave

CHAPTER ONE

I STOPPED JUST outside the ward and leaned my head against the cool wood of the doorframe. I couldn't remember when last I'd slept, or, for that matter, eaten anything more than a few biscuits now and again with a hasty cup of tea.

The Spanish Influenza had already cut down three of our nursing sisters, and two doctors were not expected to live through the night. The rest of us were struggling to keep men alive in the crowded wards and losing the battle hourly. Depressing to watch the bodies being carried out, one more soldier lost to an enemy we couldn't even see.

It was an insidious killer, this influenza. I'd watched men in the best of health in the afternoon gasping for breath by the next morning, tossing with fever, lying too ill to speak, then fighting to draw a next breath. I'd watched nurses and orderlies work with patients for days on end without showing a single sign of illness, only to collapse unexpectedly and join the ranks of the dying. The young were particularly vulnerable. On the other hand, Private Wilson, close to forty, seemed to be spared, even though he handled the dead, gently wrapping them in their soiled sheets and carrying them out to await interment. The shed just beyond the wards was filled with bodies, sometimes stacked like lumber. The burial details couldn't keep up. And those men too were dying.

The influenza epidemic was already being spoken of as a twentieth-century plague, and no one was safe. I feared for my parents—there had been no word from Somerset for over a fortnight. Even Simon Brandon hadn't written, and that was more worrying. Was he too ill? Or trying to find a way to tell me that the Colonel Sahib and my mother had died? Every post seemed to bring sad news to the wounded or the staff, and word was that people in Britain as well as France were dropping in the streets or dying before they could reach hospital, entire families wiped out. Matron had told me that the posts were delayed because so many of the censors had fallen ill and there was no one to take their place. Cold comfort, but all I had. And as time went on, I wasn't really sure that I wanted to hear.

Sister Burrows came out the door, and I moved aside. She slipped off her mask as I had done and took a deep breath of the evening air.

"Dear God," she said, and it was half a prayer. "I don't know how much more I can face. There's nothing we can do for them. Nothing. And there are the wounded to nurse as well. It's—it's rather overwhelming."

She was pale with exhaustion, dark circles beneath her eyes. A mirror of my face, I thought. If I had had the time to look at my own reflection.

"I ache with weariness," she went on after a moment. "How are you bearing up?"

"As well as anyone else," I answered. "It will have to end soon. The influenza. There will be no one else to infect."

Two officers leaning on canes limped past, nodding to us, and another man, turning his back to us, disappeared into the canteen. His shoulder was swathed in bandages, and I couldn't help but notice how stained and ragged they were. I knew I ought to hurry after him and ask to have a look at the wound, but I didn't have the energy. Let him drink his tea undisturbed, then report to Matron.

"Today we received more influenza patients than battlefield wounded," I commented as the heavy odor of French tobacco followed in the wake of an orderly carrying a mop and pail.

"I hope the Germans are suffering as badly as we are. If not, in a few weeks they'll be able to walk unimpeded to Paris."

I smiled. "If they try, they'll be struck down as well. All the lines are reporting influenza cases." On a more somber note I said, "Seeing that orderly reminds me. When he has time, Private Wilson has been carrying linens to the laundry and bringing back fresh supplies. And still we're running short."

"I'll pass the word," she said, "when he comes back this way." She cocked her head to one side. "I can hear the guns again. You'd think the Germans would have the decency to stop fighting until this influenza is over."

"There was an hour of blessed silence earlier. I even heard a lark somewhere." I pulled my mask back into place. "I must look in on the Major. His fever is soaring."

"Go on. I'll bring cool water to you to bathe his face."

I thanked her and went inside. We did what we could to help each other as well as our patients. Even Matron had taken her turn bringing round the tray of tea.

I wasn't sure whether it was in the middle of the night or early morning when Lieutenant Benson died. I had sat by his bed for an hour or more, knowing the end was near but refusing to give up. My head ached from leaning forward to hold his hand at the last as he'd asked me to do, and I was rather dizzy from missing my dinner, but there had been no time to spare for it.

Lieutenant Benson's death had not been a tranquil one—influenza never lets its victims slip easily away—and as I closed his eyes, I felt a crushing sadness.

Dr. Timmons came then and confirmed that the patient was dead. I went to ask the orderlies to bring the stretcher to our ward.

Private Wilson was on duty, as he so often seemed to be, and as he followed me back to the Lieutenant's bedside with his stretcher bearers in tow, he leaned forward and said in a low voice, "Sister, will you come to the shed with us?"

I couldn't bear the thought. "The next time, perhaps," I offered.

"Please, Sister Crawford," he said, urgency in his voice as he quickly looked over his shoulder. I reluctantly nodded. It wasn't like Private Wilson to be so insistent or so secretive.

The Lieutenant was carefully placed on the stretcher, covered by a sheet, and our wretched little party made its way between the rows of cots to the ward door.

Private Wilson passed his torch to me, and in the chilly darkness I led the way across to the shed, a distance of about forty feet. Opening the doors for the others to pass inside, I shone the torch ahead of them, trying not to think about the men who lay here, men I had watched die. I waited, uncertain why I was supposed to be in this place but still trusting Private Wilson's judgment, while the Lieutenant was added to the rows of the dead.

When it was done, Private Wilson cast a glance in my direction, then turned to his stretcher bearers. They were as hollow-eyed with fatigue as the rest of us. "Take yourselves off for a cigarette, lads. The Sister wishes to say a few words over the dead. This one was special, like."

I nearly denied it but caught myself in time. Simon Brandon would have called Private Wilson a steady man. Whatever he was about, he wanted privacy.

Grateful for the opportunity, his men touched their caps to me and disappeared in the direction of the canteen. When they were out of hearing, Private Wilson said in a low voice, "Sister, what I'm about to ask you to do won't be pleasant. But I think you'll agree afterward that it's necessary."

Mystified, I said, "Very well."

He guided me deeper inside the shed. The torch beam picked out the sheet-shrouded remains on either side of me. "This way," he said and took me to the back row in the far left corner. In spite of the disinfectant, the shed smelled of death, and I felt like turning on my heel and hurrying out again as quickly as I could. But I followed him as he added, "The burial detail will be here in an hour. And he'll be gone."

Who would be gone?

He steadied the beam of the torch and then knelt. Over his shoulder I could see a man's arm just visible in an opening in the sheet wrapping him. I was surprised. And then I realized why the sheet was unwinding—it hadn't been done up properly in the first place. Reaching beneath the corpse above, Private Wilson managed to uncover the body so that I could just pick out a shoulder, throat, and, finally, the side of a face.

"He's not an influenza victim," Private Wilson said. "Look at him."

He reached out to pull the sheet wider for a better view, shifting the body above this one and nearly starting an avalanche of the dead. I caught my breath until the swaying stopped.

He was right.

This one corpse among so many showed none of the darkening of the skin of the Spanish Influenza victim. Instead his head lolled as Private Wilson worked with him, and I realized that his neck must have been broken.

That was odd. For one thing, we seldom saw such a wound, and for another, he would have died instantly. There would have been no reason for the forward aid station to send him on to us.

"I don't understand—" I began doubtfully, then stopped as Private Wilson's torch settled on the face of the corpse.

I knew this man!

Even in the shielded light of the torch, I was sure.

And I was just as sure that he'd never been a patient here. I would have recognized him straightaway. Or if he'd been in another ward, one of the other sisters would have said something to me. They knew I was always on the lookout for anyone who served in my father's old regiment. Then why was he lying among our dead?

I stood there, my tired mind trying to absorb this shock. Finally it occurred to me that he'd indeed been wounded and that in the ambulance something had happened—a freak accident when the driver hit a deep hole, a fall from the upper berth onto the steel floor. But if that was true, where were the bruises to support it?

I leaned forward to search for an identification tag. To my surprise, there was none. And he wasn't in uniform. It was true, we sometimes got patients so badly wounded we had no idea who they were or what regiment they'd served with. A tunic already torn in the trenches, cut off in the forward aid station for a better look at the site, or removed entirely for emergency surgery, and any hope of identifying him could be lost well before a man arrived in our ward. But as a rule, the ambulance driver could tell us his unit, or there were other wounded from his sector who could give us a name and rank until the patient was able to speak for himself.

"Please, I need a little more light," I whispered, trying to see where he'd been wounded.

"We need to mind the time, Sister. The burial detail will be here soon. And we don't want to attract anyone else's attention." Still, he brought the light nearer. I couldn't find any other marks on the man's body, except for a few scars, some of them half healed, others from before the war. I looked at him again. Death had changed his features, of course, but not so much that I could have doubted the evidence of my own eyes. I hadn't been wrong. And there was only one conclusion I could draw.

I stepped back, thoroughly shaken.

"Dear God." It was all I could manage to say.

What should I do? My first inclination was to call someone and have the Major's body taken out of the shed to somewhere the circumstances of his death could be looked into.

It was then I realized that he hadn't been dead for very long. Rigor hadn't set in yet. Which meant that whoever had killed him was very likely still somewhere in the vicinity. But who could have done this? Why should Major Carson have been murdered?

There. I had put it into words. *Murder.*

Private Wilson had already come to that conclusion. He'd brought me here to be his witness.

My mind refused to function. Where to start? Matron, of course. *Begin with Matron*, I told myself.

Pulling the sheet back over the body and then the face, I said, "How did you discover him?"

"By accident," Private Wilson answered. "I was doing a count of the bodies, as I always do, for the burial detail's records, and I found there were fifty-seven, not fifty-six. I started again, and actually walked by each of the rows, to be sure. That's when I saw the arm. He wasn't put here by my men, Sister. I see to it that those who died of their wounds are on the far side of the shed, the influenza patients over here. It's been my way of doing things since this epidemic began in earnest."

"How did he come to be here in the first place? This far behind the lines?"

"That's a very good question. My guess is, it's likely whoever killed him thought to hide him here. But he didn't know how it was done, did he? How to wind the sheet properly, or which side to put him on, or that my count would be off." He hesitated. "Do you know him, Sister? Can you put a name to him?"

"I— It's been quite a few years. But he was a Lieutenant in my father's old regiment. I'd been told that he'd been promoted again and was now a Major. His name is Vincent Carson."

"I didn't wish to speak to anyone else about this business until I'd talked to someone I could trust. I didn't wish to find myself accused of putting him here. After all, I'm the one in charge of the dead, you might say."

"No, of course, I understand. Matron is finally sleeping. I'm to wake her in an hour's time. I'll tell her then. She'll know what's best to do. Can you put off the burial detail? Just for a bit? Once he's taken away, there's no hope of proving he was here, how he died, or even who he is. He'll be in an unmarked grave."

"I'll do my best. Perhaps we shouldn't wait—perhaps we should go to one of the doctors."

I shook my head. "They've got their hands full with the living. More wounded just arrived. No, Matron is the best choice. I've seen her cope in every sort of emergency you can imagine." But could she cope with murder? It was my turn to hesitate. "You do understand, don't you? It hasn't been very long since Major Carson was killed. Whoever put him here could be one of us—an orderly, someone from the canteen, you, me, one of the ambulance drivers."

"Not a pleasant thought, is it?" Private Wilson said.

He helped me finish wrapping the Major as best we could, so that he appeared to look more or less like his neighbors. I'd been dizzy before, but the disinfectant in here seemed to be aggravating it. I was finding it hard to concentrate, was eager to leave the shed and step out into the fresh air to clear my head. But duty was duty.

I stood there for a moment longer, remembering Lieutenant Carson. He'd been young and eager, his shock of unruly red hair setting him apart, and his grin had been contagious. Now his hair was short-cropped and showing signs of graying, and it was a man's face I'd looked into, thinner, deeply etched by his years in the trenches, dark circles beneath his eyes from lack of sleep and too many horrors witnessed. The face of war, my father had called it.

I felt a pang for my father when the news reached him. He'd thought highly of Lieutenant Carson, and he'd told me once that he wouldn't be surprised to see Lieutenant Carson in command of the regiment one day. Even then his knowledge of military strategy and tactics had been outstanding, and I had believed the Colonel Sahib's prediction.

"We'd best be going, Sister," Private Wilson said, urging me toward the shed doors. "We don't want to arouse curiosity, lingering here, like."

He was right. I turned and in silence walked with him to the door. "Thank you for confiding in me, Private Wilson." I shivered in the chilly air of the night as I crossed the bruised grass. "I'll bring Matron as soon as possible. With any luck the burial detail will be late anyway, but hold them off as long as you can. Tell them—tell them that Matron wishes to speak to them."

"Rather a dirty business, murder," he said grimly. "I couldn't believe the evidence of my own eyes when I found him." Then, turning to me, he asked, "Are you all right, Sister?"

"I think I forgot to eat. I'll just go across to the canteen and have some tea."

"Thank you, Sister. It was a brave thing to do, coming with me in that shambles. I'll be close by, on call, if Matron wishes to see the man for herself. And I'll keep an eye on the shed."

And then he was gone, tramping off in the darkness to where he could watch for the burial detail, as promised.

I hastily swallowed a cup of tea, then went back into the ward, stumbling on the threshold. *I must get some sleep,* I told myself. *As soon as I've spoken to Matron and we've contacted the proper authorities. I must write to the Colonel Sahib also as well—*

Just then one of the other nursing sisters called to me, asking me to help her change the bedding of a patient whose fever had broken in a cold sweat.

Glancing at my watch, I went down the ward to where Sister Marshall was waiting. It was only a little more than forty minutes before the hour was up. Not long at all now before I could wake Matron. I blinked my eyes as the face of the watch seemed to swim in front of them. Shaking off my fatigue, I smiled at Sister Marshall's patient. "This is a good sign. You'll feel like drinking a little broth later. To begin healing." I made a mental note to bring the Lieutenant a cup as soon as he was settled again.

My head was pounding as I bent over the bed to tuck in the sheets and my shoulders were beginning to ache. I ignored the pain, moving on to the next bed to hold a patient upright as he went into a paroxysm of coughing, hardly able to draw the next breath. Thirty minutes now until I could wake Matron.

When the time came, I didn't wake up Matron after all, nor tell her about the extra body in the shed.

Instead I was being carried to an empty cot on a stretcher, and I was soon fighting for my life.

CHAPTER TWO

IT WAS MY turn to be nursed, and I remember very little about it. Feverish and choking on the fluids that threatened to overwhelm my struggling lungs, I was ill for days, slipping in and out of consciousness.

Once it seemed I heard Matron saying, "She's strong, I thought she'd be all right."

I tried to rouse myself to tell her about Private Wilson and the body in the shed, but I couldn't put the words together and must have made no sense.

Another time I heard Dr. Wright speaking. I opened my eyes and saw his thin, haggard face as he bent over me to listen to my lungs. "Her father is Colonel Richard Crawford. He'll want to know."

Know what? That I was dying? But I couldn't let them down by dying! I couldn't imagine my mother's face when word came. A telegram? A letter? I couldn't hold the thought long enough to decide.

Later still, it was Simon Brandon's voice that reached me in the dim recesses of illness and pain, urging me to drink a little broth to keep my strength up. But Simon was in England, and I was in France. Confused, I let myself drift once more, wanting to cry with the agony in my chest that was threatening to kill me.

He was there again, bathing my face and hands as the fever peaked, and finally as I lay so weak that opening my eyes seemed to be too great an effort even to contemplate, his voice said bracingly, "It was a close-run thing, Bess, but you're going to live. I'm taking you to England tomorrow. Hang on a little longer, and you'll be home."

A while later, it was an Australian voice that spoke to me, and I felt my hands gripped tightly. But I couldn't respond.

I was told afterward that I'd slept most of the journey back to England. Because of that, and the fact that in Somerset it had been raining for a week or more, it was decided that the longer journey home would be too much for me. Instead as soon as we landed in Dover, I was settled into a motorcar amongst a mountain of pillows and carried by easy stages to Eastbourne, on the southern coast of Sussex. There my father had taken rooms at the Grand Hotel.

I was aware in Dover—only just—of my mother's hands touching my face and her voice saying, "My darling!" and then my father telling her, "Don't cry, my love, she's safe now."

And Simon's voice said, "She was exhausted to begin with, even before she was taken ill. It will be some time before she's herself again."

I hoped I wasn't dreaming in delirium, that they really were there.

I awoke one morning in a lovely room filled with sunshine, the sound of the sea rolling across the shingle strand a soothing backdrop to living in the present once more. As I opened my eyes, I found it difficult to imagine where I was. Not at home. Nor in London or France. Not even in the cramped little stateroom on a crossing. Around me now were the elegant furnishings and high ceilings of a first-class hotel. Or was it an hotel?

India? The Maharani's palace? But I was lying in a bed, not on silver-shot silk cushions.

Just then my gaze found my mother's face. Surprised, I said, "Hullo." My voice sounded rusty from disuse. All the same, I could almost watch the strain fade as she smiled at me.

"My darling girl," she exclaimed, and her fingers reached out to brush a strand of hair from my forehead. "Could you drink a little more broth, do you think?"

And for once I drained the cup before I lay back against the pillows, too weak to do more than watch the shadows of sunlight on water that danced across the ceiling above my head. The sea air was heavenly, the sun bright, no guns thundering in the distance too close for comfort. I took a deep breath and smiled.

As she took the cup away, my mother must have said something to my father, because he came in almost at once, taking up my hands as they lay on the coverlet and kissing them gently. "Welcome home," he said, his voice husky.

Much later I understood how hard it had been for him, this illness of mine. For once in his life, he had faced an enemy a regiment with all its might couldn't defeat.

He sat for a time by my bed, watching me as I drifted quietly into sleep again, and when I woke, it was Simon sitting there in his place.

"The Colonel is resting. Your mother as well," he told me softly. "I don't think they've closed their eyes for days."

I was sure he hadn't either, for the lines of worry in his face told their own tale.

Smiling, he fed me more broth, and held my hand as my father had done while I slipped in and out of a healing sleep.

They took it by turns, the three of them, staying constantly by my side, plumping pillows, feeding me until I could manage a spoon for myself, and talking of things that had nothing to do with war or sickness. Gradually I understood where I was and was even carried to the window to lie there for a while and watch the sea below.

When I was stronger I was allowed to sit on the sunny balcony, swathed in blankets and shawls. My father read to me sometimes, and Simon sat by me in companionable silence. My mother tried not to treat me like her small daughter recovering from measles, and that was a measure of how frightened she had been for me.

I on the other hand was unspeakably grateful that the three people dearest to me in the world had not been struck down by this merciless killer. I learned too that Mrs. Hennessey, who let the flat where I stayed in London on my leaves, had also come through unscathed. Mary, one of my flatmates, had been ill, but it was a milder case, and she had survived. Diana had been just as lucky. There was no accounting for the way the disease had chosen its victims.

One evening we were sitting together, Simon and I, watching the moon rise over the water and enjoying the milder weather. Earlier, the band had been playing in the open-air stand close by the strand, and the music had drifted up to us along with the soft whispers of the waves rolling in. There had been old favorites as well as martial tunes, and I had hummed along with some of the selections. Then, reluctantly breaking the mood, I said, "Simon. I had the most vivid dream while I was ill. It had to do with Major Carson. Do you remember him?"

"In fact I saw him in France not three months ago," he said. "What brought him to mind?"

"I'm not quite sure." Hesitatingly, I added, "He was dead, his body hidden amongst the influenza victims. I think—it appeared that his neck had been broken."

In the pale light of the moon I saw his gaze turn toward me. After a moment he said, "Fever does odd things with the mind. And you were very ill."

"Yes, I know. Still, I dreamed I needed to tell Matron about finding him, but she was sleeping, and I couldn't remember where. And I could hear the burial detail coming for him, and I had to stop it. But I couldn't move, I couldn't speak. As if I were paralyzed or strapped down to my cot. It was all rather frightening."

"I shouldn't worry about it, my dear," he said gently. "The dream will fade as you heal."

"I'm glad," I told him, smiling, grateful for the lovely evening and the peace of England. Not everyone was as fortunate as I had been.

Leaning my head back against the pillows, I watched the moon ride through a cloudless night sky before drifting into a dreamless sleep.

I awoke in my own bed the next morning and felt better than I had for weeks. But the influenza epidemic was still raging, and I knew how desperately I was needed in France. I concentrated on getting well and recovering my strength, which seemed to have flown out the window. We began to walk, my parents or Simon taking it by turns to accompany me. At first it was only a few dozen feet across Reception before I succumbed to a weakness so profound I had to lean on someone's arm to make what seemed to be an interminable return journey to my room. Determined to heal, three times a day I sallied forth, and soon I could stroll to the music stand and then nearly as far as the pier. Before very long, I could even walk out to the pier's end and then back to the Grand Hotel, without weakness or shortness of breath. The next day Simon dismissed the carriage that was paid to follow us wherever we went, in the event I tired.

When first I had brought up returning to the war, the Colonel Sahib vigorously opposed it, and I saw the fright in my mother's eyes at the very thought. And so I had said nothing more. They were right, it was too soon. Eager as I was to resume my duties and spell the overworked staff that so desperately needed experienced nursing sisters, I mustn't become a burden for them instead. Holding on to my patience, I had concentrated on recovering and regaining my strength.

A few days after Simon dismissed the carriage, my mother and I walked to the west of the hotel for a closer look at the Seven Sisters, the great white chalk cliffs that ranged beyond Beachy Head Light, the wind whipping at our skirts as my mother and I stood looking at the line of headlands. The lighthouse itself was invisible, down along the waterline and tucked out of sight. Sometimes great chunks of the cliff faces fell into the sea, but today, in hazy sunlight, they shone so white it hurt the eyes to stare at them.

I said, "I shall have to go back, you know."

Without looking at me, my mother said, "Bess. When you are stronger."

"Next week. Or the week after."

"We'll let the doctor decide, shall we?"

But Dr. Everett was a family friend and not to be trusted. If my mother asked him to keep me in England longer, he'd do it for her.

I tried another tack. "I'd be willing to spend a week in a clinic, to test my strength."

"I can feel the wind shifting. Shall we turn back?" And as we did, she added, "I'll speak to the Colonel Sahib, Bess, dear."

I left it at that, hoping that the seed was planted, and, with luck, would grow. And I hoped as well that I could count on my father to back me up this time.

But I was wrong there. Nothing was said that evening, and early the next morning a summons came from Somerset. My parents bade me a guilty good-bye and set out for home, leaving me in Simon's care for a few days

"A memorial service. I'd almost forgot, darling," my mother said, bending to kiss my cheek. "I've been so worried for you, it slipped my mind, but thank heavens the Rector sent to remind us."

"Whose service?" I asked, trying to keep a note of suspicion out of my voice at the sudden and all-too-convenient disappearance of both my parents.

My suspicion was wiped away by my mother's answer.

"I thought Richard or Simon had told you. Perhaps they felt it was too soon after your own illness. It's Vincent Carson, Bess. He's dead. He was killed just after you left France. The original service had to be postponed because large gatherings were discouraged. The family feels it's safe enough now to hold it. The Colonel Sahib is delivering the eulogy."

I was about to tell her that Major Carson was dead well before I sailed for Dover, but just in time I remembered that I had only dreamed it. It hadn't recurred—I was thankful for that—but it hadn't faded the way dreams usually do. And that was worrying.

Simon and I wished them a safe journey and watched them out of sight. He'd only just come back from London, and my father had taken him off for a brief report before setting out. And then to my surprise, without a word he walked off down the Promenade toward the pier.

I thought perhaps he wished to be alone, that something had happened in London or wherever he'd been, because I had noticed a grim set to his mouth as he and my father had emerged from Simon's room.

But when he returned to the hotel, he waved to me as I sat on my balcony. I went down to meet him, and we walked on to one of the benches set out on the lawn.

"My mother just told me that Major Carson had been killed."

"He was a fine officer. I spoke to his widow just last week. She's resigned, I think. If this war lasts much longer, there will be no one left to come home."

"How did he die?" I fought to keep the anxiety from my voice. Surely not—

"According to Julia he was struck by shrapnel and died instantly. A kindness, she said."

Everyone in England wished a kind death on their loved ones. No lingering, no crying out for mothers or wives, no pain-filled last moments. It wasn't always that easy, whatever a sympathetic commanding officer wrote to the next of kin. I'd held too many men during their last moments.

I didn't intend to carry it any further—this was not the best time to bring up the dream. Indeed I should have felt immense relief that it was no more than that. But the images in my mind, suddenly vivid and disturbing, wouldn't go away. I needed to exorcise them once and for all.

Before I could stop myself, I said, "Simon, remember I told you once that I believed I'd seen Vincent Carson's body amongst the Spanish Influenza victims? But it didn't belong there?"

"Yes. It was a dream, you said. Does it still worry you?"

"In a way. I try to put it out of my mind, but sometimes I question whether it was real or fever. For one thing, why should I dream that he'd been murdered? And I felt that his murderer must still be nearby. That it was urgent to report his body. It's that sense of urgency that makes it impossible to let go of the dream. Please, I don't want it to be true. I just wish there was some way to settle this for good. Then I could tell myself to stop being silly. I've dealt with patients who were delirious, and their nightmares fade with time. Mine hasn't. I need to know why." I made a gesture of frustration, not certain how to explain the confusion I felt.

"Part of it is my fault. I should have told you when you first mentioned it that he was dead. That might have helped. But I thought it wasn't the best time to give you such sad news."

I smiled wryly. "There's one solution. When I'm back in France, I'll find Private Wilson and speak to him. He might be able to tell me why I thought I'd gone into that shed. There will be a simple explanation."

I could already imagine Private Wilson saying in his gruff, kind way, *Sister, you fell ill just after Lieutenant Benson died. You were that upset—small wonder you imagined—*

"Oh!" I said, my hand flying to my mouth in bewilderment. "Simon—it was just after one of my patients had died that I fell ill. And when the body was removed, Private Wilson wanted me to see what he'd discovered in the shed. That part must be true. He wasn't certain what should be done about it. It still doesn't explain why I should have thought it was Major Carson."

"A dead man amongst dead men," he said after a moment. "Have you thought, Bess, that if there was someone in the shed who didn't belong there, Private Wilson has already dealt with the problem? While you were ill. And if he didn't, without your confirmation, whoever it was has long since been buried, murdered or not. If there was no identification with the body, finding it now will be nearly impossible in an unmarked grave. Sadly, there isn't much that could be done."

"You're right, of course," I said, wishing I could keep the doubt out of my voice.

"Julia told me Carson had died instantly. Was that a kind lie? Was he brought in dying of his wounds? Do you remember seeing him in the ward?"

I shook my head. "He was never one of my patients. It's just an uncomfortable coincidence that Major Carson died about this same time. As if I'd foreseen his death."

He stared at me in the sunny warmth of the morning. "I wish you'd come to me sooner. Or I'd pursued this when you first mentioned your dream. I didn't think—there has to be a way to resolve this for you."

"I can't do as I did at eight, I can't open the closet door and see for myself that no monsters live inside." I smiled, making light of my feelings.

"There's no need to wait until you're back in France. I'll look into this. What was the orderly's name? Private Wilson? He should be easy enough to find."

"Thank you," I replied, feeling a wash of relief.

"Shall I ask your father's help?"

"No, please. At least—not yet." I had other issues to face with my parents.

"Consider it done. Meanwhile, it's too fine a day to waste. We'll take a drive in the afternoon, shall we? And I'll ask the hotel to put up a lunch for us."

At a little past eleven o'clock, Simon knocked at my door as promised, and I went down with him to his motorcar.

The drive out of Eastbourne was lovely, climbing through narrow twisting lanes where trees overhung the road and cast cool shadows.

We came into the little village of Jevington, where pretty cottages lined the road and wildflowers bloomed along the low walls. I saw an elderly man, stooped and gnarled by rheumatism, hoeing between his roses.

Unexpectedly I was reminded of Melinda Crawford, who like

me had lived in India as a child, but much, much earlier, at the time of the 1857 Indian Mutiny. Melinda's mother had survived the unspeakable horrors of the siege and subsequent battle for Lucknow, struggling to keep her small daughter safe. And when it was over and she had come back to her house on the outskirts of the town, she found it burned to the ground and her English garden in ruins. She had knelt in the torn earth and wept for her lost roses. It was the only time Melinda had seen her mother cry until the death of her father.

A small link with home, that garden, and its destruction seemed to epitomize all she had suffered in a foreign country. I wondered who the old man was keeping those roses alive for through these awful years of war. A son—a grandson?

Simon took a turning to the left, up a twisting road that led to a knoll. And there before us was the church of St. Mary's, set above its sloping churchyard overlooking the back gardens of houses below it. Nearer the lane a stretch of clipped grass offered a view of the Weald, crystal clear in the noon air.

The church was partly Saxon, and we went inside to look at their stonework in the tower, and then moved down the aisle. There had been a service here only this morning, the flowers at the altar not yet wilted, the air of sorrow still lingering in the dim silence.

Outside Simon spread our rugs on the grass by the view and brought out the large wicker basket provided by the hotel. Inside were sandwiches, bread and cheese, even Banbury buns. We ate in companionable silence, and there was a Thermos of tea for me, a bottle of wine for Simon, although I noticed that he didn't open it.

We had just finished the last crumbs of the Banbury buns when he shattered the tranquil spell.

"Bess. Your parents have asked me to speak to you. They were already late starting for Somerset, but they wanted you to know that they fully understand your eagerness to return to nursing. After all, it's what you've trained for, what you do so well."

My heart leapt with joy. But he was still speaking.

"And so it's been arranged for you to be posted to a clinic in Somerset, beginning at the end of next week. It shouldn't try your strength too far. And you'll be close enough to come home occasionally—"

I stared at him, then interrupted him, not wanting to hear any more. "But—I told Mother that I'm needed in France—" Not to belittle the demands of working in a clinic devoted to convalescents, but it wasn't why I had trained to be a nurse. As long as the war lasted, I wanted to serve the men fighting and dying in the trenches.

Simon was examining the view, as if trying to memorize it, unwilling to meet my gaze. "You must understand, Bess. They came close to losing you twice. Once on *Britannic,* when she went down at sea, and again when you nearly died of the Spanish Influenza. And you came close, my dear girl, too close for our comfort." His voice changed as he said the words, and it was a measure of how I'd frightened those I loved.

"Yes, I understand, of course I do. But if I were a soldier in my father's regiment—as I could have been if I were his son and not his daughter—he would want me to return to my duty."

"Third time's unlucky, Bess. That's how they see it."

I bit my lip, then asked quietly, "Because I'm their daughter?"

"Essentially, yes. You're all they have."

"Vincent Carson was all that Julia had. He was her husband. No one made any effort to keep him in England."

"That's different, Bess, and you know it. I'm sure Julia would have tried, if she could."

"Is it different, Simon?"

I got up and walked across the lane to stare up at the stonework of the Saxon church tower. Simon followed me after a moment, standing just behind me.

For the first time I could remember, I was furious with my father. And then with my mother for not taking my part in this argument.

They had supported me from the beginning when I chose to go into nursing. Reluctantly, yes, but they had understood the call of duty. Why not now?

I knew why, of course. Simon was right, twice I'd had close calls. Nurses did die at the Front. Of illness, of gunshot wounds from aircraft that made it behind the lines—I'd had experience of that myself—of shells gone astray. Nurse Edith Cavell had died before a German firing squad. There were no guarantees. But I could have just as easily died of the influenza in Somerset, never having set foot in France.

Yes, I was their only child. But how many mothers had lost their only sons? How many wives had grieved for their husbands? How many children had lost their fathers? I needed to go back. I needed to do what I could for the torn bodies that came to the forward aid stations or to the hospitals just behind the lines. I couldn't sit out the rest of the war in what amounted to the comfort of a Somerset clinic. It was unimaginable.

Had my parents given Simon this onerous task of breaking the news to me, rather than face up to it themselves?

"They must have thought you very brave to take on this charge for them," I said over my shoulder, unable to keep the bitterness from my voice. It was almost as if Simon had betrayed me too.

"The Colonel and his lady had to leave for Somerset, Bess. Julia Carson particularly asked your father to deliver the eulogy."

"It's expecting too much," I said, turning to him. In the sunlight, framed by the rolling green land of the Weald, he looked every inch the soldier. A tall, strong, very attractive man with more courage than most.

"Give it a try, Bess. You can save lives in a clinic, you know."

"A handful. Compared to what's happening in France. You've been to the Front, you know how they are dying."

"I've seen it," he said shortly. It was the first time he'd admitted that he'd been sent into the thick of the fighting for reasons he never spoke of.

He took a deep breath.

And I realized that for the first time in all the years he'd been close to my family that I was asking him to divide his loyalties. To go against my parents' express wishes and help me do what they didn't want me to do.

I stood there waiting, all the while knowing how cruel it was even to ask.

A choice between the Colonel Sahib and my mother on one side, and me on the other.

I knew I would remember the expression in his eyes for the rest of my life.

"Bess—" he began, and then choosing his words carefully, he gave me a name. "I make no promises that your appeal to this man will succeed. Your father has more authority than I ever will. But it's worth a try."

He turned away from me, looking down the sloping churchyard with its row after row of gravestones under shady trees, and on to the rooftops of the village beyond. "My head tells me you should go back to France. No one will ever know the number of men who owe their lives to you and women like you. At the same time my heart— Bess, call me superstitious, if you like. But I don't wish to find out if the third time you come close to dying, we *will* lose you." He moved his gaze to the window high in the Saxon tower, as if looking for answers there. "When I got to France, I was told you were dying. That there was nothing more to be done."

And with that he turned on his heel and went to pack up the remains of the picnic basket, folding the rugs neatly and stowing the lot in the boot of the motorcar.

I stayed where I was, blindly looking at the church porch, wishing I could take back the words I'd spoken. Wishing I hadn't had to make him choose.

And then he was calling to me, and I walked slowly across to the motorcar, and he helped me inside.

We drove in silence all the long distance to Eastbourne.

Chapter Three

When we arrived at the Grand Hotel, Simon passed the picnic basket to one of the staff, handed me down from the motorcar, and said as I prepared to go inside, "I'll see what I can discover about Private Wilson. It may take several days."

And then with a nod he was gone.

I watched him out of sight, knowing that he had left not for an hour or so but for days. There had been someone with me ever since I had reached England—my mother, my father, Simon. I felt suddenly alone, separated from those I loved. Separated by more than distance.

Turning, I went up to my room and sat down at the little white desk between the windows, intending to write my first letter requesting reinstatement at the Front.

And I found the words wouldn't come.

Setting the sheets of hotel stationery to one side, I walked out to the balcony and for a while watched the sea, green and blue and, in the distance, almost black. There was a slight haze in the direction of the Seven Sisters, but toward Hastings and France the sky was clear. We were too far away to hear the guns. But I could imagine them. And imagine too the damage they were doing to flesh and bone.

It was difficult to go against my parents' wishes. We had always been of the same mind about important things. I could understand their feelings. I doubted that they could understand mine. Or was I being selfish and willful, where wiser heads knew better? I told myself that it was the wounded and dying who should be weighed in the balance, not my own wishes.

In the end I put the letter—or what was to be the letter but was now only a blank sheet—in the desk drawer and went down to take my tea in the enclosed veranda. Some hours later I dined alone. I couldn't have said afterward what I had chosen from the menu or how it had tasted.

There was a woman at the next table. She sat there, staring into space as if her mind were a thousand miles away, picking at her food as if it had no more flavor than mine had had. Fair and rather pretty in an elegant way, she appeared to be older than I was, and I put her age at thirty.

I hadn't noticed her here before this, whether because she had sat somewhere else or because she'd just arrived.

The headwaiter came over as she pushed her plate aside and asked, "Is everything to your liking, Mrs. Campbell?"

"Yes, it was lovely, I've no appetite, I'm afraid."

"Not bad news, I hope," he ventured, frowning. "You weren't yourself last evening either."

Bad news was more common than good these days. Yet he'd asked as if he knew her from another visit and felt free to inquire.

She laughed, but not convincingly. "No, nothing to worry about. Perhaps the sea air will improve my spirits and my appetite."

He cajoled her into trying the pudding, although it was clear to me that she wasn't hungry enough to care. And she ate a little of it stoically, then signaled the waiter again, rose, and left the dining room.

The Grand Hotel had an excellent reputation. It catered to people like my parents, and they had had no qualms about leaving me here to dine alone. I was well looked after, and so it wasn't surprising to see another woman alone.

I walked through great doors leading out to the veranda and stopped by one of the vases of fern for a few minutes to watch the waves roll in. I could sympathize in a way with Mrs. Campbell. I too needed to make a decision.

I was just on the point of turning to go up to my room when I overheard someone mention her name. There were two women sitting together just by the balustrade. They couldn't see me for that fern, but I could just glimpse Mrs. Campbell, a shawl over her shoulders, walking down to the drive and moving on to one of the benches set out beneath specimen trees. It was the one where Simon and I'd sat that morning.

"There she is," one of the women said in a low voice. "I told you I thought it was she."

"Yes, you're right. Shocking that she should show her face in such a place as this. Not after all the publicity surrounding the petition for divorce."

"Unfaithful, he said."

"Yes. But it couldn't be proved, could it?"

"Sordid, all of it. I mean to say, he's at war. You'd think she could put aside her personal feelings and remember that."

I turned and went indoors. I remembered too vividly Lieutenant Banner at Forward Aid Station No. 3, dying of his wounds and saying in a whisper that held a world of despair because time had run out, "She won't have to go through the divorce now, will she? She'll be a widow instead. I've made it easy for him, whoever he is. He'll step into my shoes without a qualm. But if he mistreats her, by God, I'll come back and haunt him!"

I shivered as I remembered his vehemence, but it had cost him his last breath, and he was gone. I wondered sometimes if Mrs. Banner's new husband had ever looked over his shoulder and listened for a footstep.

The thought followed me into sleep.

The next morning I took my pride and my courage in my hands and wrote the letter to London.

I put the direction on the envelope, took it to the front desk for stamps, and when they offered to put it in the post bag for me, I thanked them and said no.

For in spite of everything, I felt that I was betraying Simon.

I paced the veranda before lunch and after tea, and happened to see Mrs. Campbell leave the hotel, the manager himself seeing her into her hired car. Had the whispers been too much for her?

Two days later I scolded myself for my reluctance to post that envelope. My parents would be returning to Eastbourne shortly, and I would surely lose my nerve altogether once they were there to persuade me in person. I was on my way down to Reception to see to it personally when I met Simon himself just coming through the hotel door.

It had been raining somewhere along the road, for the shoulders of his coat were wet. His face was grim, and I suddenly had a premonition of bad news.

Nodding to me, he took my arm and said, "Shall we walk along the seafront? It won't rain for another hour or more. You won't need a coat."

"Yes, I— Simon, what's wrong?"

"Not here."

And so it was we walked down to the water and stopped halfway to the pier, standing for a moment to watch dark clouds building far out to sea. Lightning was playing in them, bright flickers against a gunmetal sky. The air was oppressively warm, even though the wind was just picking up.

We were out of hearing of anyone. Simon, leaning his shoulders on the parapet of the seawall, seemed lost in thought.

My mind was running through a mental list of our acquaintance. Who was dead? Why couldn't he find the courage to tell me?

"Please," I said baldly. "Don't—I'd rather you didn't try to find the right words to break the news."

He straightened and looked down at me, as if he hadn't realized that I was there. "No, it isn't bad news, Bess . . . it's . . . I don't quite know what to make of it." He turned and led me to a bench. After we'd sat down, he said, busy with his driving gloves, "I inquired of London where Private Wilson could be reached. I thought perhaps you could write to him, even if you couldn't return to France. My contact was reluctant to tell me anything at first, and I had to use your father's authority to pry the information out of him. Which was odd in itself. But then I understood why. The Army isn't eager to give out such information. It seems— I was told that Private Gerald Wilson, who was an orderly in the hospital where you were working when you fell ill—a man close to forty-one years of age, just as you'd described him to me—was found hanged in the shed where bodies were left to await burial. The doctor who declared him dead felt that his work had turned the man's mind. Fearful of falling victim to influenza himself, he'd decided to die by his own hand."

I sat there aghast.

After a moment I said, "Are you sure you were given the correct information? There must be a dozen men by that name and of the same rank." But looking at Simon's face, I could already read the answer.

"I knew him, Simon," I said earnestly. "I worked with him every day. He wasn't the sort to kill himself. He recognized the sadness of his work, but he understood too that a man of his age was more useful as an orderly than at the Front. He handled the dead— wounded and influenza victims. He knew the risks."

I realized that I had fallen into the past tense, as if I had already accepted the truth. But I refused to believe it.

"It's in the official record, Bess."

"Yes, but it's wrong, I tell you. It must be *wrong*."

We sat in silence while I dealt with the turmoil in my mind. Finally I said, "It isn't true. Yes, it may well be that Private Wilson was found hanging, that part I can't question because I wasn't there. And, of course, someone had to cut him down, which means the record is correct—as far as it went. But it wasn't suicide. He must have been killed because he'd seen that body in the shed. When I fell ill so suddenly, he must have had to speak to someone else. And so he had to die."

"Bess, you're assuming what you dreamed was real. The official report on Carson's death was shrapnel wounds. I looked into that as well. They wouldn't have got that wrong either."

"Very well. I won't go on claiming it was Major Carson I saw. But part of my dream must have been real. I must have seen a body. I must have done. And there were no other wounds. Only a broken neck. Which means whoever he was, he was murdered. Why else would Private Wilson be killed? Simon, I was thought to be dying, and so I was no danger to anyone. But he was. Someone made certain that what he'd seen was never reported. The killer was still there, waiting to be sure the body was buried."

It occurred to me just then that if I hadn't fallen ill, I might also have been killed because I'd been in that shed. What's more, the burial detail would have come and gone, and the fifty-seventh body would be well out of reach if by chance I did survive and remembered some wild and feverish tale.

Instead of relieving my mind, Private Wilson's suicide seemed to confirm that what I thought I'd dreamed was true.

I thought about that kindly man who saw to the dead with such infinite gentleness. Could he have seen too many bodies, could he have been driven to killing himself to stop having nightmares about the rows and rows of dead that he dealt with day after day?

It was possible. Of course it was. But the two deaths in tandem?

All the more reason to hurry back to France and find out.

As if he'd followed my reasoning, Simon said quietly, "Even if you go back, you can't be certain you'll be sent to the same hospital."

And that was true. Assignments were based on need, not personal preferences. Still, I'd be in France. I could eventually find out what I wanted to know about Private Wilson.

Again Simon followed my logic.

"It isn't Wilson's death that matters, is it?" he asked. "That's to say, he wasn't the primary target, was he? Carson appears to have been. If this is true, why should anyone kill him? He was a respected officer, and careful of his men."

"I have no answer to that," I said slowly.

"Who are his enemies?" Simon pressed. "Who stands to gain the most from his death?"

I sighed. "Since he died in France, it could be that someone at the Front wanted him dead. It's happened before that scores have been settled there. If it wasn't in France, then the reason will lie in Somerset, where Major Carson lived." I remembered Mrs. Campbell and Lieutenant Banner. "Do you know if the Carson marriage was a happy one? He wouldn't be the first soldier to fall in love with another man's wife. She wouldn't be the first woman to fall out of love, after a hasty wartime marriage."

"I can't believe that of either Julia or Vincent."

I couldn't help but think that neither of the Carsons would have told Simon if there was marital trouble. Or my parents, for that matter.

"I understand, but—"

"Stay out of it, Bess. The last thing you want to do is cause Julia Carson any more grief. And I've told you, there's no proof that there was anything or anyone in that shed. Or that Private Wilson killed himself. Too much time has passed."

"I would never hurt her. But what about Private Wilson's family? How do they feel about his death?" I took a deep breath. "If I don't pursue this, who will?" In my pocket was the letter I'd written. I handed it to him. "What shall I do, Simon?"

"All right. Go to Somerset and learn what you can about Carson. Julia likes you, she'll talk freely to you. And if you discover anything, come to me. Let me handle it."

"That's fair. If it's possible to clear Private Wilson's name of the charge of suicide, I'll find it. In his own way, he'd been a very brave man." A thought struck me. "What was the date of his death? Do you know?"

With reluctance, Simon told me. It was the night after I fell ill.

"Where did Private Wilson come from? Before the war?" I was ashamed that I didn't know, had never thought to ask.

"From Cheddar Gorge. Or just outside it, to be more accurate."

And Cheddar Gorge was also in Somerset. It explained, perhaps, why he had chosen to confide in me rather than go directly to Matron. I'd have sworn he didn't know, hadn't recognized the dead man. But how fallible was my memory? I hadn't been watching Private Wilson's face. What's more, he'd seen that of the corpse before I had.

The trouble was, there was so little to go on. Only my belief that Private Wilson wouldn't have killed himself and the timing of his death.

Simon waited as I digested that.

Another thought crossed my mind, and immediately I was ashamed of it. But I had to know.

I searched his face. Was this a conspiracy to force me to choose Somerset for myself? But Simon had never lied to me. He wouldn't have lied about Private Wilson's death or where he lived. Even to convince me that I had every reason to go to Somerset.

I got up and walked a little way on my own. Simon stayed where he was, on the bench by the parapet. His gaze was on the confection that was the pier, for all the world an exotic place, filled with wonders, but in fact it was only a way for those visiting the seaside to amuse themselves.

I wanted desperately to go back to France. But setting that aside, could I spend a week or two at the clinic, as everyone seemed to want me to do? It would permit me to learn something about Major Carson and Private Wilson. Going back to France sooner might put me closer to where events had taken place, but I'd be walking blindly into something I knew little about, uncertain where to put my trust. And if murder had been done, I'd be vulnerable.

It shouldn't take too long, should it, to learn what I needed to know and *then* ask to be sent back to France?

Simon had put my letter into his pocket. I didn't feel I could ask him to return it. On the other hand, if I'd written it once, I could write it again when the time came. And I wouldn't be putting Simon squarely in the middle.

I paced as far as the pier, then turned and walked back again. Simon was standing by the parapet now, his gaze on the hotel. He didn't want to read in my face what decision I had made. And I realized in that moment how worried he was, how much my return to France concerned him.

There were very few things that frightened Simon Brandon. It was a measure of how much he cared for me that he couldn't face me now.

I said when I'd reached him, "It appears that my decision has been taken out of my hands. The clinic in Somerset it is."

His relief was well concealed, but still I saw it.

"This doesn't mean that I won't go back to France, Simon. You do understand that."

"Yes" was all he said.

As he offered me his arm for the walk back to the hotel, I thought perhaps things had turned out for the best.

It was difficult to be at odds with those I loved.

But the time would surely come when I'd have to face making the decision again.

Chapter Four

Shortly after my parents returned from the Major's memorial service, we set out for the clinic in Somerset. No one mentioned my about-face on serving there. It would have been gloating, and my parents would never do that.

We spent one night at home, and the following morning it was my father who drove me to my next posting.

I asked, to pass the time, how he had felt about the memorial service.

"Difficult at best, of course. But I think it went off rather well, and it gave Julia Carson a little comfort. He's buried in France, you know. Vincent."

"I remember him before he met Julia. He was half in love with Mother for a time."

My father chuckled. "So he was. But then a good part of the regiment thought they were in love with her. Your mother has an air about her that binds men to her."

"Did you know his family well? I remember Vincent's father as a rather stern man. On one visit he found me in an upstairs passage, looking for Mother, and he quick-marched me back to the Nursery, ordering Nurse to see that I stayed there."

"Did he indeed? He was a barrister, a formidable opponent in a courtroom, but outside of it he had a stiff manner that sometimes put people off. Vincent confided to me that it was a great shock to his father when his only son chose the Army over the Law. He'd assumed that Vincent would be eager to follow in his footsteps, and for a time he blamed me for that decision. His mother, on the other hand, was from Devon, her family connected with the Raleighs in some way, I think. She was known for her good works and her flame-red hair. A beauty in her day. She was very fond of your mother. Do you remember her?"

"She'd carry me off to the kitchen, where they looked after me until Nurse could fetch me. There were small cakes, iced in different colors. And a cream cake with a rum and sultana sauce for tea."

"Rum?" he asked, his brows flying up. "I never heard of that."

I laughed. "Yes, well, I was sworn to secrecy. It was quite lovely, actually."

Odd that Vincent Carson had married just the opposite woman—pretty, but not a beauty, and a homebody. Her fame, such as it was, lay in her gardens, where she enjoyed spending hours, to the despair of her gardener. She had wanted children, a house full of them. But there hadn't been any. And wouldn't be now.

"The Major had two sisters. They were a little older than I, and treated me with kindness."

There had been some gossip about that amongst the women from the garrison in India who called on my mother from time to time. One of Vincent's sisters had married beneath her, causing a family breach. The other had married well, her husband something to do with banking in Bristol.

"Do you think—if my duties allowed—that I could call on Julia? Not right away, of course. But I'd like to do that, unless she's not receiving visitors yet."

"I think she'd be delighted to see you."

It was clear from what my father was saying that Simon hadn't told him about my belief that the Major had been murdered. I was grateful.

Medford Longleigh was a small village in the rolling country that led to the Cotswolds, and high brick walls kept the houses and shops from sliding downhill into the road. They gave a very secretive air to the village, but in fact it had been the only way the area could be settled. The clinic was in Longleigh House, which was just on the outskirts, where the twisting main road straightened itself out for a quarter of a mile or more, allowing the gates to the park to appear to be even more stately than they were. Tall, capped with stone, then curving down in a graceful sweep to connect to the walls that surrounded the grounds, they promised a grand house ahead.

And the promise was fulfilled. Three stories high with an elegant roofline, tall chimneys, and a wing set to either side, the house was lovely. Stone faced the windows, and the portico was Grecian, with wide steps leading down to the drive.

My first thought was that if I'd lived here, I'd have found it hard to give it up to the Army and the hordes of doctors, nursing sisters, orderlies, and patients who inhabited it now. Of course it was the size that had made it ideal for a convalescent clinic. It could accommodate dozens of wounded and the staff to serve them.

My father said gently as we drove up the winding drive through the park, "I'm pleased that you made this choice. Very sensible of you, my dear." Beneath the words lay the hope that there had been no lasting harm done to our relationship

Smiling in return, I assured him that I was satisfied with this decision.

And then we were pulling up in front of the house.

He came around to my side of the motorcar and handed me out while an orderly bounded down the shallow steps to fetch my valise from the boot.

Colonel Crawford was welcomed by Matron herself, as a courtesy due his rank, and we had tea in her small office. Then he was given a tour of the clinic while a young woman, Sister Harrison, took me to my quarters and settled me in.

We had been assigned to what in better times had been the servants' bedrooms, made more habitable now with odd bits from the more fashionable rooms downstairs.

"We don't have much time to ourselves," Sister Harrison was saying as she looked around my quarters. "But the bed is quite comfortable, and you'll be glad of that."

"Matron told me that the majority of your patients are orthopedic cases, with a few surgical cases as well."

"Yes, all officers, of course." Officers and men of other ranks were not mixed in clinics. "It isn't arduous work, there are enough of us to share it out. Some of the patients are difficult, others meek as lambs. But I must warn you about the Yank. He can be quite a handful." Her smile told me that she liked the man in spite of that.

"An American?" I asked, surprised.

"He joined the Canadian Army when war broke out. Didn't want to miss it, he said, while waiting for his own country to come into it. He's quite popular with the men. Someone told me he had a pocket full of medals and should have been put in for a VC. But then he's American, you see."

Victoria Crosses were not handed out lightly.

She helped me unpack my uniforms, and as I went down to report for duty, my father was just leaving. I wondered if he'd been at his most charming in order to smooth my path here. That would be like him and explained why he chose to bring me to Longleigh House rather than send me off with Simon. Not that Simon couldn't have smoothed my path as well, but rank had its privileges, and that was pointed out as Matron said, watching his motorcar disappear down the drive, "A fine man, your father."

I took up my duties just after luncheon had been served, my first assignment reading to the men. It was difficult to keep them amused, anxious as they were to return to duty if they could. Broken legs, cracked ribs, shoulder injuries, back wounds, all of them the sort of thing that took time to heal, like it or not. And Sister Harrison was blunt about it.

"A new pretty face is just the thing," she told me, handing me a Conan Doyle mystery. "And light fare. Nothing heavy-going, sad, or reminding them of the war."

When I walked into what had once been the drawing room of the house, I found some forty patients there waiting for me. Their expectant faces told me that word had already made the rounds regarding a new Sister being assigned to the clinic.

A tall, fair man with a welcoming smile stepped forward, limping, to hold my chair for me, and as I sat down, I wondered if he was the American. He lacked the reserve I was accustomed to in British officers, his manner open and rather cheeky, I thought.

I read the story, and for the most part my audience was attentive. I saw two or three men gingerly stirring in their chairs as if in pain, and made a note of it. One fell asleep almost on the first page, which I took to mean he had been given medication before the midday meal. His face was slack, as if the relief from suffering was a blessing. The others applauded Mr. Holmes's acumen in solving the case, and then it was time for exercises. Patients were divided into groups where the affected limb was strengthened.

I assisted the doctor in charge of one such group, helping men work on the muscles in damaged arms, clenching and unclenching their fists, gently encouraging their bodies to remember how to respond to lifting and carrying without dropping things, and to learn anew the skills to compensate for weakness and the pain they were still experiencing.

Next I made the rounds with the sister in charge of giving medicines. After that I walked with three men recovering from broken limbs, their canes tapping across the drive as we headed toward the park. We moved slowly, chatting as we went, and I learned that one had been wounded by shrapnel, another had had a bullet through his knee, and the third had broken his tibia in a fall down a shell hole, catching his boot in the loose earth, and bending his leg back in such a way that the bone snapped.

After dinner, where I fed several patients who hadn't yet

recovered their dexterity with fork and knife, I was asked to help change bandages for the night. For the most part, the wounds were healing well, although I could see Dr. Gaines's concern over one patient whose wound was still draining.

"I don't want to operate again," he muttered to himself. "No, that wouldn't be at all wise. Still . . ."

By the time I got to bed that first night, I was very tired and all too aware of the fact that I was not yet healed enough myself to keep up the pace. I wondered how I would have managed in France, where we were chronically short of staff and sometimes worked four-and-twenty hours without relief.

Still, I settled into my routine easily and soon discovered what Sister Harrison meant about the American.

He was polite, always there to open doors or carry heavy burdens, though his limp grew more pronounced when he did, and I scolded him for not taking proper care of his injury.

He smiled. "I'm bored to tears, Sister. And you shouldn't be hauling those baskets of linens down to the laundry. There are orderlies to handle the heavy work."

It was true, of course, but the orderlies were busy enough that I sometimes preferred not to wait for them.

"And I shall be blamed if you inflame that wound while being chivalrous."

He grinned. "My mother," he said, "taught me to treat the fairer sex with deference and courtesy. Whatever the cost."

"Yes, well, she wouldn't be best pleased with me, Captain, if your leg has to be amputated because you were being silly."

But there was no discouraging him. "My leg," he said loftily, "is healing better than expected. I'll be back in France before the summer."

His name, I soon learned, was Thomas Barclay. His father had made a fortune in railroads, especially running lines north through the state of Michigan, and then he had had the foresight to realize that a ferry could carry the new flood of holidaymakers across to Mackinac (pronounced, I was informed, Mackinaw) Island to the famous hotel there, or to the Upper Peninsula, which abutted on Canada. Railroads, shipping, even a monopoly on the horses used in lieu of lorries and even motorcars on the island had been quite lucrative, and a yearly regatta (which he claimed he'd won more than once) brought even more guests to the north. This explained to some extent his decision to join the Canadian forces, as did the fact that he and his father had often gone north across the border to hunt with friends living there.

Sister Harrison said one morning as she settled her cap over her sleekly brushed auburn hair, "You have made a conquest. The Yank follows you about like a forlorn puppy."

"Have you looked at his leg? He refuses to let me see it. I'm rather worried about him."

"Don't be. Dr. Gaines gives him a tongue-lashing when he doesn't take care of it properly. I think he rather likes making you fret over him. One way to be certain of your attention," she added with a grin.

The next day was my free afternoon, and I had given some thought to my plans. It was not more than twenty miles to where Julia Carson lived in a village called Nether Thornton. Twenty miles was farther than even I could manage on a bicycle.

Dr. Gaines owned a motorcar, which he kept in an outbuilding on the grounds. I had been told this in passing by one of the officers, and I had seen it as well when he drove to London with a patient to consult a specialist.

I went to his office and asked respectfully if I could borrow the motorcar for a few hours, explaining that an officer in my father's old regiment had been killed recently and that I should like to offer my condolences to his widow, having been unable to attend the memorial service.

He peered at me over the rims of his glasses. "Ah. You had the

Spanish Influenza," he said, as if that was how he remembered who I was.

"Yes, sir."

"Can you *drive* a motorcar, Sister? I shouldn't like to lose mine at the hands of a well-meaning novice."

"I understand, sir. I've driven motorcars, ambulances, and even lorries."

"Yes, that's in France, I think, where roads are rather poorly defined, and there's room for error. This is Somerset, where brick walls and hedgerows tend to hem one in."

I smiled. "I have driven in England, where the roads are often nearly as narrow, twisting, and ill made as in France."

"So they are. Well. I shall allow you to borrow it this time. On the condition that you take someone with you."

I didn't want anyone with me while I spoke to Julia.

"Humor me, Sister," he said, reading my expression all too clearly. "It will give me peace of mind to know you are well protected should any problems arise. Matron would not enjoy informing your father that we have misplaced you or injured you on our watch."

Reviewing the patients I had come to know, I cast about for a suitable escort. But Dr. Gaines had already made up his mind.

"Take the Yank with you. He's impatient, trying to push his recovery. An outing of this sort will do him good. And he's presentable enough. You needn't worry about upsetting the family."

The last person I wished to have with me.

But it was clear that I shouldn't be allowed to take the motorcar at all, if I insisted on going alone. And there weren't many patients, for that matter, well enough to accompany me. I tried to put as good a face on it as possible and thanked him for the use of his vehicle.

And so it was that Thomas Barclay and I set out for Nether Thornton in early afternoon. Captain Barclay was in good spirits, glad to be free of Longleigh House for even a few hours.

"My father's great-grandfather was English," he said happily, as if this forged a bond between us.

"A great many Americans have English forebears," I replied repressively, turning out of the drive onto the main road. "After all, it was once a British colony, was it not?"

"There are Germans living in Michigan," he informed me. "Lutherans, most of them. I find it hard sometimes to think that the Germans I'm ordered to shoot aren't their cousins or former neighbors. When we take prisoners, I can't tell the difference."

I too had met Germans who were not the ogres of the popular press. "Yes, I understand. My father told me once that nations are often at war, but people are not."

"A wise man, your father. Army, is he?"

"Yes. His regiment was sent to India shortly after I was born, and my parents took me with them. I was educated there, rather than being sent home to school. I'm very grateful to them for that decision."

"I'd been to Canada, of course, but otherwise I was never out of the States until I sailed for France. Still, I've traveled widely in my own country. My father saw to that. He had many interests in railroads and shipping, and my mother and I went with him as often as not. I know Charleston and New Orleans, San Francisco and New York, Denver and Boston. Ever been to America?"

"I haven't."

"Well, when the war is over, you're invited to visit. My mother and sisters would like you. They'd take you to Mackinac Island. You'd explore on horseback, sit on the famous veranda to watch the sunset over Lake Michigan, and have a real English tea in the lobby. I think you'd enjoy that."

"Thank you."

He was relaxing in his seat now, and I realized that he'd been quite tense after we'd reached the main road, waiting for me to overturn the motorcar on a curve or run us into one of the high walls in the surrounding villages. Smiling, I said, "I do drive well. I was taught by Simon Brandon, who never does anything by halves."

"You must have been," he replied, grinning sheepishly. "Neither of my sisters drives." There was a pause, and then he asked, "Who is Simon Brandon?"

"A family friend," I said, not wishing to go into the whole of my relationship with Simon. He had been my father's batman when he first joined the regiment, and later rose to the post of Regimental Sergeant-Major. He and my father had always been close, despite the difference in their ages, for Simon was nearer to mine than to his. I had known him all my life. He lived in a cottage near our house in Somerset, and like my father, retired from active duty, he was often employed by the War Office in matters that were never discussed. They disappeared for hours or even days at a time, came home weary, sometimes bloody, and often grim.

"From the way you said that, he must be more than simply a family friend," he pointed out.

I turned to him. "Are you jealous, Captain?"

I expected him to deny it, but he said slowly, "I think I am."

We drove in silence the rest of the way to Nether Thornton, and on the outskirts I said, "I'm here to call on Mrs. Carson. Her husband was killed recently." I explained the connection and was casting about, trying to think of a kind way to ask him not to come in with me, when he solved the problem himself.

"Then you don't want a stranger underfoot. Just ahead—the pub, The Pelican. Drop me there. Just don't forget to retrieve me when you're ready to go back to Longleigh House."

I smiled, grateful. "I shan't forget. Dr. Gaines would be furious if I lost my minder. And I should like to borrow the motorcar again."

"Anytime, Sister. Just ask me." He paused. "Can you use the crank? Or would you prefer that I come to fetch you? Either way, I shan't say a word to the good doctor."

"Thank you, but I can manage," I assured him. The Colonel Sahib had taught me the safe way to use a crank.

I drew up halfway along the High Street, setting the Captain down in front of the handsome half-timbered pub. He had more difficulty descending from the motorcar than he'd had getting into it. I looked away as he struggled, knowing he wouldn't take kindly to an offer of help. Finally, standing straight, his cane in his hand, he said, "I'll be as sober as a judge whenever you come for me. You needn't worry." And with that he walked in front of the motorcar and entered the pub. I was beginning to learn how much effort such bravado required on his part. And the cost in pain.

I drove on through the center of the village and to the house close by the church where the Major had lived after his marriage.

Leaving the motorcar by the front gate, I walked up to the door. Black silk draped the knocker, and I let it fall gently against the brass plate.

After a moment the door was opened by Tessie, who had been with the family from the time of their marriage. Tall and rawboned and kind, she said, "Miss Crawford! It's so good to see you. Mrs. Carson will be delighted that you've come. Are you feeling stronger? You look quite yourself, you know."

"And I am." I explained about the clinic as she ushered me inside and down the passage to the sitting room.

Julia rose from her desk as I came in, exclaiming as Tessie had done and coming to embrace me. "I'm so happy to see you. How are you? Your father told me you'd had quite a severe bout with this terrible illness."

"I was one of the lucky ones," I responded. "It quite ravaged France."

"Come, sit down. Tessie will bring us tea. I was glad that Vincent died quickly. We also lost our cook to the influenza, and it was a terrible death. Nineteen people died here in Nether Thornton, and we were told we had only a mild outbreak. But we were warned that it could return because of that. The possibility doesn't bear thinking about."

We sat and reminisced for a bit, and then when the tea was brought in, she said, "I thought my world had ended when the news came about Vincent. His commanding officer wrote to me. A Colonel Prescott. A lovely letter, assuring me that Vincent hadn't suffered, and how much my letters had meant to him to the very end. He must have known my husband well. Little things are such a comfort at a time like that, and he told me that Vincent was liked by his men and that they had been brokenhearted by his death. That they had asked to see his body and pay their respects before it was taken away. Vincent cared for his men. It would have meant so much to him."

All this was very interesting to me. How could Colonel Prescott have known so much about the Major's death in the lines? Unless it was true. I felt a twinge of doubt.

"It was indeed thoughtful. Er—had he served under Colonel Prescott for some time?"

"Well, there were the censors, of course, and he seldom mentioned names in his letters. It was Private J. and Captain H. and Colonel R. He kept a journal too, and he used the same code, so to speak, in that. In the event he was taken prisoner and the Germans could use the information against us. I'm told journals are discouraged for that very reason."

Piecing together such small bits of information could sometimes lead to a picture of a regiment's strength and position.

"Did Colonel Prescott send his journal home with the rest of his possessions?"

"I don't believe he knew about it or he would have looked for it. It wasn't in the box of his belongings. I wept when they came. They still carried the scent of Vincent's pipe tobacco. Do you remember? He had it made up for him in London. I could bury my nose in them and feel that he was close again. There was the pipe, his Testament and his shaving kit, and so on. Two of his books, one a volume of poetry, another a history. His other uniforms. So few things to mark a man's life and death."

I had to agree with her. Her husband had been an energetic, intelligent, and caring man. Hard to capture those qualities in the small packet of his possessions.

Still curious about the journal, I brought the subject back to that. "Did he ever show you his journal? When he was on leave?"

"He read to me bits and pieces, the parts that he said wouldn't disturb me. The pages on his short leave in Paris were wonderful. He promised to take me there after the war. Well, after France was herself again. And he read me a section about his first crossing to France, and some of his feelings about leaving me and facing death. I remembered those lines when the news came. 'I vowed to love, honor, and cherish Julia until death parted us, but this separation feels like a small death. If it should come to the worst, and be the real thing, if I am capable of carrying any thought into the grave with me it will be, I shall love you until the end of time, just as if I'd been at your side until we were old and gray and still slept in each other's arms.'"

The tears came then, and I chided myself for being the cause of them. But she said as I comforted her, "I find I do well for the most part. And then suddenly I am bereft and I find myself crying uncontrollably. It's so silly."

"It isn't silly at all." Indeed, it showed me that there was no trouble in this marriage. "You miss him terribly, and I won't promise you it will get any easier. But with time, it will be a different pain."

She looked up at me. "Your mother said something like that to me. I was so grateful for her understanding."

When she was calmer, I asked, "Was there anyone in France that Vincent was particularly close to, someone he confided in?"

"He and Andrew were close—they were at Sandhurst together. But Andrew died early on, at Mons. After that, Vincent was reluctant to make friends. It was too painful to send them into certain death. The price of promotion, he called it, when he had to give such orders himself."

I'd heard other officers who felt the same way.

"Was there anyone he particularly disliked?"

"What an odd question!"

"Not really. Vincent was always such a good judge of character. And as I remember, he wasn't one to suffer fools lightly."

She smiled at that. "No, he wasn't, was he? I asked him once— well, war is rather terrible, isn't it, people wounded and dying in front of one's eyes, and I thought perhaps petty things no longer mattered. He answered that whatever a man was before the war, he usually brought with him to France. Good or bad. But he particularly disliked those who let down the side, who couldn't be counted on in pinch." A frown replaced the smile. "It's odd, now that you've brought this up—there was trouble with one of his sergeants. Vincent was very angry with the man. I never knew what it was about, just that later he was angry with himself for having lost his temper. Fortunately soon afterward, this sergeant was shifted to another part of the line. Vincent seldom lost his temper, but when he did, he could be quite furious. It went with his red hair, I think. His mother also had a lively temper."

I laughed, agreeing with her. And to my surprise, she added, "There was also that brother-in-law of his. Sabrina's husband. Vincent called him a slacker. A disgrace to the uniform."

"He wasn't in our regiment, as I recall."

"Oh, no. He joined the Royal Engineers. God knows what they saw in him. But he has been serving under Vincent, something to do with mines. He *had* been serving—" She caught herself and changed the tense. "I can't seem to stop thinking that Vincent's death was confused with someone else's, and he'll write soon to tell me he's well and not to worry."

I had stayed as long as I should in politeness, and so I set my teacup back on the tray and took my leave. Julia begged me to come again, if I could, and I promised I would. "Were Vincent's sisters at the memorial service? I haven't seen them since your wedding. I hope they are well."

She made a face. "Sabrina didn't come. She's very likely poor again. You never know with that man she married. I think he must gamble or something of the sort. They always seem to be short of money. But Valerie was here. She and Vincent were only a year apart. She stayed with me, and we comforted each other."

"I'm glad."

With another embrace we said good-bye, and I drove Dr. Gaines's motorcar sedately back to The Pelican, where the Captain must have been watching for me. He came out at once, smiled as he nodded toward the crank, and said, "Well, well."

"Don't be silly."

He got in beside me, and I saw the grimness of his mouth as he settled into his seat. This outing had tried his leg. As impatient as he was to leave the clinic and get back to the fighting, it was clear to both of us that he wasn't ready yet.

Perhaps, I thought, this explained why Dr. Gaines had sent him with me—to measure his readiness in a way that he could face, rather than listening to a doctor telling him a hard truth.

I found myself with a new respect for Dr. Gaines.

We drove out of Nether Thornton in silence, mainly because Captain Barclay was in no mood for light conversation. But as his leg stopped throbbing quite so viciously, his spirits returned and he said, "Was it a good visit?"

"Yes, indeed." Julia had unwittingly given me food for thought.

My confidence had been shaken by Colonel Prescott's letter. And yet there was the evidence of Private Wilson's death. And what had become of Vincent's journal? If it was in his tunic pocket when he was killed, someone should have discovered it and put it with his other belongings. A doctor wouldn't have undressed him if he had died instantly of his wounds. Sadly there was no time for the dead, because there were so many living in need of attention.

"Penny for your thoughts," Captain Barclay said after several miles of silence.

I smiled ruefully. "Sorry. I was distracted."

"This wasn't simply a courtesy call, was it?" the Captain asked after a few minutes. "There's something on your mind. Why *did* you go to visit Mrs. Carson?"

That was too close to the truth for comfort.

"Actually I was thinking about Major Carson's journal. He kept one, according to Julia. She'd seen it, he'd read her a few passages from it. But it didn't come home with his other possessions."

"Is it important?"

"I—don't quite know. For Julia it is."

"It could have been lost when he was wounded and every effort was being made to save his life."

"He died instantly, according to his commanding officer."

"It's what we're taught to write. No mother or wife wants to hear that a loved one died screaming and writhing in agony. When he was hit, his men would have done what they could, and whatever falls into the unspeakable muck in the bottom of a trench is lost forever. Or it could have been buried with him."

"True," I said doubtfully, unable to tell him that it could all have been a lie, how Vincent Carson had died.

"You don't believe me. Why do women fix on tangible things? He could have given instructions for the journal not to be sent home. It's possible he wrote what he believed to be the truth at the time, but still words that perhaps it would pain his wife to read after he was dead and unable to explain. Or perhaps his commanding officer read enough to feel it was unwise."

"Yes, I do believe you," I said, threading my way through a flock of sheep that was taking up the road. "Thinking about it in that light." But it once more raised the specter of marital problems.

There was nothing about Julia even to hint that she was glad to be free to marry someone else. But if Vincent had fallen out of love with his wife and there was someone else, he could have written about his struggle with himself. A very good reason to order it destroyed if he was killed.

"Good. Anything else worrying you? I'm always happy to make your burdens lighter."

I had to laugh. For the rest of the journey we talked about him— how he'd come to join the Canadian Army, when and where he was wounded, and what he hoped to do when the war finally ended.

We had come within sight of the gates to Longleigh House when Thomas Barclay said again, without warning, "Tell me again who Simon Brandon is."

CHAPTER FIVE

I WROTE TO Simon that evening in the quiet of my room. A storm was blowing up, and I listened to the distant thunder, reminded again that I ought to be in France.

By telling Simon what I had learned, I was able to put it in better perspective.

Was there anything really suspicious in what Julia had told me? Or was it my imagination looking to support my own belief about how Major Carson had died?

I sealed the letter and set it out for the post, then went to bed.

I was kept busy over the next few days. One patient was on the brink of developing gangrene, and with my battlefield experience Matron asked me to work in the surgical theater with Dr. Gaines.

When I went to read to the ambulatory, Captain Lawrence had been scanning a newspaper, and as he set it aside, I glimpsed a photograph on the page turned up. It was Mrs. Campbell. I couldn't see the full caption, but the first part read DIVORCEE ARRESTED FOR—

For what?

When the hour was over, I was summoned to the surgical theater again. An abscess required draining. As the patient was being taken away for recovery, Dr. Gaines said to me, "You really ought to be in France, you know. Your skills are wasted here."

Surprised by his praise, I said, "My family was frightened by my illness. I think they pulled strings to keep me in England."

He nodded and said nothing more. I realized I'd been too honest, but I didn't want him to believe that I had run away from the nightmare of nursing there. Pride, I told myself, sometimes had much to answer for.

But then my ancestress, who had sent her husband off to face Napoleon at Waterloo and danced through the night to conceal the fact that experienced officers had been called to duty, would have appreciated my dilemma. She had helped keep the townspeople of Brussels calm and unsuspecting. It was her duty to the cause, even though she knew she might never see her husband alive again. Perhaps I had inherited a little of her strength. I'd like to think so.

The following day we faced a long and very difficult surgery as we fought to clean a suppurating wound and save a man's leg. It had been a near run thing, and the smell of the infection had filled the tiny surgical theater, nearly sickening us, but when the last stitch had been taken, the wound dressed, Dr. Gaines nodded to me and walked out of the room. I could see how exhausted he was, but I was impressed with his skills and dedication. It would have been much easier simply to amputate the lower part of the leg and be done with it. There was always the shadow of gangrene hanging over such cases. But he had done what he could to leave the patient whole.

I had hoped this morning might bring Simon's response to my letter, but there was nothing for me in the post. Instead, summoned to Matron's office as I finished changing into a fresh uniform, I found him waiting for me there.

Matron said, "Your father has sent a message by Sergeant-Major Brandon. I'll leave you to speak to him in private."

Simon thanked her, waiting until the door had closed behind her and the sound of her footsteps had faded down the passage, before saying to me in a low voice, "Will you walk in the park with me?"

"Is anything wrong?"

"Not at home," he said briefly. I nodded, and we left Matron's office and went out into the park where we couldn't be overheard even by chance.

"The only Colonel Prescott I could find in the lists is an officer in the Royal Engineers. As you'd expect, he never commanded Major Carson. I can't say whether or not they ever met, but I doubt it. Carson's commanding officer was Colonel Travers."

"Julia must have been mistaken," I said doubtfully. "But she was impressed by his kindness in his letter, and surely she'd have got his name right when she spoke to me."

"This tends to support your dream. I'm beginning to believe there was indeed a murder."

"Have you said anything to my father about this matter?"

"No. He'd order an immediate inquiry, and I don't think we have sufficient proof to make this public. Besides, it would be cruel to upset Mrs. Carson if none of this turns out to be true. Early days."

"I should think that letter of condolence to a family giving false information about an officer's death would be a place to start."

"To start, yes. I'd like to see this carried to a conclusion."

"Yes. But, Simon, what about the journal? He read portions of it to Julia. It must exist!"

"There's no certainty that it has anything to do with his death."

"I know. One can hope. There must be answers *somewhere*. I must speak to Private Wilson's family. Not that I expect to learn anything from them, but if they also find it hard to believe that he killed himself, then it supports my own feeling."

"I did one other bit of research while I was in London. Remember Sabrina Carson, who married a reprobate? Your mother told me she wasn't at the memorial service. Whether it's against his will or not, William Morton is in the Army. Most likely called up and threatened with desertion if he didn't appear at the proper time." There was contempt in Simon's voice. He had no sympathy for a man who refused to serve his country in its hour of need. "His wife is living on a private soldier's pay. That may explain why she couldn't afford to travel to the memorial service."

"Or to dress appropriately," I added. "That would matter to her."

"I hadn't considered that possibility. Nevertheless, Morton was in a Wiltshire regiment that was depleted, and it was combined with ours. It could have caused friction between the two men."

"But Julia told me he was in the Royal Engineers."

"Sabrina could have lied to her. Wasn't he an actor, and not a very good one at that? Attached to a third-rate touring company that barely stayed one step ahead of the bailiffs? I shouldn't put it past him to tell his wife what she wanted to hear."

"My mother told me once that he reminded her of the snake charmers in India, luring unsuspecting girls out of their homes the way the snake charmer lured the cobra out of its basket."

"Depend upon your mother to make an apt comparison."

"What am I to do now?"

"Nothing. Let me explore several avenues, and see what I can discover. London has sent for me, and I'm on my way there now. Give me a few days to attend to that, and I'll be back in touch." We had nearly reached the house in our walk. "I wouldn't make too much of this yet, Bess," he warned me. "But Morton might not have passed up a chance to rid himself of his brother-in-law."

"I'm torn," I admitted. "I'd rather not have to tell Julia that her husband was murdered."

"Remember that you're the only other person to have seen that body," Simon reminded me. "Take care. At this stage, I'm damned glad you *aren't* in France."

I sighed. "There's that. All right. Be safe, Simon, whatever it is that London wants. Is my father summoned as well?"

"I won't know until I get there."

And he was gone, in a hurry to reach London because he had already taken precious time to come and speak to me.

I watched his motorcar out of sight, then turned to find the Yank standing in the doorway behind me.

"The family friend Mr. Brandon, I presume? Why isn't he at the Front?"

"It's a long story," I said. "And not for your ears."

He followed me inside. "Sorry, I was more than a little jealous. You don't hang on my every word the way you hang on his."

I turned. "Did *you* just arrive with news of my family?"

"I did not. I misjudged the visit. Why do I seem always to be apologizing to you?"

"Because you tend not to look before you leap," I retorted, and left him standing there.

On my next free afternoon, I once more asked Dr. Gaines to allow me to borrow his motorcar.

He didn't quiz me on my skills as a driver—apparently he'd received a good report from Captain Barclay—but again he insisted that I take an escort with me.

And once more it was the American Captain waiting for me at the door when I came down from changing into a fresh uniform.

"Where to this time?"

I glanced over my shoulder, but no one was within hearing. "We're going to see one of the wonders of Britain. Cheddar Gorge. It's a deep natural ravine slashed through stone. Amazing, really. I'll drive the length of it and show you. But first there's someone I'd like very much to visit."

"Another widow of an officer in your father's old regiment?" There was an undercurrent of suspicion in his voice, as if I found that to be a handy excuse for my assignations.

"The family of a man I served with just before I was taken ill. He's dead." I had to smile to myself at the thought of the Captain feeling jealous of Private Wilson.

But he only nodded as we set off down the drive, as if time would tell.

As the crow flew, Cheddar Gorge was not all that far from Longleigh House, but the crow didn't always fly the way the road makers went. It was a twisting, turning route that led us to where we were going.

The Gorge is some three miles long, narrow at some points, wider at others, with towering limestone ramparts on either side. Quite a spectacular drive, really, through a place where it was said early cave dwellers found sanctuary.

As we approached the Gorge, I could see the small house that sat to one side. If this was not where Private Wilson lived, the occupants could tell me where to look. Old and weathered, the house must have been freshly painted shortly before the war because it appeared to be in better condition than some of its neighbors. Behind it rose a small barn, and I glimpsed several sheds as well. There were black-and-white cows grazing quietly in a meadow on our left.

"This is where Cheddar cheese comes from," I told the Captain. "It was aged in the coolness of the caves you'll see in a bit, after we've finished here."

"I thought Cheddar cheese came from New York," he told me with a grin. "That's where we buy it, at least."

"There's no pub that I can see just here," I said, ignoring his attempt at humor. "But would you mind terribly waiting for me in the motorcar? Mrs. Wilson will be shy enough finding me on her doorstep. You'll frighten her."

"Don't worry. Go speak to her. I'll be fine."

I thanked him, got down, and went up the walk to the front of the house. Marigolds bloomed in clay pots on the steps, and a cat slept on a cushion by the door.

It rose at my approach, stretched and yawned, then waited to be let into the house when Mrs. Wilson answered my knock.

She wasn't quite what I'd expected. A pretty woman in her late thirties, she said pleasantly, "Are you lost, love? The entrance to the Gorge is just down the road over there."

"My name is Sister Elizabeth Crawford. I've come to see a Mrs. Wilson. I knew her husband in France. I was a nursing sister in the aid station where he served as an orderly."

"I'm Joyce Wilson," she said after a moment. "Will you come in?"

"Yes, thank you." I followed her into a neat parlor where nothing was out of place except a yarn ball that obviously belonged to the cat. It had come with us into the room and jumped into a tall rocker that stood by the cold hearth.

"That was my husband's favorite chair," she told me, reaching down to touch the cat's head. I could hear it purr from where I stood. "Toby remembers and often sits there of an evening. He's company, he is." Her Somerset accent was nearly impenetrable.

"Do you have children?" I asked.

"A daughter. I've sent Audrey away to live with my sister. I didn't want her to hear what was being said about her father."

It was my opening. I had wondered how to bring up such a difficult subject.

"For what it's worth, Mrs. Wilson, I cannot in good conscience believe that your husband killed himself. I worked with him day in and day out, you see, and I knew how he felt about what he was doing. Yes, it was depressing work, sad work, often heartbreaking work, tending to the dead. But he took pride in doing it well and with respect."

I hadn't meant to be so forceful, but as I sat in that tidy parlor with a woman whose husband had been branded a suicide, I couldn't stop myself.

Her face crumpled at my words. She said after a moment, her voice husky, "I never believed it myself. Not Jerry. He knew he was too old to fight, but he felt he could do something to help stop the Hun. Even as an orderly. When did you see him last?"

"I was nursing our influenza patients as well as the wounded, and then without warning, I myself was stricken with it. I remember a soldier named Benson dying and your husband bringing in the stretcher bearers to carry the—er—him out to the place where we took the dead while they were awaiting the burial detail. He was himself that evening, and I saw nothing in his face or his bearing to warn me that he was distressed in any way or worried about his own health. There were many people—sisters, doctors, orderlies—who worked with the ill and never fell ill themselves. He had no reason to think he might be the next victim."

"I'm grateful to you for coming so far to tell me this, Sister. It was very kind of you. I shall take comfort from it. I've had precious little of that since Jerry died, I can tell you. But why would anyone report my husband hanged himself, when neither you nor I believe he would or even could?"

"I don't know. There must be times when there are so many dead and dying that the rolls are confused. It's all I can offer you as a reason." It wasn't true, but I wasn't prepared to add to her burden the possibility that Private Wilson was murdered.

"Yes, but he hasn't written to me, so he must be dead. How did he die then?"

"From overwork—exhaustion. We weren't sleeping at all, and we ate only when we remembered and there was time. It took a toll on all of us. And Private Wilson was nearing forty, wasn't he?"

"He was forty-one his last birthday."

"That could explain it."

"I still don't see how a mistake could have been made," she insisted.

"I don't know myself. But I'm going back to France as soon as possible, and I'll find out what I can. You may not hear immediately. But I shall write after I've spoken to Matron and some of the others he and I served with."

"I'll be forever in your debt, Sister, if you could do that for me. For him. It isn't fair for him to be treated like a leper if he did nothing wrong. Or for Audrey to be singled out as the daughter of a suicide."

"There was nothing at home—you or your child—to worry him?"

"Nothing at all. We've done better than most, having only a small farm, too small to have our crops taken from us. We eat what we grow, and we manage very well. There's hardly anything to buy, is there, with shortages everywhere one turns. And so his pay was enough for us. I don't know as I get a pension, under the circumstances. What worries me now is finding someone to help with the cows and the milking and general handiwork, what Jerry always did. I can't pay now, you see. And there's other farms that do."

All the more reason to get to the bottom of what happened to Private Wilson.

Aloud, I said, "Did he write often, your husband?"

"His last letter came barely a week after he died. It wasn't anything out of the ordinary. He sounded like himself, though tired, as you'd expect, and he gave me advice about matters here on the farm, as he always did, remembering what time of the year it was. I was that shocked when the word came. I sat here until three o'clock in the morning, trying to take it in. Except for Toby, I told no one. And cats don't talk, do they? But soon enough word got round. I don't know how they found out, but people did. And so I sent my daughter out of harm's way. That left just Toby and me to do all that needs to be done. But we'll survive somehow. Our kind always does."

It was a sad commentary on the future.

We talked a little longer, and at one point she said, "I'd give anything to have my man back again. And then that woman in London behaves so badly she's divorced. It doesn't make sense, does it? Why couldn't *her* husband have died, if she was so eager to be free? Not wishing him harm, you understand, but let me keep mine."

I did understand. I rose to leave soon after, and she went with me to the door, thanking me again for coming to tell her what I believed.

I walked to the motorcar with a heavy heart.

Whoever had killed Private Wilson had much to answer for.

As promised I drove the rough track that passed for a road running through Cheddar Gorge. The limestone walls, often sheer, rose over four hundred feet high and in places were honeycombed with shallow crevices or deep caves. The entrance was half hidden by cheese shops, tea shops, and souvenir stalls, most of them closed for the duration, but beyond we could crane our necks and see the tops of the ramparts. I'd always found it an impressive sight, even though I'd viewed the great peaks of the Himalayas. The deeper into the Gorge we went, the more wild and mysterious it seemed to be, only the sounds of our motorcar breaking the silence and the calls of a crow that resented it. Even as we drove out into lower but still hilly countryside, I felt as I always did, that people had lived here for a long time. It would have offered sanctuary in a time of uncertainty.

Beside me Captain Barclay stared about with interest, and I thought for once he had been struck speechless, this American who had an answer for everything.

When finally we reached the far side of the Gorge where the land evened out, I turned to him and said, "Isn't it a marvelous sight?"

He agreed, although his praise was rather subdued. I was pleased I'd brought him here.

On the way back to Longleigh House, he cleared his throat and said, "Sister, if you want the truth, there's really nothing like this in Michigan, although there's a small ravine on Mackinac Island. But I've been to the Grand Canyon, you see, and it's stunning. Your Gorge, for all it's fine enough, can't hold a candle to the one in Arizona. I just didn't want to belittle yours by comparing them."

Put out with him all the same, I said nothing. He grinned. "You have to remember," he said, "that England's a *little* country."

Later, before taking up my evening duties, I wrote to Simon, telling him what I'd learned talking with Joyce Wilson, and reminding him that it wasn't just Major Carson whose fate needed to be clarified.

I expected to hear from him any day now, hoping that he'd been able to find out more information somehow, something that would lead us to the next step. But there was no news.

When it came, the letter I did receive shocked me.

It was from the headquarters of Queen Alexandra's Imperial Military Nursing Service.

And inside were my orders to return immediately to France.

CHAPTER SIX

I REALLY DIDN'T know how to respond to the news. It was what I had wanted from the moment in Eastbourne when I felt well enough to consider my future.

Had Simon pulled strings to make this possible?

I couldn't imagine my mother and father having a change of heart.

And what was I to tell them, when these orders hadn't been any of my doing?

I went to Matron, to speak to her about my concerns, but when I broached the subject, she smiled warmly. "Ah. I see they've come through. I didn't wish to say anything until we could be sure. We shall be very sorry to lose you, my dear, but Dr. Gaines spoke to me, and I must say, I agreed with him. You should be in France, not here. And so he wrote to the proper people, expressing his feelings in the matter, and I am glad to learn that they decided in your favor."

I could only sit there, stunned.

It was as if a godmother in a fairy tale had granted a fervent wish, but left the recipient to deal with the aftermath of that wish being granted.

"You seem surprised, Sister Crawford. I should have thought you would be delighted by such news."

"I am," I told her truthfully. "I—it's just that I'm not sure how to break it to my father."

"He's been a serving officer all his life. He'll understand the importance of duty, if anyone does," she said bracingly. "Now to particulars. You'll finish the week with us, take three days of leave to visit your family and prepare for this posting, and then report to France."

It occurred to me that I had promised Julia Carson that I would come to see her again, and now there would be no opportunity.

"I'm very grateful, Matron. It's such a surprise, it will take some time to get used to."

The smile returned. "Of course. And I needn't ask you not to tell your patients until the last day. We find that staff leaving often unsettles them."

"I'll say nothing," I promised.

But where was Simon, and what would he think when he came here to see me after finishing whatever it was that had taken him to London, only to find me out of reach? And how would I learn whatever it was he might have discovered, given the censorship of the post to and from France?

There was another worry. Would I be in danger? But no one knew what I suspected. At least I hoped no one knew except for Simon and Private Wilson's widow.

Changing the subject, Matron was now discussing a patient, and I forced my thoughts back to the present.

When I was dismissed, I knew I should seek out Dr. Gaines at once and thank him for his intercession. Instead I went outside to the park where Simon and I had spoken privately, and as I walked I tried to think.

I couldn't turn down my orders. They had been cut, and even the Colonel Sahib, as my mother and I called him, would find it difficult to cancel them now. I should have to make the best of it, go to France and do what I did so well: help save lives.

I met Dr. Gaines as I was walking back to the house. He'd come in search of me, and he said as I approached, "There you are. Matron tells me your orders have been cut."

"Yes, thank you, Dr. Gaines, it was very kind of you."

"Nonsense. You're a good nurse. Now come inside and we'll unwrap that leg and have a look. Tell me what you think."

He was being polite, of course. But I went with him and the Lieutenant's leg was looking much better. We cleansed it again and put on fresh bandages. Dr. Gaines nodded to the owner of the leg, who had been watching us with such anxiety that my heart went out to him. A Yorkshireman, he said little, but his eyes spoke for him. "You'll keep it, Lieutenant, and live to fight another day. If you follow instructions for the next few weeks."

We made rounds, looking at Captain Scott's damaged shoulder, Lieutenant Fraser's badly fractured hand, Major Donovan's shrapnel-shattered hip, and a dozen more cases the doctors were watching closely. When we'd finished, I was released from duty and allowed to go up to my room.

Halfway to the stairs, I encountered the American. He said without preamble, "You're leaving."

"You shouldn't be listening at doors," I informed him. "You seldom hear the truth."

"It's something in your face," he said. "Never mind, I'll be back in France before you know it. Keep watch for me."

"Captain. Don't be silly. You'll lose that leg if you aren't more careful. How many times does Dr. Gaines have to warn you?"

"I know. I have an incentive now to take my exercises seriously. *And*," he added with a gleam in his eye, "Simon Brandon will still be in England."

Without waiting for me to reply, he hobbled away.

Dr. Gaines himself drove me home when the time came. I was rather surprised by that, but then I remembered what I had told him about going back to France. I expect he felt that his presence would in some fashion soften the blow for my parents.

I hadn't called to warn my parents that I was coming. I saw my mother's face as she opened the door and found us standing there. The succession of emotions touched my heart. Surprise. Fear. Anger. Resignation. They were all there. I presented Dr. Gaines, and she took us to the drawing room, rather than to her sitting room, a measure of her feelings. But she was politeness itself, apologizing for the fact that the Colonel Sahib was away at the moment, asking the doctor about the clinic, and carefully channeling the conversation away from the reason for my being there.

Finally, when there was nothing else to be said, Dr. Gaines cleared his throat and told my mother precisely what had happened and why.

She didn't argue with him. Instead she thanked him with apparent sincerity and asked if he'd care to stay for dinner.

"Alas, no, I have my evening rounds, and I shall be late for them as it is. But thank you for your kindness." He turned to me and wished me well. "Write to us if you will. I know that Matron, the staff, and the patients who know you will be delighted to hear how you are faring. And one patient in particular who asked me only this morning to find a reason to keep you at Longleigh House."

I smiled in return. "I shall," I promised. And with that, and a last glance at my mother, he was gone.

She closed the door behind him and said, "Well. As I have always said, things have a way of working out."

"I didn't ask Dr. Gaines to intercede," I assured her.

"Darling, I know. And he made that quite clear, so that there would be no doubt in our minds." She put her arm around my shoulders and pulled me close for a moment. "Love sometimes sees the future crookedly. It tries to convince us we know what's best. When the call came from France—it was that Australian of yours. Sergeant Larimore. I don't quite know how he learned that you might be dying, but he felt someone would wish to be with you at the end—I couldn't quite think what to do. Your father was in London, he wouldn't be home for another four-and-twenty hours, and I didn't have the proper papers to allow me to go to France on my own. Simon had just landed in Dover, and so we sent him to you. I don't know what mountains he and your father moved to make it possible for him to go at once. When he got word to us that you would live, it was a miracle. As if God had granted us a reprieve at the last possible moment when all hope had gone. It took some time to recover from that shock. Perhaps we were wrong to want to keep you safe in England, but we too had to heal."

I hadn't known all this. I had assumed that ill as I was, and being the Colonel's only child, I'd been sent back to England to recover properly.

I had attended Sergeant Larimore in the winter, when he was wounded, and because of him I had learned firsthand how swiftly word could travel at the Front. I felt a rush of gratitude for what he'd done.

It was a measure of my parents' fear that no one had told me until now. As if it would bring back for them what must have been long, terrifying hours of not knowing.

If I had been in France and was told that one of my parents was dying, I would have felt much the same helplessness. And so I could understand. Indeed, there had been a fortnight when I had had no news and feared the worst.

"We must consider what to have for dinner," she said bracingly, changing the subject before we were both brought to tears. "I was planning to dine alone, and now here you are. Let's talk to Cook and see what's possible."

I left Somerset before my father came back from whatever mission had taken him away this time. My mother made the best of what she must have considered to be a bad bargain and sent me off with freshly ironed uniforms, a packet of sandwiches, and her love, as she'd always done.

When I reached Portsmouth after a long and wearing journey on the train, shunted from siding to siding as troop trains hurtled through, given precedence, I was walking through the dark and crowded port to find my own transport when I saw a tall figure in uniform making his way toward me.

It was my father, calling to me as he recognized me, enveloping me in an embrace that expressed, more than anything, his belief that he wouldn't be in time.

"There you are!" he said. "I've moved heaven and earth—and more to the point, the War Office—to get here before you sailed, and I thought I'd missed you in spite of everything."

"How did you know?" I asked. "Did Mother reach you?"

"Someone from the Canadian Army reached me. He told me where to find you."

That ridiculous American, I thought, *hoping to stop me from leaving by summoning my father to meet me here.*

But I was wrong about his motives.

My father was saying, "God knows how he found out where I was. I am most grateful he did. Of course I shall most likely be sent to the Tower for leaving London so precipitously. He must know people in very high places. Perhaps he will also arrange my pardon."

I laughed, as I was intended to do. "I never told him that you were away. I wasn't aware of it myself until Mother told me."

"You know him, then, do you? This Canadian?"

"It's a long story. And he's an American serving with the Canadian forces. I can't think why he should even guess where or how to find you."

Somewhere down the quay a blast of a ship's horn, muffled but still loud in the damp night air, reminded me that I hadn't yet located my transport.

"Look, there isn't much time. Simon told me about Vincent Carson. I don't want you involved with this business, Bess. Leave it to us. I have ways of finding out what we need to know about this Colonel of his. And if I can track down his grave, I can ask to have the body exhumed in the hope of discovering the cause of death. Are you quite certain that his journal wasn't there when you found him?"

"He'd been stripped of his uniform, and there was no way to know even what rank he held or in what regiment. The burial detail would have no choice but to put him in a grave marked UNKNOWN. What's more, there were no possessions to be sent to his family. If I hadn't recognized him when Private Wilson showed me the body, no one would have known the truth. We'd have believed he'd died in the trenches, just as it was reported."

The Colonel winced at that. "And as far as Simon could discover, Private Wilson never officially reported finding the Major's body. Which means if he did speak to someone else, it cost him his life. Listen to me. If anyone approaches you, trying in any way to discover what you know—even someone you believe you can trust— send word at once but let them believe your high fever erased any memory of what happened the evening you fell ill. Ignorance will keep you safe, my dear. Remember that."

"Yes, I understand," I told him, and only a few minutes later, he was waving to me from the quay while I stood by the rail, watching until the crowded docks blocked him from view.

Why had Simon chosen to tell the Colonel Sahib about Vincent Carson's death?

There hadn't been time to ask, but I could think of two reasons— Simon needed my father's authority to open doors shut to him.

Or he was going into danger and felt that the time had come to protect me by bringing my father into the picture. Pray God this was *not* the reason. But it had been too long since last I heard from him, and in ordinary circumstances he would have found a way to get in touch.

And it worried me as well that Captain Barclay had reached my father. Even my mother had had no idea where he was.

* * *

Although I was offered a cabin, I had too much on my mind to rest. And so I remained at the rail of *The Mermaid,* a former ferry turned transport ship, and watched the long, dark shape of the Isle of Wight slip by in the night. The wind was unseasonably cold, coming off the water, and I looked up at the bridge to see the watch scanning the seas for German raiders. All lights were out, and the only sounds beside the wind were the engines, a deep and reassuring throb.

I was not the only recovered invalid on board. A good few officers and other ranks I saw on deck were in my opinion still too pale and too thin to return to active duty. But there was that other driving force a soldier understood only too well: the need to be there with those he'd had to leave behind for the duration of his recovery. I read it there later in the intensity of their gaze watching for the first faint blue haze that was France looming on the horizon. The determination not to let the side down, even if it meant dying with them.

Someone found a chair for me, and I sat there, waiting patiently for the journey to end. I was not going back to the hospital where the body of Vincent Carson had been discovered by Private Wilson. Still it was possible for me to get there if I looked for the opportunity. Patient transfers, picking up supplies—there was always traffic of some sort between forward aid stations and those behind the lines.

And then the buffeting of the Channel ceased, and we were moving up the Seine, our destination Rouen. I stood at the rail, picking out landmarks. Gripping my valise, I watched men on the quay bringing *The Mermaid* in close and tying her up. Then we were ordered to prepare for disembarkation, troops to report in companies. One of the officers nodded to me, indicating I should be among the first to land. But the way had no more than been cleared when the tall, fair Australian who'd contacted my mother appeared out of nowhere, coming up the gangway in long, swift strides to enclose me in a huge embrace, swinging me off my feet.

"You're alive. I had to see it for myself," he said. "Your mother, bless her, is a rare lady."

Laughing, I commanded him to put me down.

Behind me, an English officer said angrily, "I'll have you on report for that, Sergeant."

Sergeant Larimore set me down, turned to him, and said blandly, lying through his teeth, "She's my English cousin, sir." And then leaning closer to whisper in my ear, he said, "I'm that glad you're alive, my lass. I couldn't contemplate a world without your shining face. Now I know you're safe, I must report to my unit. I've been on leave without permission for the past two days, watching for you."

And he was gone, disappearing into the crowded quayside before I could say a word or ask him who had told him I was even sailing to France.

It must have been my mother. The American didn't know about Sergeant Larimore.

"Cousin, indeed," snorted the officer behind me.

"Alas, sir, the black sheep," I replied. With that I nodded to the ship's officer and walked sedately off *The Mermaid* and into Rouen.

I was back in France at last. As I made my way toward the American Base Hospital, where I was to meet my convoy, I could hear the guns in the distance. Someone jostled my shoulder, apologized in rough French, and another man, appearing to be in a great hurry, brushed past me, nearly causing me to drop my valise. I realized all at once how vulnerable I was, alone in a city of this size. I hadn't really taken thought to the danger I might be in until now, where I was surrounded by people on their way to market or the port or the waiting trains. I didn't know the face of my enemy, if he was that. But it occurred to me that I could disappear here, and even my father, with all his authority, couldn't find me in the muddy bottom of the river.

* * *

I was glad to see my next transport waiting just beyond the port—an ambulance packed with supplies to replace the depleted stocks of aid units closer to the Front. The driver was someone I didn't know, a taciturn man who told me his name was Sam and we were late already, Sister, so don't dawdle, please, Miss.

I took the seat beside the driver, my valise tucked into a tiny space in the back, and we set out, steadily moving north as the roads, the traffic, and the terrain allowed. I asked what news he had of the war, and he said, "The Germans are winning all along the line. That's what it feels like, Sister, when I drive the dying here."

It was a bleak assessment, and I hoped that it was wrong. The Americans were supposed to be turning the balance toward the Allies. We fell silent and I watched the trains of mules and guns and columns of troops making their way toward the shooting, and the line of wounded being transported to the rear in Rouen. There had been heavy rain the day before, according to Sam, and the roads were a morass. We bumped and jerked and skidded over them until my head was beginning to ache from all the jolting. There was nothing for it but to endure.

At length we were close enough to the trenches that in the darkness I could actually see the muzzle flashes. The noise was deafening. When we reached the aid station, I could pick out the long line of wounded standing or lying on stretchers outside the nearest tent, and a doctor with a haggard face looked up anxiously as he heard the rumble of the ambulance coming in, and then shouted to me, "Hurry!"

There was no time to find my tent or change my clothes. I left my coat and valise in a corner, borrowed an apron from someone, and began to sort the cases as they arrived. The driver was offloading supplies, and hands were reaching for bandages and septic powder almost as quickly as they were unpacked.

Hours later, when I was finally replaced, I walked out into the pale light of another dawn.

Working those long hours had cost me dearly, for my parents were right, I wasn't at full strength yet. The clinic had been almost too easy, with its regular hours and quiet evenings. And now, too tired to sleep, I nursed a cup of tea in the cool of sunrise and considered the problem of finding the elusive Colonel Prescott.

I could hardly go about asking officers who came to the aid station if they had served under him. I knew too well how quickly word got around.

Whoever he was, how could he have known when he wrote that glowing letter to Julia that Major Carson was dead, unless he had had something to do with whatever had happened? Why else would he have written it, except to allay worry at home? It had sounded genuine enough, compassionate, sympathetic. And of course it had had to sound that way, in order not to arouse suspicion. After all, Julia Carson had the regiment behind her, and my father, once its Colonel, as well. If the Major simply disappeared, questions would be raised.

And then there were the men under the Major. What had *they* been told?

I was to have my answer to that a few days later.

We had been busy all morning and well into the afternoon. Then there were a few blessed minutes of grace, and I went to my quarters to change my bloody apron for a fresh one when a woman's voice called my name. I turned to see Diana hurrying toward me.

Because our own homes were scattered across England, four other nurses and I had taken a flat together in Mrs. Hennessey's London house, converted to flats for the duration of the war. A widow, Mrs. Hennessey was strict with her young ladies, and it was a comfort to know that we were in good hands when one of us arrived late at night, tired and thankful not to have to find an hotel or face a longer journey elsewhere when we had scarcely twenty-four hours of leave.

Diana threw her arms around me, crying, "I can't believe it's you! Bess? We were so worried. When your mother wrote to say you were recovering, I was afraid to open the letter for two days." She scanned my face. "Still a little tired, I see. I was afraid you might come back too soon."

I held her at arm's length. "You're absolutely blooming yourself."

She blushed a little. "Bess, wish me happy! I'll be married this time next year. I wasn't sure you'd seen the announcement in the *Times*."

"But that's tremendous news. I wish you both a glorious life together. You deserve it."

"Thank you. I'm so grateful you didn't want him for yourself. You could have had him, you know."

I laughed. "Diana. The instant he saw you, I was forgotten. Love at first sight, if ever I witnessed such a thing. And how are the others? Mrs. Hennessey?"

"She is flourishing, Mary is back in France after her bout with influenza, and the others are due for leave any day now."

"I'm so glad."

"Your family? My dearest Simon?"

It was a long-standing joke between us. Simon sometimes took her to dinner when I wasn't in London, and Diana swore he did it to make me jealous. And I could see that she thoroughly enjoyed those invitations. Perhaps more so than she had been willing to admit until another man had come into her life. "They're well, thank goodness." I hoped it was true in Simon's case. I was still waiting for word.

We exchanged news of other friends, and then Diana said, "Wasn't Major Carson in your father's regiment?"

Surprised to hear her bring up his name, I replied warily, "Yes, indeed. In fact, I called on Julia Carson, just before I returned to France."

"What I'm about to tell you won't be for her ears, but the Colonel might wish to know. There's a whisper going around. That he's deserted."

She was using the present tense. As if she hadn't heard that Vincent Carson was dead. My shock must have been reflected in my face. "I—I can't imagine such a thing. Major Carson? No, there must be some mistake . . ." I let my voice trail off, encouraging her to go on.

"The story I overheard was that he was pulled from his sector for a special assignment and never made his rendezvous."

"Good heavens." It was all I could think to say. Collecting my wits, I added, "He—he's such a very conscientious man. There's even talk that one day he'll follow my father as Colonel. I can't think what would cause him to desert."

"Yes, well, you know how gossip is. The only thing I could think of was shell shock, and that he has no idea who or where he is. I met him at that dinner party your mother gave just after war was declared. If he hadn't already been married to Julia, I'd have set my cap at him."

"The two of you would never suit," I said drily, grateful she'd changed the subject.

"True. Well, I must drive an ambulance to Rouen. The man who should be doing it collapsed two hours ago. Pneumonia. And then I have ten days' leave. I could fly to Dover at the very thought."

I said quickly, "Could you carry a message for me? If I was quick about it? I don't want it going through the censors."

"A love letter? Bess, who is the lucky man? I'd heard there was an Australian in your life. Is he history now?"

"This is to Simon. I have to get information to him and have been racking my brain to find a way."

"I have less than two minutes."

"Yes, of course." I ran to my quarters, scrabbled in my valise for pen and paper and an envelope, then scribbled what Diana had told me on the sheet. There was no time to reread it. I sealed it in the envelope and wrote the direction on it, praying that he would be at his cottage to receive it. If he wasn't, my parents always collected his post in his absences, so that no one would realize he was away so often.

Breathless, I hurried back to Diana, gave her the letter, and watched her drive off with her usual care for the patients in the back, one of them the regular driver.

Quickly changing, I went back to my duties, regretting only that Diana and I had had so little time together. I'd have liked to hear more about her wedding plans and remind her that I would like to be included in the wedding party.

I was dazed with fatigue when I finished my shift, and collapsed on my cot, falling into a deep sleep.

Toward morning I dreamed that I had gone into the shed where the dead were taken to look for Major Carson, anxious to find his body before the charge of desertion was brought against him. Certain that if I could show his broken neck to his commanding officer, I could clear his name. But what I found instead was Private Wilson hanging there, his body already limp in death, his face gorged with blood, making him nearly unrecognizable. I'd had to peer at him, and as the corpse swung at the end of the rope, his hand touched me and I screamed.

Sister Colter said, "Really, Bess, you told me to wake you at six."

I came awake with a start, looking up at her. "I'm so sorry," I managed to say. "I must not have heard you calling me."

"You were so deeply asleep you wouldn't have heard a cavalry charge," she agreed, and was gone, leaving me to wash my face and put on my uniform.

I was still shaken by the dream as I gulped a cup of tea, then hurried to deal with the line of men waiting for attention.

There was still no response from Simon by the end of the week, and I wasn't sure where he was. A letter had come from my mother, letting me know that everyone was well, and there had been no mention of Simon being away so long. Either he was at home and safe, or she was being circumspect.

And then the next morning as I walked into the surgical tent, I saw his tall figure just ahead of me.

Simon was making his way down the row of severely wounded men, stopping at each cot, speaking quietly to the men who were conscious, simply looking down at the ones who were not. When he reached the end of the line, he turned back and saw me.

According to my mother, both Simon and my father visited the wounded often, and without fanfare, wherever they happened to be.

There was something about both men that made them popular wherever they went, and their compassion for the ill and the dying was infinite. They had been soldiers with impressive records themselves, but it went beyond that. War seemed to forge a brotherhood that made someone like Captain Barclay claim he was healing even when it was a lie. Even when he knew that going back to France might well end in his own death.

I watched as Simon had a word for each man, making one or two of them smile, and he offered comfort to those who were suffering in grim silence.

I waited until he came up to me. Nodding, he said, "Outside?"

I followed him into a dusk lit by artillery flashes. Once or twice, I could see bursts of machine-gun fire. He turned his back to that, saying, "I must be brief. I'm supposed to be in Dover. I got your message. It seems that orders came down from HQ to send Carson as liaison to the French forces. He must never have reached the meeting with his opposite number—but the odd thing is, whoever that was, he never reported Carson missing. What's more, no one can be certain where the order originated. The signature is a scrawl."

"That explains how his murderer got to him, doesn't it?" I responded softly. "Once out of the lines, following a guide he didn't know, he could have been lured to his death. But why? Why kill Major Carson?"

"There are bodies and wounded men everywhere. No one notices one more."

"Private Wilson did. And was killed because of it."

"I want you to make a list, as comprehensive as you can, of everyone who was in and out of that aid station."

"Simon, do you realize how impossible that is?" I expostulated.

"I don't mean the dead and dying. Orderlies who were there for a week or more are not likely candidates either, and a Sister couldn't break Carson's neck. He was too strong, too tall."

"Private Wilson would have known such things." I shut my eyes. Searching faces in my memory. After a moment I shook my head. "I may not have seen him. This killer has no face so far," I said finally. "I'll keep trying, but it's a needle in the proverbial haystack."

"And possibly the only lead we'll have."

He touched my shoulder in a comradely gesture. "Take care, Bess, whatever you do. I don't want to have to explain to your mother how it was you got hurt."

And then he was gone, disappearing into the night.

When the next ambulances went south with wounded who could be moved, I asked if I could be the nurse in charge. Dr. Hicks looked at me, said, "You could use a few hours of respite," and it was arranged.

I rode in the last ambulance, prepared to do what I could if we were forced to stop and attend to one of the men. It was a hard, jolting ride through mud and craters and ruts deeper than most axles, and was warm enough for the miasma to rise and envelop us with the unforgiving smells of the battlefield. I held on for dear life to avoid being shaken to death. But we reached our destination without mishap, blessedly everyone still alive.

Here was where I'd fallen so ill. Here was where Private Wilson had died. Had the staff changed? How many of them had survived?

I felt a wave of relief when I saw that Matron was the same woman I'd served with. She would be able to tell me about Private Wilson. After I'd turned my charges over to her, she invited me to her room for a cup of tea.

I hadn't expected the rush of emotion that I'd felt as the aid station had come into view. I couldn't help but wonder if matters would have been very different if my collapse had come an hour, even two, later and I'd had an opportunity to speak to her about what Private Wilson had shown me in the shed. Would he be alive now? Or would I simply have put Matron at risk too?

I tapped at her door, was admitted, and offered a chair.

"I can't tell you how good it is to see you healthy once more," she said warmly. "You gave us a terrible fright, you know." In the lamp's light I could see how worn she looked, and how tired.

"I'm so sorry."

"I've read about the great plagues of history," she said. "I never dreamed I would experience one. We lost so many good people."

"Did Private Wilson survive?" I asked, and immediately felt a surge of guilt for letting her assume I knew nothing about his death. "He handled so many bodies. I often wondered."

"Haven't you heard, my dear? He's dead."

"I wasn't told," I answered, which was true—I'd asked Simon to find out what had become of him. "He was always ready to do whatever we asked. Such a good man. Was it a lingering death or a kind one?"

Frowning, she said, "Odd that you should ask." She looked down at the chart in front of her, then raised her eyes to meet mine. "After you were taken ill, he came looking for you, but you were too feverish to answer whatever question he had intended to ask. Instead he left a message for me. I'd been awakened early—there was an emergency, you see—and before I was free to speak to him, one of his stretcher bearers came rushing into my office to say that Private Wilson had hanged himself in the shed. Dr. Harrison suggested that he'd begun to feel ill, that's why he'd sought a nurse. Then as his symptoms progressed, and he realized what lay in store, he decided to end it while he was still able. I was there when he was cut down, and I myself closed his eyes."

"Did you agree with Dr. Harrison's view?" A surgeon, he'd worked mainly with the wounded.

Looking away toward the door, she said, "I must say, as far as anyone knew, he didn't appear to be presenting symptoms. No fever, no aches, no dizziness. And so I've wondered, you know, if I'd been available, rather than having to put him off, perhaps I could have done something for him—given him an opportunity to tell me what was on his mind. I don't know if I could have helped, but I'd have tried. I did wonder if there was a problem at home. Several people asked for compassionate leave when their wives or a child died of the influenza."

But there had been no problem at home. I'd spoken to Mrs. Wilson.

"I don't know that anyone could have helped him," I said gently.

"Do you remember the onset of your symptoms?" she asked, turning back to me.

"Not really. Great fatigue, but we were all unbelievably tired, weren't we? A headache, I think. Dizziness."

"You told Sister Burrows that you felt cold, unable to warm yourself. And then you fainted. Your temperature climbed rapidly."

Surprised, I said, "I don't remember fainting. Or being so cold. But perhaps Dr. Harrison is right. Private Wilson knew what was coming and that he had to act quickly."

"I've tried to comfort myself with that thought. But there will always be that little niggling doubt."

There was no way I could assuage that sense of guilt. Not without telling her the whole truth. I could only agree that he was the last person I could imagine doing such a thing.

"We can't read minds, can we?" She took a deep breath. "I was glad it was not my duty to write to his wife. Dr. Bennett broke the news as gently as he could. "

"I don't remember Dr. Bennett," I said.

"No? He'd hardly arrived here when he was ordered to another station. Three of their doctors died in the epidemic." She finished her tea. "I must make my rounds," she said. "And you are needed elsewhere. It was good of you to come and see me, Sister Crawford."

And five minutes later, the ambulance, washed down and ready to go back the way we'd come, was there at the ward door

I had remembered nothing useful by coming here, I thought as we bounced and skidded over the broken ground. All I had confirmed was that Private Wilson had indeed killed himself. Or so it appeared. And perhaps he had, after all.

And then as if once I'd stopped trying, the memories crowded in, memories I hadn't looked for because I hadn't remembered they were there.

The man with the bandaged shoulder. I'd been standing outside the ward for a moment on that last evening before I fell ill. Another Sister had joined me there, both of us struggling with exhaustion and hoping to find in the fresh air, away from the odors of death and disease, a brief, desperately needed renewal. Yes, and I could almost see again how stained and frayed the bandaging was. The man had gone into the small, makeshift canteen, and I'd wanted to stop him and tell him to see to that wound before it turned septic beneath the filthy dressing.

Had he?

For that matter, was it truly a hasty field dressing? Or was it a disguise? There were so many men coming and going, all of them wounded, that one more hardly warranted notice.

With two sisters standing not twenty feet away, why hadn't he come to either of us to ask for help?

Sister, I've been waiting two hours or more, and nobody's had a look at this shoulder. I'm fair famished for my tea, but it's hurting like the very devil—begging your pardon, Sister—and I'm that light-headed from the pain . . .

We could have brought him his tea while the wound was being seen to. Why had he turned away?

There had been two officers passing by, limping.

Were they the reason he'd turned aside? Because he wasn't wounded after all and had just put a dead man in the shed, where he should never have been found by Private Wilson or seen by me?

It was a shocking possibility.

"Stop!" I said to the driver of the ambulance. "We must go back. I—I've forgot to pick up something for Dr. Hicks."

We had not come so great a distance that we couldn't turn back, but ambulances were badly needed at the Front, and as the driver was reminding me, I ought not be using one for personal errands. But the question I needed to ask Matron would only take a moment, no more. Unless, of course, the Sister was still there.

Grumbling, my driver did as he was told, motioning the remainder of the convoy to continue on its way and reversing as soon as he could. I sat there, trying to recall which sister I'd been talking with. So much of those last few hours before my collapse seemed to be shrouded in a haze.

Sister Burrows, that was it. I'd liked her. We'd worked very well together.

The driver stopped not far from the ward where Matron had her office, and said, "I shan't turn off the motor."

A reminder that time was passing. I splashed through the muddy, torn yard and scraped my shoes before knocking at her door.

"Come," she called, and I stepped in.

"Sister Crawford?" she said, surprised to see me. "Is there an emergency?"

"I had forgot—I have a message for Sister Burrows." It was the only thing I could think of to explain my returning so impetuously.

Matron frowned, emphasizing how much these last weeks had aged her. "Didn't you know? She died of the influenza not a week after you left us."

I didn't know what to say. Stammering, I finally replied, "No. I hadn't been told." Remembering my hasty improvisation, I added, "Nor had the young Lieutenant. I'm so very sorry."

"She was a fine nurse," Matron agreed. "She kept you alive, I think, until the crisis came. It was devotion to duty more than hope, but here you stand, living proof of her skill."

"Did—did nursing me contribute to her own illness?"

"I doubt it. Like you when the influenza struck, she had been on her feet for nearly thirty-six hours working with a new convoy of the infected, although the doctor had told her to take a few hours for sleep. They had turned the corner, most of them, when she fainted outside my door. That too is to her credit."

"I shall write to her family," I said. "Thank you, Matron."

I had turned to the door when her next words stopped me in my tracks. "You're the second person this week who has asked for her."

I forced myself to turn again slowly. "Who was he?" I asked.

"How did you know it was a man?" Matron demanded, the frown returning.

"I assumed it must be a patient. Or a former patient."

"Yes, I see. It was rather odd. His name was Prescott, he said. Colonel Prescott. He told me Sister Burrows had nursed his son, and that he'd come to thank her. It's always possible, of course, that he has a son in the Army. But Colonels seldom arrive without an entourage." She regarded me. "Not related to your young Lieutenant, by any chance, is he? I'd feel more comfortable if he were."

The last thing I wanted was to claim a connection with him. "I think not. My young Lieutenant was named Hennessey, and he came from her village." I could feel myself flushing as I lied so boldly.

"I expect Sister Burrows is the only one who could have told us what this was about."

"Do you recall what he looked like? The Colonel?"

"Prescott? Mustache. Dark hair. Very cold gray or perhaps blue eyes. I noticed them in particular. Possibly an inch or so short of six feet. A bulky man."

I tried to remember what I'd seen of the man with the bandaged shoulder. Surely he'd been fair?

I shook my head. "I don't think I remember a Prescott in our ward. Perhaps the son was one of those she nursed after I'd gone to England. Did you look at the lists?" We kept records of our patients. I was praying she would tell me he was there.

"No, the Colonel explained that his son was carried to the aid station where Sister Burrows had served before coming here. He'd had difficulty tracking her down, that's why it had taken so long to speak to her, he said."

"That could be true," I replied, thinking aloud. "Still, I'd have thought he was too busy to come in person."

"I wondered myself. But it's possible he's a better officer than he gave me the impression of being."

I could hear the ambulance horn sounding now. I'd been here longer than I'd expected.

"I wonder if his son could have confused Sister Burrows with someone else," I suggested, for Matron's sake. I didn't want her to be too curious about this Colonel Prescott and find herself his next victim. "Wounded men are so often in and out of consciousness—"

"I should have thought of that myself. It makes sense. Take care, Sister Crawford," she said. "Don't work yourself into a relapse."

"I promise."

And I was racing back to the ambulance, slipping quickly into my seat almost as the driver let in the clutch, and we were off.

This was the second appearance of "Colonel Prescott." I needed to pass the information along to Simon or my father. But it wasn't the sort of thing I could trust to the censors. He and my father had access to the military pouch on occasion, but I didn't.

I couldn't ask for leave. With the warming weather the influenza epidemic seemed to be waning, for we were beginning to see more wounded than feverish patients. Still, we were working around the clock, and nurses couldn't be spared.

But what to make of this visit from Colonel Prescott, whoever he was?

When I reached the forward aid station I was told I wasn't on call for six hours. And I was grateful—I could feel every mile in that ambulance in the stiffness of my body from clinging to my seat. But instead of sleeping, I found myself lying there, mulling over what to do. Simon had assured me that there was no Colonel Prescott presently on the rolls. He was seldom wrong about such things. The fact that there were rumors that Major Carson had deserted explained why his own commanding officer hadn't written to Julia. Why had a Colonel Prescott? And why had this same Colonel Prescott come looking for Sister Burrows? Had she seen him later that night when I'd been taken ill? Spoken to him?

I was finally drifting off into sleep when I remembered the orderly carrying a mop and pail.

Hadn't Sister Burrows promised to speak to him when he came by again, to ask him to bring a basket of clean linens to our ward? And if I'd come asking questions, she might have remembered that, especially if he'd never brought them. She could have described the man, surely.

But why had he risked coming openly to speak to Matron?

Because she would have no way of connecting him to that night.

The next thing I knew, someone was shaking my arm, trying to wake me out of a deep sleep.

I said, "Is it six o'clock already?" For it was still very dark outside as far as I could tell.

"Dr. Hicks wants you at once," Sister Hanby told me. "Hurry, it's an emergency."

I dragged myself out of bed and into my clothes before I was fully awake, running across to the tent where emergencies were dealt with. Dr. Hicks was standing in the doorway, waiting for me.

"There's a patient here who claims he knows you. You'd better come quickly, he's in a bad way."

My first thought was the Australian sergeant, wounded again. But when I saw the face of the man on the stretcher, his uniform cut off and dark blood pulsing from the wound on his shoulder in spite of what the nursing sister could do, I felt the world spin around me and thought for a moment I was going to faint.

Chapter Seven

Steadying myself by an effort of will, I crossed to the stretcher and looked down into the dark, pain-filled eyes of Simon Brandon.

I could see him relax as he recognized me.

"Be glad the Hun is a damned poor shot," he said quickly, and then lost consciousness.

I took over the pressure bandage as Dr. Hicks prepared to operate, saying as he worked, "The bullet is still in there. That's the trouble. Keep the pressure just there while Sister Evans prepares him." He hadn't even asked me how I knew the man lying in front of him or why he had demanded to see me.

We worked for an hour or more, but Dr. Hicks was good at what he did—he'd had long years of practice—and he managed to remove the bullet and find the tiny bit of uniform that had gone into the wound with it, probing carefully without adding to the damage already there. For the shot had clipped a corner of Simon's lung, and we were fearful that it had clipped an artery as well. But the bleeding stopped as we began to close the wound, and his color was better.

Next would come the fight against deadly infection, although we had cleaned the wound as thoroughly as we could.

What was he doing here, wounded by a German bullet?

I was just putting the final touches to the bandage that covered his chest and shoulder when Simon opened his eyes. They were dazed and confused at first, and then as the ether continued to wear off, he quickly regained his senses.

"Hello," he said hoarsely, recognizing me again. "I thought I'd dreamed you."

"Not likely. How did you come to be shot? I thought when I saw you last that you were on your way to Dover."

"A convenient lie," he murmured.

I knew better than to press for more, but thinking through where our aid station was located—how close to the firing it was—and where in this particular sector we were, it suddenly occurred to me that Simon had gone behind enemy lines. It was the only explanation for his getting shot. I felt cold. If the Germans had captured him, he would have faced a firing squad. Simon would consider that a lesser problem than being caught by some of the tribes of the Northwest Frontier in India, but he would have been just as dead, although not as quickly.

The Gurkhas, the fiercely trained and ferocious little men of the King of Nepal's Army, were often sent behind the lines, because they could move in the night like the wind, barely heard and always unseen.

If they had brought him here, they had not waited to see how he fared. And that was not unexpected either.

Simon knew the Gurkha officers—always English, not Nepalese—and there could well have been a mission that required someone of Simon's experience and skill to accompany the native soldiers—or to guide them—wherever it was they had had to go. There were whispers about their prowess. I'd heard a few myself. That they brought back German officers for interrogation. That they took out snipers or machine-gun nests that couldn't be reached any other way, even that they crawled to the lip of the German trenches and listened to the conversation of the unsuspecting occupants. If only half the stories were true, they were remarkable.

Almost as if he'd followed my thinking, Simon added, "Get me to England, fast as you can."

"You've just had very serious surgery. You can't be moved."

"Doesn't matter."

I knew that he would find a way somehow, whether I helped him or not. That's when I gave him something without his knowledge that made him sleep for five hours. My conscience was clear. Whatever it was Simon knew or had learned, it could wait. His life was more precious to me than his service to England. And for a Colonel's daughter, brought up to put the regiment first, above all else, even one's own feelings, this was tantamount to treason.

My ancestress at Waterloo would have been appalled. My mother would have understood completely.

It was several days before we could move Simon, and his fever fluctuated enough that we were afraid to do so even then. In addition to my own duties, I kept the bandages clean, kept the wound itself as antiseptic as I could, and saw to it that he slept as much as possible. It wasn't until the third day that he realized I'd been giving him something to keep him asleep.

He was absolutely furious with me, insisting that his information was critical, but I let his anger wash over me without answering him, and when he had exhausted himself I told him that I had sent word straightaway to the Colonel Sahib, telling him—obliquely—what had transpired.

It did little to pacify him, for as he told me—rightly enough—my father might not receive my news for a week or more.

Therefore I was both relieved and glad when my father came striding into the aid station just after dusk followed by four tall Highlanders.

He greeted me with a nod, and turned to Simon.

"You look like the very devil, Sergeant-Major."

"Thank you, sir."

"I've brought people with me. If the good doctor here gives his consent, we're to carry you by easy stages to Rouen, thence to England."

It was the way I'd been taken out of France.

My father was gone in an instant, and I turned on Simon Brandon. "And you were saying, Sergeant-Major, about my decision to write the Colonel Sahib?"

He gave me a sheepish grin, weak but with something of his old spirit showing. "You did well, Bess. Bless you. But this truly is important."

"You frightened me, Simon," I told him, unable to stop myself.

"Then we're even." And I realized how worried he'd been on that slow, uncertain progress to the ship as I lay so ill.

I looked around and saw that we were alone. Still, I leaned close to his ear and told him what I had learned from Matron.

"He's tidying up," Simon warned, fighting to stay awake and coherent. "It must mean he knows you're back in France. Watch yourself, don't ask too many questions. Damn it, Bess, did you give me something again?"

"This time it's your body trying to heal. You mustn't think you can go haring off to London as soon as you reach England. My father can deal with any matters for you."

"Yes. All right."

"Simon. Promise?" I demanded.

"I promise," he said faintly.

And then they were bundling him up in bedding and carrying him out to the waiting ambulance that my father had somehow commandeered. It would be a rough journey. Simon would be wishing for release by the time he reached Rouen.

My father came to me, rested his hand on my shoulder, and gripped it strongly. "Thank you, my dear. And this is from your mother." He bent his head and kissed my cheek.

"Keep me informed. Please? Don't let me worry."

"We'll do our best," he told me, and then they were gone.

As the ambulance drove slowly past me, avoiding the lines of wounded, Dr. Hicks said from just behind me, "I gave him a little morphine. He'll not remember the journey. What's more, he will not reopen that shoulder fighting to avoid the jostling. Stubborn man, Sergeant-Major Brandon. What was he doing here in France in the first place?"

I said, as offhand as I could, "He's responsible for training recruits. I expect he comes sometimes to see firsthand how to do it better."

Satisfied, Dr. Hicks nodded. Then he said, "Don't stand there staring after them, Sister Crawford. There's work to be done."

And there was.

A letter came from my mother quite soon after my father had reached England, sent in one of the HQ pouches that were secure. I collected it while on a run to replenish supplies.

Still, she was circumspect, saying only that "our dear neighbor" was slowly recovering after a small relapse, and I was not to worry. She went on to talk about ordinary household matters—how Cook had not smoked the bees sufficiently before stealing a little of their hoard of honey for our table, how the new calf was faring, how the roses had bloomed beautifully this spring, reminding her of the summer of 1914, and how she hoped that I was not overextending my strength, cautioning me that a relapse on my part was still possible.

And then she added a few lines that I knew must have come straight from my father.

Thank you, my dear, for your latest news. Your letters are always so precious. And that reminds me, we've just learned that your cousin is being sent back to France. We thought you'd want to know. That nasty broken leg has mended sufficiently for him to

*return to light duties. If you run into him, he brings our best love.
I know you'll be happy to see him again, although we shall miss
him sorely. He's always such a joy to have around, isn't he?*

The dear neighbor was, of course, Simon, whose cottage was
just across the back garden and down the lane from us. I wasn't
surprised to hear he'd had a small relapse, for the journey had been
hazardous from the start.

My latest news meant that Simon had managed to remember
what I had told him about Colonel Prescott and Sister Burrows.

But who was "our cousin"?

I had no cousins, not now. One had died in India many years ago
of cholera, and the other had been killed at Mons early in 1915.

Clearly, whoever he was, he was coming back to France in spite of
still recovering from a broken leg. I was confused by the reference to
light duties. There were no light duties in the trenches. I ran through
our acquaintance, came up empty-handed, and read the last para-
graph again.

And then I realized that my father was alerting me to the fact
that my news was worrying enough that he was sending someone to
keep an eye on me and make communication easier until Simon was
well again.

Not a real cousin, then, but someone I knew and, what's more,
knew that I could trust. Someone who wouldn't stand out or draw
attention to himself or, more important, draw attention to the fact
that he was guarding me.

In spite of Simon's warning, I was aghast. This had all begun
as an attempt to find out who had murdered Major Carson and
perhaps even Private Wilson. But now it was possible that I was in
danger, not only because I'd seen the Major's body but also because
I could have seen the man who killed him. Whether I actually could
identify him or not, all that mattered was that the killer believed
I could. He had come in search of Sister Burrows, if the man who

presented himself to Matron was one and the same Colonel Prescott who had written that spurious letter of sympathy to Julia Carson.

I couldn't imagine what Major Carson's death was all about, which made it easier for me to make a mistake or put my trust in the wrong person.

What's more, when I looked over my shoulder in the dark, I had no way of knowing if the person I saw in the shadows of a tent or lurking behind an ambulance was friend or foe. And that was truly disturbing to me.

While I was looking for Colonel Prescott, whoever he was, the man in the stained bandage might be standing just behind me. Or the orderly carrying the mop and pail might be the man handing me fresh bandages. Because I couldn't be sure I'd know either of them.

As I drank the last of my tea and finished the thin sandwich that was my dinner, I asked myself what in the name of God Major Carson had done that had set all this in motion.

Vincent Carson was one of ours. My father would move heaven and earth if he had to, to find the captain's murderer. It would become a personal obligation, a matter of honor.

But where to begin? How were we ever going to know what it was that had put the Major in danger in the first place? And what about the rumor that he'd deserted? Was it true, what Simon had said, that this meant whoever was behind the Major's death was indeed tidying up?

I watched the shell flashes as the ambulance crawled over the rutted road toward the forward aid station, listening to the bombardment that presaged an attack.

What part—if any—had Sabrina's husband, William Morton, played in any of this? Where was he? If he and his brother-in-law had never seen eye to eye, had this escalated to the point that it had led to murder?

The staff was waiting for our supplies, and I was busy for hours working with the latest influx of wounded. It was shortly before moonrise when the last of the men had been examined and a decision had been made about their treatment.

Dr. Hicks, straightening his back, then arching it, as if it ached, said, "Go on to bed, Sister. We've done all we can. I'll rouse Dr. Timmons and Sister Clery. They can take over."

He was right, we had done what we could do. And that was saying a good bit. I said good night and trudged out into the darkness, wondering if the time would ever come when I could say with any confidence that I had had enough sleep while I was in France. Certainly since Eastbourne and even Longleigh House, I had not.

I made a detour to wash up before going to bed, entering the empty line of latrines and basins, listening to the sound of my footsteps echoing on the thin boards that kept our feet out of the foul mud below. A single candle in a dish gave me enough light to see the bucket standing under the water lorry, and I filled it just enough to take out my handkerchief and wash my face and hands. Water was precious, but so was cleanliness, when dealing with patients.

I had closed my eyes to splash water over my face. It smelled strongly of brine and faintly of petrol, but it was cool enough to feel the fresh morning air on my wet skin. I leaned my head back to bathe my throat.

Just as I did, an arm came round my neck from behind, hard enough to choke off my breath, and I had a flash of thought—that this was how Private Wilson had been found hanging—before I reacted. I wasn't about to be choked into unconsciousness and then a rope pulled around my neck. Private Wilson had been taken unawares. I was as well, but I had a little history to guide me. I hadn't grown up in an Army post without learning something about self-defense. Subalterns had vied to show off—and show me tricks sure to protect me.

As the candle sputtered, my booted foot kicked out at the water bucket, connecting with such force that it went bouncing and clanging down the boards. My hands went not to claw uselessly at the arm of my attacker and the heavy fabric of his uniform sleeve, but at his vulnerable sides, digging in my nails and raking upward, finding the soft skin beneath his tunic and shirt. It caught him by surprise. As he twisted to protect himself, I tramped down on his instep with my other boot. And these weren't the pretty shoes of a London season; they were designed to survive the Front.

He relaxed his arm briefly, swearing and jerking back in pain. I spun out of his grip, and as soon as I could fill my lungs with air again, I screamed. Furious, he shoved me toward the lorry, and I stumbled as I tried to keep my balance, hurting my wrist as I went down.

He reached for me again, pulling me up, trying to get a hand over my mouth, no longer hoping to make my death look like suicide. Now he was intent on simple murder. I cried out again before he succeeded in cutting it short.

There are only a handful of women this close to the front lines, and my first scream brought men racing from every direction. By my second, they were converging on us. My assailant flung me against the offside wheel of the water lorry with some force. I threw up my hands just in time to protect my head and face. He ducked beneath the lorry and disappeared into the shadows on the far side.

By the time the first orderly reached me, I'd scrambled to my feet, alone and furiously angry in my turn.

I could have tried to pass off the attack as female fears and an overwrought imagination in the shadowy, poorly lit latrines.

Perhaps it would have been better that way. But my hair was tumbling down my back, the side of my face where I'd scraped it on something was already an angry red in the light of the torches blinding me, and the strap of my apron had been torn off the bib. There was no disguising the fact that I'd been in trouble.

Their first thought was an attempt at rape. And why should they even consider murder?

Dr. Hicks was pushing the other men aside, leaning forward to get a better look at me. He swore as he took in the damage.

"Are you hurt anywhere else?" he demanded, his face like a thundercloud.

"My wrist—I think it banged into the pump as I broke away. Nothing a cold compress won't help." In spite of the effort I'd made to get myself under control, even I could hear the shock in my voice. Nor could I do much about the fact that I must have looked like a thundercloud myself.

Everyone seemed to be there in the darkness behind the ring of torchlight. Sisters, orderlies, ambulatory patients, ambulance drivers. I quickly scanned their faces searching for—what? A stranger amongst them, anyone who could fit Matron's description of the man who'd come looking for Sister Burrows. But of course there was no one who by any stretch of my imagination could have attacked me. There was only genuine concern for me. And by coming so quickly to my aid, they had unwittingly allowed my assailant to escape.

Dr. Hicks seemed to realize that in the same moment. He half turned to the orderlies and ambulance drivers, saying grimly, "Don't stand there—start searching the aid station. Top to bottom. Find out who did this!"

That done, Dr. Hicks marched me off to the surgery tent to bathe and dress my face, then find a compress for my wrist where a bruise was fast turning to an ugly red.

"Did you see who it was, Sister Crawford? Can you give us any description?"

"I tried. But he came from behind, out of the shadows, and I think the candle went over as he reached for me. I didn't even know he was there until he put his arm around my throat." I didn't add that his other hand had been locked in the palm of the hand suffocating me, bringing all his strength to bear on cutting off my air. He had known what he was doing, there was no doubt in my mind about that.

"Did you mark him in any way?"

"Not where it could be seen. There was no chance," I said as he tilted my head to look at my throat. "I couldn't have reached his face, I was nearly sure of that, but where I dug my nails into his sides, there must be marks."

"You kept your head," he said, nodding in approval, "but sooner or later the shock will catch up with you."

"He must have lined up with the walking wounded, then slipped away when no one was looking."

"Yes, that chest wound—we were so busy. It must have been then."

The soldier had been dying from blood loss when he was brought in, and somehow, miraculously, Dr. Hicks had found the source of the bleeding and stopped it. The boy—he seemed no older than that on the stretcher—was sent straight back to the Base Hospital, with a fifty-fifty chance of surviving. We'd all applauded when Dr. Hicks had stepped back and nodded, his hands and arms covered in blood. I wouldn't have believed it possible if I hadn't watched it for myself.

In that moment of success, someone could have stepped out of line, walked to the latrines, and waited for me. He must have seen me clearly as I sorted the cases, but I'd been too busy to see him.

"I'll strip every man in here if I have to. You were damn—very fortunate," the doctor was saying to me as he considered the marks on my neck. "I won't have this sort of thing on my watch."

And he stormed out to do just exactly that.

But of course he didn't find my attacker or anyone with a mark on him that would correspond to my struggle.

Soon after that, he came back to escort me to my quarters, saying only, "He's not here. Mind you, that doesn't mean he wasn't. Or that he won't come back. If not for you, then for one of the other sisters. And I'll see that word is passed. This won't be tolerated."

He stood outside my tent until I was inside, and I found it

comforting, despite my certainty that there wouldn't be a repeat attack. At least not while the guard of the entire station was up.

I didn't fall sleep for a long while. My body was still tense, the feel of that arm choking me still too fresh. Every little sound in the darkness seemed overly loud and menacing, even though I told myself to ignore it.

Where, I thought, lying there, was the "cousin" who had been sent to keep me safe?

Wherever he was, he'd nearly been too late.

Another search was made at first light, but there was no sign of my attacker. Dr. Hicks excused me from my morning shift, but I went to him and asked him to let me work. As frightening as the experience had been, I knew that I was safer and less likely to dwell on what had happened if I kept busy.

Everyone was sympathetic, and I noticed that someone was always within call, wherever I went.

But what to tell my father? And if Simon got any inkling of what had occurred, he'd be in France before the day was out, still bleeding or not.

In the end, I decided to say nothing to them. For all I knew, it had indeed been an attempt at rape, not murder.

I was walking across to my quarters that night when I heard Dr. Hicks just behind me say sharply, "Who the devil are you?"

I turned to see him challenging someone who was only a black silhouette against the faint light of the distant shelling.

"The new orderly," the voice said. "I walked up. There wasn't any transportation."

"Then you'll damned well stay there until I can take a good look at your orders."

I knew that voice, didn't I? But I couldn't quite place it, for coming out of the darkness, half muffled by the big guns, I couldn't quite make the connection. I needed more to jog my memory.

"I'll wait until you have sorted him out," I told Dr. Hicks, hoping to catch a glimpse of the man's face as they repaired to the small tent where the doctors kept their paperwork and whatever medicines we had under lock and key.

But he said, "No. Wiser to go inside and leave me to deal with this."

Nodding, I did as I was told, and as soon as I was safely in my quarters, he was gone.

The next morning Sister Clery said, "Have you met the new orderly?"

"A glimpse, nothing more."

"Well, I can tell you he isn't like the rest. Wait until you see for yourself."

"More to the point, is he good at his work?"

"Wasted," she said firmly. "Remember that hand that we thought might be turning septic? We had to take it off this morning, and Corporal Dugan was fighting us for all he was worth. Barclay held him for us until we could get the ether mask over his face—"

I didn't hear the rest. I had placed the voice now, as well as the way the man had been standing as he spoke to Dr. Hicks.

What was Captain Barclay doing in France at a British aid station masquerading as an orderly?

CHAPTER EIGHT

I SAW HIM coming out of the canteen, a cup of tea in his hand, grimacing as he drank it without sugar or milk.

I called, "You're the new man, are you? Barclay?"

"I'm never going to learn to like tea," he said plaintively, approaching me.

"Sorry. It's all we have. There's a shortage."

"So I've heard." He glanced around, then said swiftly, "Bess. You don't know me." With that, he walked off.

But wherever I was, it seemed that Captain Barclay—Barclay the orderly—was somewhere close by. He seemed oddly out of place to me in his khaki orderly's tunic with the red cross on his sleeve. I'd seen him in his own uniform, and he wore it with an air that suited his rank. Still, everyone else took him in stride, and his attempts at rank-and-file humility were successful, although sometimes I caught a gleam in his eyes that belied them. Working with the wounded, to his credit he did the most menial task from emptying bloody basins to carrying away an amputated limb with the grim stoicism of a seasoned orderly. He'd been in the trenches, of course, he'd seen and dealt with worse, but it was not something anyone grew accustomed to, however hard the shell put up to keep one's sanity in the face of such horrors.

I couldn't help but think in the dark hours of the night that he'd appeared right on the heels of the attack on me. And then I'd remind myself that the Colonel Sahib had sent him, and the Colonel Sahib was seldom wrong in his judgment of a man's character.

I could also see Dr. Gaines's fine hand in all this. Captain Barclay had been pressing to return to his men, ready or not. This would be a lesson in a different kind of humility—forcing him to listen to his doctors.

In a way his presence was comforting. In the first place it freed me to work without looking over my shoulder. In the second, I'd been concerned about someone *hovering,* in my way at every turn. But apparently he'd been ordered to keep his distance, close enough to protect me but without being underfoot. I'd have given much to discover why my parents had turned to Captain Barclay as the safest choice to watch over me. He was, as I knew only too well, a very persuasive man. Still, his wound helped him carry off his charade. That must have carried some weight.

What little I learned about his "story" came in bits and pieces from others.

He was Canadian, had joined the British Army because he had been living in Britain when war was declared, but he was rejected because of a leg injury that refused to heal properly—hence his limp—and so he'd become an orderly instead. (His time in the clinic had given him a good background to make that believable. He talked about his duties there with the ease of experience.) He wasn't married (this from Sister Clery), and his father was in the merchant marine—which was close enough to the truth. I asked where he lived, and I was told he'd been an orderly at Longleigh House in Somerset, had served in Dover, on several patient transport ships (which had aggravated his bad leg), and was now with us.

Dr. Gaines again, I thought. And he'd also been responsible for my own return to France.

Several evenings later, Dr. Hicks sent me to the Base Hospital for supplies—we'd been running short for three days, but he hadn't been able to spare anyone. With a brief respite in the fighting—the guns were silent and lines of fresh troops were making their way to the Front to relieve those who'd endured a week of heavy shelling—we had only a trickle of new patients.

We took with us three badly wounded men who were due to be sent back for more treatment, and Barclay was assigned to drive.

It was a more or less uneventful journey, although once a nervous company of raw troops fired on us from a distance before their sergeant got them under control again, shouting at them in a Glaswegian accent that made half of what he was saying unintelligible.

We delivered our patients and saw to it the instructions accompanying them were duly signed for, then collected the list of desperately needed medicines, bandages, needles, sutures, and so on that Dr. Hicks had requested. An hour later, the ambulance carefully stocked, I got into the seat beside Captain Barclay after he'd turned the crank.

"Wait until we're out of sight," he said in a low voice, turning out of the racetrack and picking up the road to the Front.

And so I waited. Last night the sun had set in a blaze of gold and red, sliding behind a bank of deep purple clouds. Now it was pitch-dark without the flickering light of the shelling, and the only way we could be certain we were on what passed as a road were the wide swaths of deep ruts left behind by the lorries. Our blacked-out head-lamps were woefully inadequate, casting shadows that only made it harder to judge anything in time to avoid another bone-wrenching jolt. About two miles out we spotted the single chimney and broken wall of a farmhouse. It had become a marker of sorts, and we all knew to watch for it. The rest of the village was little more than rubble, with no way of judging where the streets had been, much less the houses or shops that once had lined them. How this single chimney and wall had survived God alone knew.

The ambulance rocked and swayed over the debris, and I feared we would never extract it again just as Barclay turned off the motor and silence fell. I could have sworn I heard a cricket somewhere, it was so quiet.

"All right," he said, turning to me, his face a pale mask in the darkness and oddly sinister. "I'm sorry there was no chance to explain before this. I was told I didn't know you. I suspected the Sergeant-Major's touch there. Necessity or precaution or jealousy." The mask split into a white grin in the shadows.

"How is Simon?" I asked anxiously.

"I didn't see him, to tell the truth."

And that worried me. Surely if he were well enough, Simon would have been consulted.

"Then how did you become involved in this? What did they tell you? Dr. Gaines and my father?"

"Dr. Gaines had been sent for. He must have told your father that I'd accompanied you to Nether Thornton and then to the Gorge."

"But you'd spoken to my father once. When I was sailing to France. You told him where to meet me."

"That was sheer luck. Bess, I called the War Office. They found him, wherever he was, and passed on my message. Apparently they thought I was the Sergeant-Major. The Colonel had a few words to say about that when we spoke again."

I could just imagine how annoyed my father was. The relationship with Simon was sacrosanct. He wouldn't have appreciated Captain Barclay's efforts, however well intentioned.

"At any rate, your father asked if I was fit enough for duty and if I'd take on a hazardous assignment. I was to report directly to him. Or if I couldn't reach him, then to your mother."

I'd told Simon about my companion on those journeys. Was it he who'd remembered?

"What did they tell you? How did they explain that I might be in danger?"

I still wasn't prepared to trust this man.

"The Colonel told me the truth. At least I had the feeling he did."

"What did they tell you?" I asked again, trying not to sound impatient.

"That someone had been murdered and you were the only witness who could testify to that. The trouble was, the killer knew you, but you couldn't identify him as easily. That you were in danger. Well, by God, they were right. I heard about what happened just before I got there, and if I get my hands on that—on whoever it is, I'll kill him myself." The grin had disappeared like the smile of the Cheshire Cat, and I could feel the tension in the man across from me, a deep-seated anger that was like a flare of warmth in the ambulance.

"At any rate," he went on after collecting himself, "when they spoke to me, I jumped at the chance. I'd rather be back with my men, but if that's out of the question, I'll use this assignment to prove that I'm ready to fight again."

"Going over the top is not easy with a bad leg," I said. "You know that as well as I do."

"Yes, I can get others killed if I'm a burden," he said impatiently. "That's been brought home to me. But your father saw to it that I was given a background that wouldn't make anyone suspicious. And your father asked me to give you this."

He moved in the darkness and his hand stretched out toward me. In the palm lay the little pistol that Simon had given me once before. I recognized it immediately.

"My father? Not Simon himself?"

"I never saw the Sergeant-Major, Bess."

I bit my lip. Once before I'd been afraid that bad news was being kept from me. I had that feeling again. Had Simon not lived to reach England? Had he lost that arm?

I looked down at the little pistol. Nurses were not permitted to carry weapons, but this time, remembering my feeling of helplessness when that arm had come around my throat and how lucky I was that I'd been able to kick the water pail, then scream, I touched it with my fingertips and then settled it carefully in the pocket of my uniform.

Captain Barclay was saying, "Better to wing him, Bess. Your father wants him alive."

"But who is he?" I asked. "Why did he—what reason could he have for attacking me? I've never made an official report of any kind." I wanted to know precisely how much my father had told the Captain.

"It appears he killed one Major Carson, who was in your father's old regiment. And that he's willing to kill again to protect himself. That woman. The one who lived near the Gorge. Apparently he'd killed her husband as well. The orderly who had discovered the Major's body."

Finally satisfied, I nodded. "He must be in the Army. He would have to be to reach the Major and then to attack me. One can't simply take the next ferry across the Channel."

"Yes, that was your father's theory. They don't know what rank he actually holds. But it's easy enough out here to kill someone and steal a uniform. One unmarked grave more or less wouldn't be noticed."

But one couldn't murder a Major without a flag going up. He'd be missed. A private soldier wouldn't.

What's more, whoever this was had been able to carry off the masquerade as Colonel Prescott. Both in person and in the contents of the letter he'd written Julia Carson. I wondered how many roles as a military officer William Morton had played on the stage. Shakespeare was filled with them, seventeenth- and eighteenth-century plays as well. Gilbert and Sullivan had created lively military characters. Productions had come out to India and were amazingly popular.

But then Matron had questioned Colonel Prescott's manner—something had made her uneasy. Of course until I asked questions, Matron had kept her doubts to herself. Had I allayed her

suspicions—or would she at some point bring them up with someone else?

Matron. I felt a chill. She'd seen his face. But he'd made no effort
to harm her. Why? Had there been no opportunity? Or did he think
she could wait?

Captain Barclay was adding grimly, "Something could have happened in the trenches between this man and Carson. Not everyone
out here is a gallant soldier serving King and Country."

I'd heard stories of shooting unpopular officers in the back when
the opportunity presented itself. Charging across No Man's Land is
a chancy business at best, and it would be easy, firing at the enemy,
to find one's nemesis in the crosshairs.

If Sabrina had been cut off without a farthing when she married
her actor, there could very well be hard feelings against Vincent for
not doing more for her when the elder Carson died.

But Vincent hadn't been shot in the back; his neck had been
broken.

Captain Barclay gingerly climbed out and restarted the ambulance. "We've delayed long enough. They'll begin to wonder, up
ahead."

The overworked motor coughed and struggled for several seconds before finally turning over properly. Captain Barclay reversed
gingerly, the wheel jerking in his hands, and then we were safely
back on what passed for a road. I stopped a sigh of relief, but I had a
feeling he felt the same way.

We traveled in silence for a time.

I said, "Someone knew I was at the aid station. I don't see how he
could."

"It shouldn't be that difficult." He turned to me in the darkness.
"'My sister's at a forward aid station.' Or 'I served under Colonel
Crawford before he retired. Is it true his daughter's a nurse out
here?' Word gets around."

And so it had last winter, when I'd asked for information about convents that took in French orphans. The answer had come back to me in the most unexpected way.

"Then I'm still at risk. But he won't try to kill me at the aid station here. Not again. For one thing, I'm carefully watched. All the sisters are. But my next posting—or on the way to it—I'll be vulnerable."

"Quite. But I wouldn't write off someone stopping this ambulance and killing both of us," he said tightly.

I shivered at the thought, and touched the weight of the little pistol in my pocket. Simon had reminded me that it wasn't of a caliber to kill or maim. But it was better than no protection, and it could make enough noise and cause enough pain to stop my assailant until someone came to my rescue.

With that thought in mind, when we had reached the station, I slept more soundly in what was left of that night.

Barclay was always in sight, wherever I was, and I wondered when or if he slept at all. He looked tired, and some of that I put down to his leg still being weak. His limp seemed to be worse, but he never complained.

Sister Clery, sitting down beside me as I ate a hasty dinner before returning to my duties, eyed me with interest. "I think," she said after a moment, "that you have a beau. And he really is handsome, even though he's not an officer. He ought to be. Perhaps there's something mysterious in his past that prevented him from joining the Army under his own name."

Realizing she was speaking of Barclay, I laughed. "He's actually a rich American in disguise, and he followed me to France because I've refused his proposals of marriage nine times."

She laughed with me. "I tell you, Bess, if that were true, I'd volunteer to mend his sad and broken heart myself."

"Alas, I fear it's beyond mending."

"Ah, well. But I've noticed that everyone has been keeping an eye out for us. I don't mind telling you, I was badly frightened when you were attacked."

"Whoever he is, he's well away from here now," I assured her, and hoped that it was true.

New orders came for me before the week was out. Dr. Hicks informed me of them when he and I had finished working to stabilize an abdomen torn by shrapnel before taking the risk of sending the patient on to Rouen.

"I shall miss your steady hand and good eye," he said. "But my loss is another station's gain."

"Thank you, sir." And then, with a sense of foreboding, I asked, "Could you tell me who ordered my transfer?"

"I spoke to him by field telephone this morning. A Dr. Percy had requested you."

I'd never worked with a Dr. Percy. "Was it Dr. Percy on the telephone?"

"No, no, I could hardly hear the Major, there was so much interference. But he confirmed you are to leave at once and the paperwork is to follow by the end of the week."

"But that's unusual, isn't it?"

"True, but apparently they're shorthanded outside of Ypres, and they can't wait for the orders to come." He studied my face. "Are you worried about this transfer, Sister Crawford?"

"I—yes, I must admit that I am," I said, speaking frankly.

"I can assure you it was all straightforward. I made sure of that."

"Could you try to reach Ypres and make certain that this was not a mistake?"

"Is it the attack on you that has made you so wary? My dear, you will probably be safer in your new posting than you are here, so close to the lines. I shouldn't worry, if I were you."

"Thank you, sir." I couldn't protest any more than I had.

Yet this was what I had dreaded—a new posting I knew very little about. I'd been sure Dr. Hicks would keep me, but someone had been insistent and convincing. I had no choice in the matter.

I went back to my tent, trying to think of a way to send word to my father. I'd seen Captain Barclay no more than an hour ago, but now he was nowhere to be found.

Troubled by his continued absence, on my first break I finished packing my possessions as ordered. If I could reach Rouen, surely I could find a way to contact the Colonel Sahib. But when I changed my apron, I made certain that the little pistol was in my pocket.

Outside I could hear the grumble of ambulance motors as they prepared to leave for the Base Hospital.

Just then Dr. Hicks came to say good-bye.

"Be safe, Sister Crawford. Did I tell you that there will be accommodations for you tonight at the American Base Hospital? Your transport to Ypres, as I understand it, will leave tomorrow morning from there."

"Thank you, sir."

Sister Clery also came to say good-bye, and several of the others who weren't busy with the wounded. But still there was no sign of Captain Barclay.

Sister Clery, seeing me look around a last time before taking my seat, smiled and said, "I'll tell him you'll miss him, shall I?"

"Don't bother," I said, trying to convince myself that he had gone ahead to look into the transfer.

The ambulances followed the usual track, stopping at one other aid station to take on three more patients, and then finally, when my spine felt like a washboard, I could see the lights of Rouen ahead.

We discharged our patients, handed in the lists of names, and the drivers went away to hose down the ambulances.

I said to the sister in charge, "I've received a new posting, but the paperwork hasn't come through. Oral orders for Ypres. I'm told you have a bed for me tonight."

She glanced at my valise, then raised her eyes to my face. "Sister Crawford? I don't think—let me look at the roster."

My heart sank, but I smiled and waited patiently.

After a moment she shook her head. "No, sorry. There's nothing here."

I knew then that this was not an official transfer. "Do you have a bed? I don't believe my transport leaves until tomorrow morning."

Again she shook her head. "We've got no space, Sister. We had beds for eight hundred and we've got nearly sixteen hundred patients. I've moved in with another nurse myself, we're that cramped. I'm so sorry."

I put the best face on it I could.

"My transport expects to find me here tomorrow before dawn. Could you leave a message that I am in Rouen and will meet it on time?"

She wrote a message and clipped it on a board by her desk where there were some twenty or thirty others. "I won't be on duty tomorrow, but the nurse who is will see the message. Will that do?"

I could tell she had more on her mind than dealing with my problems. But there was one more question I wanted to put to her.

"There's one more thing," I said with a smile. "I'm being sent to work with a Dr. Percy, near Ypres. I hear he's something of a Tartar. Have you had any dealings with him or his patients?"

"Near Ypres? Most of those cases go directly to Dover."

I could only push the matter so far. I thanked her and walked out of Base Hospital's Reception.

So much for my attempts to find out anything useful. Communications were sketchy at best here in France. The military used runners and motorcycles when contact was imperative. Radio telephones were not always dependable. And so it wasn't too surprising that someone here in Rouen wouldn't know a doctor on the coastal sector of the Front. Unless of course he had a reputation that fed the rumor mill. I'd have to wait until morning and see what sort of transportation showed up.

Ordinarily I'd have sorted out the problem of where to spend the night without a second thought. Rouen was not a small town; it was a sizable city, and wandering about in it alone—something I'd done a dozen times before this—was no longer something I cared to do. Under the circumstances.

And what had happened to Captain Barclay? I'd convinced myself that he'd come ahead to prepare the way. After all, he could hardly openly desert his duties by leaving the aid station when I did. But there was no indication that he'd even reached the Base Hospital; otherwise he'd have left a message for me. Was he even in Rouen? Now I wondered if he was alive, because he took his duty to me seriously, and yet he had vanished without a word. What's more, the ambulances that had brought me here had already pulled out for the Front, and there wasn't even a possibility of sending word back to Dr. Hicks, much less getting his answer before I myself left the city.

I stood there on the street, thinking fast. Hotels were not the best choice for a woman alone. But there was one place I was assured of a bed: the convent I'd visited last winter and several times in the early spring before the influenza epidemic took hold.

I'd always brought something with me—money, medicines, soap, food—to help with the care of any ill or wounded children. This time I had only myself.

And so I found myself on the doorstep waiting for the porteress to answer the ring of the bell. The convent had little comfort to offer a stranger at their door, but they greeted me warmly and shared what they could.

The youngest nun came in quietly to wake me at three o'clock, and I dressed by candlelight in a room that held the night's chill from the river. Then I slipped out into the predawn darkness to make my way back to where my transport should be waiting.

I wasn't particularly frightened in the dark, narrow streets where the sounds from the docks echoed and the sporadic shelling at the Front was a counterpoint in the background. No one knew where to find me, and there was no one else about. It was too early for the milk wagon or the lorries bringing in foodstuffs from the outlying villages, too early for the ships to arrive from England with new recruits. I knew the city and could find my way without difficulty, only my own footsteps echoing.

I was within sight of the racetrack and the American Base Hospital, when I glimpsed the outline of a motorcar some thirty yards on the far side of the hospital entrance where summer bushes were thick and dark. My driver? Why hadn't he halted under the lamps where I could see him better? But of course I was a little early. He was probably sleeping at the wheel after his long drive.

Still, I was uneasy. After all, I had no idea who he was, and I'd already decided to ask for some form of identification. If I wasn't satisfied, I would have the Base Hospital verify that he'd come from Dr. Percy.

Should I wait where I was? I was vulnerable here, if the wrong person knew I was expecting to meet transport this morning—and even if the transfer was legitimate, in spite of the fact that no accommodations were waiting at the hospital, it would be the perfect opportunity to find me alone and unprotected.

Or approach?

What if the driver was already dead behind the wheel, so that he couldn't raise the alarm if I didn't die quietly?

For that matter, what if that motorcar wasn't for me after all?

Standing there in the shadows of a building, I debated what to do. At this hour of the morning, it was easy to believe in danger of any kind, with my own breathing the only sound I could hear, and not even a bat swooping through the darkness to distract me from my thoughts.

I decided not to wait where I was but to move closer to the Base Hospital, where I could be heard if I had to scream. If all went well, there would be nothing to worry about. If it didn't, I hoped I could count on help sooner. I'd taken only one step in that direction when there was a sharp movement just behind me. My valise was in my right hand, but before I could swing it at my assailant, it was snatched out of my grip. I was spun into the deeper shadow of a doorway, a rough hand over my mouth.

I realized in that instant that I had stepping unwittingly into a trap, that the motorcar had held my attention while the driver had come up behind me.

Biting down on the hand over my mouth, I began to fight.

I'd just managed to force my hand down toward the pistol in my pocket when a voice whispered savagely, "Damn it, Bess, if you kick me or shoot me, I'll never take you to the Grand Hotel."

Captain Barclay. I stopped struggling. He held me close for a moment until he was sure it wasn't a trick.

As he let me go, I demanded angrily in a whisper of my own, "Did you have to frighten me like that? Why couldn't you simply tell me who you were?"

"Because," he said shortly, "you must not get into that motorcar. Or let the driver see you."

He still had one arm around me, holding me in the shadows of the doorway. I didn't know if the driver of the motorcar had seen me or not, or if he was even there. It was too hard to tell. It was still a quarter of an hour before I was to meet him, and it was possible that he had gone into a café for coffee to keep himself awake.

"Who is he?" I asked, keeping my voice low. "Did you see him? For that matter, where have you been?"

"It was more important to watch for you and stop you—look! He's just coming out of that alley across the way. Pay attention to his manner of walking. Do you recognize him?"

But the man who had just appeared was hurrying away, coughing once or twice, as if he had been ill. He disappeared into the darkness beyond, with only a last cough to tell us where he had gone.

"I don't think—that can't be him. How long have you been here? Do you know if he's inside the motorcar?"

"It was there when I got here. I've been watching it. Nothing."

"Then let me go. I won't get in, I promise you. But it's important to get a good look at him. We may not have another chance."

"No. That's not safe. Bess, I'm no match for him right now!"

"I have the pistol."

"No, I tell you. It isn't worth the risk. Wait. See if he shows himself. He'll grow impatient. He might even walk as far as those lamps by the Base Hospital."

But he didn't. Where was he?

As I heard the clock in a nearby church tower strike four, I broke away from Captain Barclay's clutches and stepped out into the street. Walking sedately toward the motorcar, I took my time. I could now see that one wing was dented, but that not surprising. Most of the motorcars anywhere near the Front were dented and rusty. When I was some ten or fifteen feet away, I stopped, looking around, as if expecting to find my driver.

"Hallo?" I called after a moment. "Anyone there?" I took a step or two nearer the bonnet, and then—apparently uncertain—I turned and took four back the way I'd come. This gave me a chance to look around me, scanning doorways and the windows of a café just down the street without appearing to be suspicious.

I was almost facing the motorcar again when, without any warning at all, out of the corner of my eye I saw movement behind the windscreen, as if someone had been lying out of sight across the seats. In the same instant the great, bright headlamps came on, their black paint gone, and I was pinned in their glare, startled and unable to see or move.

But I could hear the motor as it was gunned, and the headlamps were speeding toward me.

Behind me I heard Captain Barclay shout, but I knew that if I moved too soon, the driver behind the glare of the lights could see where I was leaping, and compensate.

I almost left it too late.

Prepared to spring to the left, where I had the whole street in which to maneuver, I realized that he too could use that space to swerve toward me. And so without hesitating, I flung myself right, into the ragged line of unkempt shrubbery that marked that side of the road.

He swerved too, just as I had feared, but in this direction he had no room—he dared not come too close to the shrubbery, or at that speed he'd lose control and crash into it. Still, he cut it close. I felt the force of his passage, the leading edge of the rusted wing brushing my hip, catching my apron, and nearly dragging me under the rear wheels before the cloth ripped and freed me. I cried out, catching at the prickly, scrubby branches of the shrubs to keep my balance.

The pistol was in my pocket, and I scrabbled for it, trying to reach it in the folds of my uniform, but I already knew it would be impossible to bring it out in time to fire at my tormentor. All the same, I was frightened and angry enough to do just that.

I twisted to take a hard look at him. But his face was half covered by a muffler, a dark striped length of woolen cloth that must have been hot this time of year. All I could see were his eyes.

Matron had said they were gray. But in the reflected light of the lamps, I couldn't be sure. For they gleamed so palely it was almost as if there were no eyes at all under dark, heavy brows.

A very pale blue? A clear gray like lake water in moonlight?

And then he was gone, roaring off down the street, narrowly missing Captain Barclay, who was already rushing toward me as fast as he could.

It was in the light of the headlamps that I saw Captain Barclay clearly for the first time.

He was disheveled, his uniform torn and bloody.

I hadn't asked him why he had disappeared, but now I had a feeling that I knew.

Captain Barclay reached me, pulling me out of the shrubbery, brushing at my coat where leaves and twigs had caught, all the while cursing me in words as vivid as any I had ever heard in the Army.

"What the hell were you thinking?" he demanded in the next breath. "Were you trying to get yourself killed? Damn it, Bess

Crawford, that was the most brazenly foolish thing I've ever seen anyone do."

"But I had to see his face. I had to be sure. And he has gray eyes, Captain, just as Matron had said he did. Or very pale blue. I could see them above the muffler. You can change a good many things, but not the color of your eyes. What's more, I wasn't entirely convinced he was inside the motorcar. He could have killed my driver and waited for me somewhere nearby. Just as we were concealed in the shadows! When he came out he'd have to face me, and I'd have had a clearer view of him. Even a clear shot, if need be."

He shook me, his hands gripping my shoulders. "And he nearly killed you. A few inches closer, and he could have hurt you badly. If you'd slipped, you'd have been under his wheels. I couldn't believe you would do anything so rash. Your father warned me you were headstrong, but I never dreamed—"

He released me suddenly and I nearly stumbled into him before I got my balance again. "Come on," he said, and taking my arm firmly enough to keep me by his side, he started walking. "It isn't a good idea to stay here. He could decide to swing back this way. And I've told you I'm in no shape to do battle."

We walked as quickly as we could down the street, then at the first corner took the next street and then the next. We finally came to a small church in a cul-de-sac, and he strode toward the door. Finding it open, we went inside, greeted by the smell of musty walls, incense, and stone. Cold and dark as it was, I felt vulnerable, even though I knew logically that there was no possible way we could have been followed here. As my eyes grew accustomed to the gloom, I could make out the baptismal font, a line of pillars leading down to the altar, and the faint glow of the altar lamp. All of them familiar things that pushed away my initial anxiety.

Captain Barclay found a row of chairs and we sat down. Wincing, he thrust one leg out in front of him, as if it ached unbearably.

"Are you badly hurt?" I asked after a moment, and saw him

shake his head. "What happened? Where were you? I looked for you before I left the aid station."

"He was clever. I never saw the blow coming. The next thing I knew, I was out in the middle of nowhere, near one of the relief trenches. I fell into one of them while I was still dazed, then had to make my way back. You had already gone, and I set out on foot for Rouen. I got a lift from a lorry coming back from the Front, carrying the dead. I've been waiting there for you, in the shadows of that doorway, for hours. I saw the motorcar arrive, and I went on waiting, knowing you had to come. Where were you? They told me at the Base Hospital that you weren't given a room there."

"I'd been told they were expecting me, but they weren't. I stayed in a convent I know of."

"Well, at least you were safe. For all I knew . . ." He shook his head helplessly.

"What are we to do now? I'm supposed to report to an aid station south of Ypres, but if what's happened here in Rouen is any indication, they have no reason to expect me there. And I don't have the proper authorization to return to Dr. Hicks. Or to leave France."

He was still nursing his grievance. "I couldn't believe you'd gone away without waiting for me. It could have been a hoax. In fact it was. A trick to lure you away from the protective Dr. Hicks. To Rouen, for instance, where if anything happened to you, you wouldn't be missed straightaway."

"Yes, but there was the message."

"Anyone who knew how to use a field telephone could have sent that," he scoffed.

"Dr. Hicks assured me the request was genuine. I asked him. He'd spoken to an officer, he said. And so I didn't have much choice, except to leave with the convoy. When there was no room waiting at the Base Hospital, I couldn't turn back. It was too late." I shook my head and felt my hair tumbling down. Quickly putting it up again, I said, "I shall have to get word to my father."

"It's more urgent to get you back to England. Bess, you can't stay in France. Don't you see? One attack can be put down to luck on his part. Two? A damned close call. Let's not wait for three."

I was reminded of Simon telling me that he was superstitious enough not to want to see me come close to dying a third time.

Captain Barclay was saying, "I thought I could protect you. I even told your father that I could. But I was wrong. Falling into that trench was the last straw."

"I don't want to go home to England. If I do, whoever this is will slip away and we'll never find out why he killed Major Carson."

"I don't know that it's important to find out," Captain Barclay said wearily. "Not if it puts you in danger like this."

"If I could find a way to return to Dr. Hicks and tell him that the message he received was only a ruse, he'd be happy to keep me there. And I'd be safer there than anywhere else. The only alternative is to go on to Ypres and let them decide what should be done about me."

"England, Bess. For your own sake. Or if not for your sake, then for your father's."

I sat there, trying to think. If I went to Ypres, whoever was out there would know where to look for me. If I returned to the forward aid station that I'd just left, he'd still know.

Perhaps it would be wiser to go to England, after all. Out of reach. But it went against the grain to see a murderer go free. To leave the patients I believed I could help. I had the sinking feeling that I'd be letting down not only Major Carson but Private Wilson and his wife as well.

What was that old saying?

He who turns and runs away lives to fight another day.

All very well and good. But if I ran away, who would I find to fight on that other day?

If the man with those pale eyes couldn't find me, then I couldn't find him. Could I?

CHAPTER NINE

ONCE AGAIN, THE decision was taken out of my hands in a very unexpected way.

We left the church finally, for there was no place here to rest. I couldn't take the American to the convent to stay for what was left of the night. It would have required too many explanations as to why I was bringing him with me, and the elderly nuns there would have felt uncomfortable if I simply told them that he too needed somewhere to stay. A British nurse didn't arrive with an attractive young man in tow, orderly or officer.

We found a small hotel on one of the streets not far from the cathedral, and Captain Barclay went in to bespeak a room. When I was certain he was being given one, I removed my telltale cap and apron, then hurried through the dark, empty streets alone, back to the convent. I reached for the knocker to summon someone inside.

It was several minutes before anyone appeared.

Surely even at this hour someone was awake, acting as porteress.

I knocked again, glancing anxiously over my shoulder. And I was just in time to see a figure sliding quickly into the deeper shadows of another doorway some four houses away.

More frightened than I cared to admit—for myself and for the nuns inside—I tried to think what to do. Screaming wouldn't help, and if I left the convent, I would be vulnerable with nowhere to turn.

I was on the point of leaving when the convent door opened at last and the elderly nun standing there said, "My dear," in French. "We were at our devotions. Is anything wrong?"

I glanced again at the spot where I'd seen the figure disappear. And at that same instant, he stepped out of the shadows and lifted a hand in salute before turning back the way I had come.

Captain Barclay had followed me—and while I was in a way glad of his protection, I was also angry with him for not staying safely in the hotel where I'd thought I'd left him.

"Who is that man?" the nun asked, peering after him.

"He's an orderly. He wished to be sure I was safe, late as it is. As it turned out, my transport was delayed."

"How very kind of him," she said, nodding. "But do come in, my dear, out of the damp air. It will do you no good."

I smiled and thanked her, and followed her into the kitchen, where a light still burned. There she saw me clearly for the first time and said, shocked, "But what has happened to you!"

I had forgot how disheveled I must appear. "A motorcar came along," I answered, trying to stay as close to the truth as I could, "and in my effort to avoid him in the narrow street, I slipped and fell into a shrubbery."

"You must wash your face and hands. And brush your hair. I will see to your garments. You can't leave us in the morning, looking like this. It would not be proper."

I thanked her again, and very shortly afterward, she saw me to the room I'd used earlier, offered me a warmed nightdress again, and gently closed the door.

Feeling a little better, I thought I might sleep. Instead, I tossed and turned, my mind unsettled over what to do.

I refused to eat breakfast in the morning, knowing how little the nuns had to spare, and hurried back to the hotel where I had left Captain Barclay. In the early light I could read the sign—L'HOTEL DE LILLE—and I stepped inside to find the clerk, a heavy man in his late fifties, just coming back on duty.

I said briskly, "Would you please tell my orderly, Private Barclay, that Sister Crawford is waiting for him in Reception?"

The clerk smiled, offered me a chair, and went up the stairs. After a few minutes, he came down again.

"The Private is not in his room."

"Not—has he come down for breakfast already?"

"I regret to say, it appears he has not slept in his room. I opened the door when there was no response." He shrugged. "He was not dressed properly. I thought perhaps he was . . . not what he appeared to be."

Taking that in, I said, "May I see for myself?"

"But of course, Mademoiselle." He escorted me up the stairs to the second floor and a room that overlooked the street. It was simple—a bed, an elderly wardrobe, a chair, and a table that could be used for meals or as a desk. The bed hadn't been turned down, and even the counterpane was smooth. No one had even sat down upon it. I could see that for myself.

"When did you last see my orderly?" I asked.

"He took a room, went up the stairs, and in a moment had come back down again, going out at once."

To follow me through the streets.

"And then?"

"I went to bed, Mademoiselle."

"Yes, of course."

I thanked the clerk and went down the stairs again, thinking furiously.

What had become of Captain Barclay? Surely he hadn't been set upon in the streets after leaving me safely at the convent door!

Was he lying hurt somewhere? But I'd taken the same route from the hotel and back to it this morning. I hadn't seen anything to arouse my suspicions.

Outside once more, I debated, and then finally went to the nearest police station, to ask if there had been any trouble in the area during the previous night.

"My orderly was to meet me this morning. He's missing," I explained.

But there had been no trouble, no arrests, no calls for assistance. The gendarme in charge assured me that it had been a quiet night. "They often are, Mademoiselle. There is little money for drunkenness and even less to steal."

I nodded, then asked where someone would be taken if he had been found injured on the street. "If he was English, Mademoiselle, he would most likely be carried to the American Base Hospital."

"Yes, of course."

Once more I was back in the street, this time on my way to the American Base Hospital in what used to be Rouen's handsome racetrack.

The orderly minding the gates was yawning prodigiously as he stretched, as if it were past time for him to be relieved.

I asked him if an American or British or Canadian soldier had been brought in during the night. "Someone found injured on the street, perhaps?"

"There's been a convoy of wounded, Sister, but only nine men this journey. All from sector aid stations. No one else has been brought in since well before midnight."

Then where had Captain Barclay got to?

I thanked him and went to find the officer in charge of the port.

He couldn't help me at first, and then he spoke to his sergeant, on the off chance there was any information that hadn't yet been officially reported.

The Sergeant, eyeing me with interest, said, "There was an orderly who couldn't account for himself wandering the streets last night. He's been taken up for desertion. I've sent to the Base Hospital to ask if he's one of theirs and what we should do with him. So far there's been no answer. And that's been several hours."

"Taken up for—" I exclaimed. It was the last thing that had crossed my mind. "Could I see this man, please?"

"It's a military matter, Sister," the officer told me politely. "He isn't the person you're looking for."

"Yes, I understand about the military matter," I said. "But I must also locate my missing orderly before I report to my own sector. If you have him, then I can explain why he isn't with me."

"What was he doing in the streets of Rouen, then? If he'd come in with the wounded, why didn't he say as much?" The officer was losing patience with me.

"I don't know. He'd been hurt himself."

"In a fight most likely," the Sergeant muttered. "We had a—there was a spot of trouble bringing him in."

I stood there, waiting. Finally the officer said, "All right, Sergeant Brent. Take her to him. If she does know him, we'll have a name, and then we can find out what he's running from."

I wanted to tell the Major that this particular man was resisting arrest because he was to meet me in the morning at the Hotel de Lille. But that would never do.

The Sergeant led me through the maze of the port to the small square building where miscreants and deserters were held until their situation could be determined. As I neared it, the odor of urine, stale spirits, cigarette smoke, and unwashed bodies struck me.

Three of the men incarcerated here were, the Sergeant told me, drunk and disorderly. He asked me to wait outside, and after a moment he brought out a reluctant Captain Barclay, who blinked in the watery morning light and then recognized me. There were new bruises and scrapes on his face, but I read the message in his eyes quite clearly.

Watch yourself.

I took a deep breath before I spoke.

"What's to become of him, Sergeant?"

His gaze never leaving the Captain's face, he said with some satisfaction, "He doesn't have the proper papers to be in Rouen. Desertion is a capital offense, and so is spying. And if you ask me, he looks more like a blood—a German officer than an orderly. He doesn't even sound like an Englishman."

"Yes, well, I expect that's because he's Canadian. He's an orderly, one Private Barclay, and Dr. Hicks can vouch for him."

"And who is Dr. Hicks when he's at home?" the Sergeant demanded, turning to look at me. I was suddenly grateful for the nuns' care in cleaning my coat and cap. The Sergeant was prepared to think the worst.

I told him, but it made no difference. Dr. Hicks wasn't here, and he wasn't likely to leave his post to come here and identify this man, much less explain why he had no pass.

We were getting nowhere.

I said, "Very well, take me back to the Major. He'll have to deal with this matter."

Turning on my heel, I started back the way I'd come, and the Sergeant was hard-pressed to usher Captain Barclay into his cell and still catch me up before I reached the Major.

I said, as I was summoned to his presence, "The man you have in custody is one Private Barclay, a Canadian. If you will contact Colonel Crawford through the War Office, you will be told why Private Barclay is in Rouen."

"Sister Crawford? Any relation to this Colonel?" he asked, dubious.

"That's not the issue here. Please contact the Colonel immediately. It's urgent business, and he will not care to have this man in your custody any longer than absolutely necessary."

"How is it that you know so much about this matter?"

I said, showing my exasperation, "I was asked to provide a reason for Private Barclay to pay a brief visit to Rouen. He was the driver who accompanied me when I was transferring patients from the forward aid station to the Base Hospital here."

He didn't believe me. But I thought perhaps he was just curious enough about what was going on to contact London.

The Major said, his voice sour, "And if that's the case, why wasn't a pass provided?"

"You must ask Colonel Crawford the answer to that. I expect there was no time to see to it."

"Why Rouen? And why weren't we told?"

"I'm not Colonel Crawford, Major. You must ask him. I'm overdue at my own post, and must make arrangements to return. I wish you a good morning."

Before the Major could think of a reason to detain me as well, I left his untidy office and walked away from the port with some misgivings.

And what was I to do now? I was hungry and it was starting to rain. I had no papers assigning me to transport to England, and I wasn't likely to be given them by this officer. I still had no way to reach my father. My best hope was that the Major would indeed contact him, and once the Colonel Sahib heard that Captain Barclay was in difficulty, he would assume that I needed help as well.

The only thing left to me, then, was to go to the Base Hospital, beg paper and pen, and then haunt the port until I found a Naval officer I knew by sight. With a smile and some excuse such as not having had time to write before this, it might be possible to persuade him to carry my letter to Portsmouth and post it there.

The American nurse in charge this morning looked askance at me when I was ushered into her tidy office. The small board on her desk identified her as Nurse Bailey.

"Sister Crawford? What can I do for you?"

"My transport back to the aid station hasn't come," I said pleasantly. "Is there somewhere I could sit and write letters? They will reach England sooner if I can hand them to someone at the port."

I could see that she was of two minds about offering me space. She was new to me, a small woman with light brown hair and a thin scar on her cheek. Pursing her lips, she considered me.

"The convoy back to your sector has already left," she told me primly. "You came in with wounded, I think? I was just going off duty."

I held on to my patience. "I've been posted to Passchendaele. Ypres. I was to meet someone here to transfer me to that sector. But he hasn't come."

"On the contrary. He was here looking for you at six o'clock this morning."

She lifted a sheet of paper from a basket to one side of her desk and read what someone had written there.

"'Driver arrived for one Sister Crawford. He was informed that she was not staying with us, and he left. No message.'"

"Indeed!" I said, repressing the urge to look over my shoulder. "Who took that down, may I ask?"

"Nurse Saunders, I believe. She would have been on duty."

"Would it be possible to speak to her? It's rather important."

"It is not possible. What are we to do with you, Sister Crawford? It would seem—and I must say your appearance rather bears it out—that you have mislaid your driver, rather than the other way around."

I lost my temper. It had been a long night, I'd had a fright, dealt with the recalcitrant port authorities trying to release Captain Barclay, and now this woman was treating me as if I had spent the night carousing and found myself too late for my transport. I'd only come here for pen, paper, and an opportunity to write to my father.

I said coldly, "If you care to look into my movements, I suggest you send someone to the convent where I spent the night. The nuns there will be happy to confirm that I chose to stay with them rather than go to an hotel as a woman alone. Now, will you allow me to write my letters or not?"

"I think not, Sister." She reached for paper and took up her pen. After a moment she considered what she had written and then said, "Your nursing service has very high standards, Sister Crawford. I am sending you to England for proper disciplining. One of our orderlies will escort you to the port, see you aboard the first available ship bound for Portsmouth, and hand this letter to the First Officer to be delivered to the proper authority as soon as you land at your destination. Do I make myself clear?" She was reaching for an envelope as she spoke, inserting the letter into it and sealing it.

I had to bite my tongue at the reprimand. I was getting what I wanted, actually, an opportunity to sail to England straightaway. Once there I could deal with these charges easily enough. And I could reach my father by telephone when I had landed, and set Captain Barclay free even sooner than I'd expected.

And then I had a brilliant notion.

I said, in as petulant a tone as I could muster, "It's not fair that I have to be sent home. What about the orderly who got me into this trouble? The port authority is holding him, but is he being sent home in disgrace? I think not! You are a woman, Nurse Bailey. Do you think it right that he escapes scot-free? He's in the Army Medical Services just as I am. Because he's a man, should his dereliction of duty be seen in a lesser light than mine?"

I watched her eyes. They narrowed as I was finishing.

"I have no authority over the port officials."

"The Major there would most likely honor any request coming from the American Base Hospital."

She was tempted.

"At the very least, you could try," I pleaded. "He's quite handsome, Barclay is. I tried to withstand his advances, that's why I went to the convent, but he followed me from the Hotel de Lille. Thank God he was stopped and asked for his papers! I don't know what he would have done."

She considered me for a moment, eyes narrowing again. Finally she rose from behind the desk, asked the direction of the convent, ordered me not to leave the room, and for good measure locked the door behind her as she went out.

I sat there fuming for over an hour. Had she believed any part of my story, or had I only succeeded in ruining my own reputation for no purpose? Time was passing, and I was locked in here.

Halfway through the long wait, I felt a spurt of horror. What if she'd gone in search of my driver instead? If he came here, promised to deliver me to Ypres as ordered, would she feel that I had learned my lesson and remand me into his care?

Surely not. He had gone long before this.

When I finally heard the key turn in the lock, I tried to make myself look frightened and contrite.

Nurse Bailey came in accompanied by a man dressed in the uniform of an orderly, but he was older, and I guessed—correctly as it turned out—that he was in charge.

I was told that he would escort me to the ship waiting on the river even now, and that he would deliver the letter Nurse Bailey had written to the First Officer, as she had intended from the start.

I didn't protest when he took my arm and led me out of the small room, through the passages, and out the gate of the hospital.

We walked together to the port. I was escorted up the gangway and handed over to a young officer who looked at me as if I were carrying the plague. Disgust was writ large in his face, and whatever he'd been told, he'd believed every word of it. I was conducted to the quarters of one of the officers and once more locked inside.

After a while I heard the sounds of the ship weighing anchor, then moving with the tide as it prepared to follow the river to the sea.

I'd failed to get Captain Barclay freed, but I'd be in Portsmouth in a matter of hours.

My worry now was, could I reach my father once I got there? Or was he off on one of his mysterious forays and out of touch for days on end? What could Mother do in his stead? Was Simon even well enough to attend to this?

CHAPTER TEN

IT SEEMED TO take longer than usual to reach the mouth of the river. More often than not, unless I was assigned to duty with the wounded belowdecks, I stood at the rail, watching our passage downstream. Instead, here in this stuffy little cabin, I tried to picture it in my mind as a distraction.

Finally I could feel the swells as we left the river behind and met the Channel. That much closer to England. Somewhere in the narrow ship's passage outside my door I heard someone begin to retch, and then the sound of feet rushing toward the companionway.

I was a good sailor, and I stood at the porthole, the lamp behind me turned off, and looked out at gray water meeting a gray sky. There was always a chance that we would encounter a German sub, and if the weather was good, the chances were doubled. But from my vantage point, there could have been half a hundred out there, and I'd have no way of guessing.

With a sigh, I closed the black curtains and sat down, not in the mood to relight the lamp. I was tired enough to sleep, but tempting as the bunk was, I wanted to stay alert if I could.

I'd just stifled a yawn when I heard the click of the key in the lock, and my door opened a very little.

I reached for the lamp, lit it, and stood there, waiting in its pool of light.

A familiar face peered around the edge. I recognized an officer I had sailed with before on a number of occasions.

"You aren't about to throw the inkwell at me, are you?" Captain Garrison asked with a grin.

"I promise," I said, and he stepped into the tiny cabin.

"I was just informed you were on board. Locked away like a common miscreant. What happened, Sister Crawford?"

"It's a long story," I told him wryly, "but I've transgressed, I'm told, and I'm being shipped home in disgrace to face my hour of judgment."

He laughed outright. "Good God, Bess, did you take a shot at the First Lord of the Admiralty?"

"Nothing so grand. I was accused of fraternizing with an orderly and in consequence missing my transport to Ypres." My hand went of its own accord to my pocket. What if I'd been searched and Simon's little handgun had been discovered?

"I don't believe it! Hang on—is that the other felon we have in irons belowdecks?"

"Unless he's an American, I wouldn't know."

"Yes, he must be. He told one of my men that his ancestors had shown us a thing or two at Yorktown, and he was ready to have another go at it himself."

It was my turn to laugh. But what was I to tell Captain Garrison? I decided on the truth. Well, part of it.

"We were both assigned to Ypres. But something went wrong with our transport, and I spent the night in a convent I knew of in Rouen. On his way back to the hotel where he was staying, Barclay was picked up for not having the proper papers. I tried to explain the situation to the harbor police with no luck, and when I went to the Base Hospital in the hope of finding pen and paper to write to my father, a nurse there decided I looked disreputable enough to have been up to something nefarious, and she sent me back to England. I begged her to let my betrayer be punished as well, and I expect that's why he's in irons below."

"You were deucedly lucky this was my ship. There are letters in my safe that must be meant for the Inquisition. I was told under pain of death not to open them but to hand them over along with you when I reached Portsmouth."

"Yes, well, I do understand in part. There's always the fear of spies in a place like Rouen. You've got people coming and going in every direction, speaking I don't know how many languages, and there are warnings everywhere to report any suspicious activity. I doubt Nurse Bailey has been in France very long. She put the worst possible interpretation on the situation. I'd have done the same in her shoes."

"No, you wouldn't have," he said. "You'd have got to the bottom of it. Wait here, I ought to let your American out of the brig before he thinks of a way to scuttle the ship. I've enough on my hands with the Germans."

With that he was gone, and it was some time before he reappeared. "I've offered Barclay my cabin to clean himself up a bit. He was all right once he knew you were safe. I need to go to the bridge and keep an eye on things." He reached into his pocket and took out two letters. "I'll leave these with you." He hesitated. "Barclay strikes me more as an officer than an orderly."

"He is. He was so eager to get back to France he was willing to take any position available. I think his doctor back in Somerset was trying to teach him a lesson, that his wounds haven't healed sufficiently to return to his regiment. A little humble pie, as it were."

Nodding, he went on his way. I folded my arms on the makeshift desk, put my head down on my arms, and went to sleep.

I'd consider what to do once we approached Portsmouth Roads.

I must have slept soundly. It was the rumble of the anchor cable feeding out that brought me awake, startled and confused. I tried to make myself presentable and settled my cap on my hair. My valise was by the cabin door. But I stayed where I was. It was one thing to be treated as a guest by Captain Garrison and quite another to appear on deck prematurely and place him in an awkward situation.

I could hear the wounded being carried off the ship, and then the tramp of many feet as the next contingent of troops came aboard.

Finally there was a tap at my door and Captain Garrison was there. "All clear," he told me. "I think it's safe enough to go ashore. There was no welcoming committee out there, and my officers won't talk. I've procured passes out of the port for you as well. I'm afraid after that, my authority stops."

"You've been more than kind," I told him warmly. "I don't know how to thank you for all you've done."

He brushed that aside. "I'll look forward to seeing you on another voyage, this time not under duress."

We walked together to the deck, where I saw Barclay, looking far more himself now, waiting for me. Without a word we disembarked and made our way along the docks to the gates. The Captain was several steps behind me, as was proper, but once we were in the town itself, he caught me up.

"Do you know everyone in Christendom, Bess Crawford?" he asked, a repressed note of disapproval in his voice.

"You forget," I said. "Since *Britannic,* I must have made the journey to France and back half a hundred times. It would be strange if I didn't know most of the ships' officers. Which makes it all the worse when they go missing. The First Officer is new, replacing a man who lost his leg during the winter. And the Third Officer is new as well. His ship was sunk on convoy duty and he's learning the run to France—"

I broke off, watching a motorcar coming toward us. I stopped stock-still as I recognized it.

"What is it?" Captain Barclay asked, tensing.

But by that time it was near enough for him to recognize the driver. My father.

As he greeted us I asked, "How did you know I was coming in?"

"I was having dinner with the Port Captain when you arrived. Captain Garrison sent a signal. He didn't specify my daughter was on board, but he did say wounded and nurses. Not sisters. And a signal never includes hospital staff—it's assumed they're aboard with the wounded. I thought I ought to have a look. But we hadn't finished our Port, and Mackenzie insisted that I stay until it had been round once."

Then he turned to greet Captain Barclay, making no remark about the torn uniform or the scrapes and cuts on his face, not to mention his knuckles.

"Thank you for bringing her home safely," he said.

Captain Barclay grimaced. "Not without difficulty."

The Colonel Sahib ushered us into the motorcar, and we said very little as we drove through the narrow, twisting streets toward the main road north through Hampshire. Clear of the city, we picked up the first showers of rain. My father settled to a steady speed and then nodded to me to begin my account of events, interrupted from time to time by the Captain. As I spoke, he listened with a grim expression clearly visible even in the cloudy darkness.

"Good God!" he said when I had given him all the details. "I'll see what I can do to set this business to rights. I think it might be best if Barclay the orderly simply disappeared, and Captain Barclay returned to the clinic for further treatment of his troublesome wound after his brief furlough to London."

Captain Barclay opened his mouth to argue, thought better of it, and said only, "Thank you, sir."

"I'm afraid my reputation can't be repaired quite so easily," I said ruefully.

"Perhaps Nurse Bailey can be thanked for helping you smuggle one of our spies safely out of France and back into England."

"I think," I said, considering the suggestion, "she might be happier if I had helped capture a notorious German spy."

"God help us if that got back to the wrong ears. No, we'll offer our sincerest gratitude to both of you for unspecified services to the Crown."

I wanted to ask the Colonel Sahib if he thought I was safe now. But I was reluctant to broach the subject so soon. And how was I to get back to France until this whole business was settled? It was a dilemma.

As the rain turned into a downpour shortly after we'd crossed into Somerset, we stopped briefly for a late supper until it blew over.

My father had said nothing about Simon, and I had been afraid to ask, for fear he was not healing as he should. It was one of the drawbacks to being a nurse. I knew too much about wounds and a man's chances of survival. Finally I took my courage in my hands and said, "Is Simon all right?"

"A deucedly poor patient. Your mother has had her hands full." And that was all he would say.

The conversation turned to Major Carson, and I asked my father if he'd ever met William Morton.

"Actually I haven't. He and Sabrina eloped, and after that her father never spoke to her again. I thought that rather harsh. It left her with nowhere to turn in the event she was ever unhappy. And so, as far as I know, she has stayed with her actor."

"A pity." I took a deep breath. "Julia told me that in one of his last letters, her husband was angry with someone in his company but didn't mention a name because of the censors. But soon afterward the offending soldier was sent to another sector. Do you think that soldier could have been William Morton? It's a pity we don't have the journal the Major kept. It might give us some answers."

Captain Barclay interrupted. "Who is William Morton?"

My father said, "He married the Major's younger sister. The family didn't approve of him. It would be interesting to see what sort of war he's had."

"He could have lured the Major to that false rendezvous. But why wait all these years?" I asked.

"A good point. Still, there's no accounting for a long-harbored anger. It can spill over unexpectedly," my father said.

"Which reminds me, Julia told me when I visited her that Sabrina didn't come to the memorial service. That she was poor again. Her words."

"She can't live as she's used to on a private soldier's pay," my father agreed. "There could have been an argument over settling an allowance on her."

"But how would the Major have felt about that? I know he was closer to his other sister, but surely he didn't carry on his father's feeling that she made her choice and must live with it."

"He never discussed it with me," my father said as the chargers of food were set before us. Shortages or not, it smelled heavenly, and we set to with an appetite. "And of course by rights he shouldn't have. It was a family matter."

"Julia might know," I said doubtfully, finishing the ham and turning to the last of the roasted potatoes on my plate. "But the same difficulty applies. Could you speak to the Major's solicitors?"

"I'd rather not make it quite so official. There's the other sister. Valerie. You could call on her. She might be able to shed some light on Sabrina's situation and her brother's handling of it. She lives in Gloucestershire. Not all that far away."

"I don't know her as well as I do Julia," I reminded him. "I shall need a better reason than to offer my condolences at this late date."

"Your mother will think of something."

Captain Barclay said casually, "I shall be glad to accompany Sister Crawford, sir. If you like."

"I can drive myself. If you remember," I told him.

We finished our tea and then set out once more. The rain had stopped, and after a while the moon followed us up the drive to the house.

Two mornings later—still encumbered with Captain Barclay but armed with an excuse provided by my mother—we set out for

Gloucestershire. Valerie and her husband lived on the outskirts of Gloucester, within sight of the castle.

She had married a man in banking who now served with the Navy.

She received me cordially, and I gave her a set of embroidered baby clothes, with a cap and a matching pram coverlet done up in lilac and palest green, for she was expecting a child in three months' time. Julia hadn't mentioned it, and when I said as much, Valerie said, "I expect she was wishing she also had a child on the way. But how kind of your mother to remember! I shall write to her at once, but you must tell her I shall treasure this gift."

"I shall. Does Sabrina have any children? I don't remember."

"A little boy. The most adorable child. I went to see her in Oxfordshire this winter as soon as I heard the news. Our old Nanny wrote to me."

"Did you tell Julia or the Major?"

"I wrote to Vincent. I don't know if he ever received the letter. He didn't answer. But they do get lost, don't they? Letters to the Front?"

"Yes. Sadly," I answered.

"I can't believe he's dead. It's just not possible. And it makes me anxious for George now. He's at sea, you know. We don't hear, his mother and I, for weeks on end."

"When they're at sea, there's nowhere to post a letter," I said, and she smiled.

"I never thought of it that way."

"Sabrina eloped, didn't she?"

"Yes, our father had forbade her to see William again. I wished at the time that I'd had the courage to attend the ceremony, but I was rather afraid of what my father might do or say."

"Did she ever send you any photographs? Of the happy couple?"

She frowned. "I never liked to display them. I didn't want to annoy my father."

"I'd like to see them. I don't believe I've seen Sabrina since Vincent left Sandhurst."

"I'm really not up to searching for them. Another time, perhaps."

"Is he dark or fair? William? My mother thought she'd seen him in a play once. Molière? Or Sheridan, perhaps."

"It was so hard to tell. They weren't very good photographs, I'm afraid." And she pointedly changed the subject, clearly not interested in her sister's husband.

We talked about her pregnancy and her garden, and then it was time to take my leave.

When I met Captain Barclay in the pub where I'd left him, his first question was "Did you learn anything?"

"Only that she doesn't wish to talk about her sister's husband," I said when we'd reached the motorcar.

"Not surprising."

"But her sister has a child. A little boy, born sometime in the winter."

Captain Barclay whistled softly. "This man Morton might not have fought for his wife, but he would for his child, wouldn't he? And he'd have been furious with his brother-in-law for snubbing him. It must have seemed rather callous, I should think, to be met with a refusal to do anything for his family."

Defending Major Carson, I said, "We don't know that he did, do we? It's possible that William Morton wasn't satisfied with his offer."

"That's true," Captain Barclay replied thoughtfully. "And there's only one way to settle that—if your father is successful in discovering any provisions in the Major's will. If he's taken care of the wife or the child—or both—then Morton is out of the running."

"I did ask Valerie if she had a photograph of her brother-in-law. But she's feeling her pregnancy and wasn't particularly interested in making the effort to find one. She didn't seem to think any of them were very good, anyway."

"What about the man's old theatrical company? Did they have posters and the like? As you said in Rouen, eyes never change."

"I don't know if they still exist or how to contact them. Sabrina might have something of that sort. Or a photograph of her husband in uniform. Every wife wants one. In case . . ."

"In case," he agreed.

A silence fell, and I found myself thinking about Simon again, all the way home.

When I told my parents about Sabrina's child, they were surprised. No one had mentioned the boy to them. They were of the same mind, that if Major Carson had been murdered, his brother-in-law could have the best possible motive.

My father said, "It's not like Vincent to be as vindictive as his father was. I don't understand it. I'll look into the will. I can be quite frank, I think, and ask the solicitors if the boy was provided for. If not, I can suggest that Julia might care to make amends."

"I'm not sure she will," I said, considering my conversation with Julia. "She doesn't seem to be as fond of Sabrina as Valerie is. I wish I'd thought to ask Valerie about the will. She must have been there for the reading."

"Hardly something you could bring up, without a very sound reason," my mother said. "But getting back to what happened to Vincent, it's possible that William Morton chose to badger him after the baby was born, and he wouldn't have cared for that. Even if he'd already included his sister in his own will, he would have resented being pressed that way. And so the two of them quarreled, and Morton went away with the worst possible view of Vincent's intentions. Morton was worried about his family, and Vincent had more than enough on his mind, keeping his men alive. They didn't like each other to begin with. This could only have made matters between them even more tense."

"She has a point," Captain Barclay put in. "With a big push coming, Morton would have been anxious to know the matter was settled. Either one—or both—could have died. One of my men asked for leave to see his widowed mother. He wanted me to sign the request before we fought. I did, but he was killed in the second wave."

"I must go up to London tomorrow," my father said. "I'll see what I can discover."

Simon hadn't been in the house, much to my surprise. What's more, my mother had put me off when I had asked to go and visit him in his cottage. She was also rather vague about his condition.

And so when my father took the Captain off to the clinic the next morning and my mother went to see a woman who had lost her husband at Passchendaele, I slipped out of the house and walked through the back garden and the wood to Simon's cottage.

It was small but comfortable, and it had suited him well. Filled with well-read books and memorabilia from his years in the Army, it had a masculine air that I'd always found pleasant.

Coming up the walk, I kept an eye to the windows, expecting him to see me approaching and pretend not to be at home. My mother was right; men were often not very good at waiting to heal, impatient and eager to be about their business again. And I suspected that he probably wouldn't be pleased to have me know he had not taken as good care of himself as he should.

I tapped at the door, waiting to be admitted. But he didn't answer the summons or come to the door. I tapped again, in case he was sleeping, and when he still didn't open the door to me, I was angry enough to open it myself, and standing on the threshold, I called his name.

"There's no use in hiding," I added. "I know you're here."

But my voice echoed in the cottage, and I knew it must be empty. Simon wasn't there.

Disbelieving, I walked in and searched. The bed was made up, there were no newspapers neatly stacked by the table where he ate his meals, and when I looked in the wardrobe, I saw that his valise was gone.

Frightened, I went out of the cottage and shut the door behind me before almost running back to the house.

When my mother came in an hour later, I was waiting for her.

"Where is Simon?" I asked. "He's not here, and he's not in the cottage. What is it you're keeping from me?"

She set down her basket, her expression suddenly kind, and I had the most dreadful premonition.

I wanted to cover my ears or tell her not to answer my question. But she was already saying the words, and there was no way to stop them now.

CHAPTER ELEVEN

MY DEAR, HE'S been very ill—"

"I was there when he was brought in, I know how serious his wound was. I thought—I was told you were nursing him. I took that to mean that he was here, or at the cottage."

"He did come here when he was well enough. He signed himself out of hospital and a driver brought him to Somerset. But there was infection, you see, and his arm—we thought for a time he would lose it. Dr. Gaines cleaned it as best he could, but Simon is still running a fever. He doesn't always remember where he is."

"Dr. Gaines? Then Simon is at the clinic."

"Yes, but he specifically asked—I wasn't to tell you."

"Why did he sign himself out of hospital? He knew the risk he'd be taking."

"There was some pressing matter he had to deal with. He came here to use your father's telephone. He didn't have access to one in Portsmouth. Too many ears, he said."

I remembered his urgent need to reach England, and how I had given him morphine to keep him quiet. Biting my lip, I considered all the possible outcomes of gangrene.

"I'm going to Longleigh House."

"Bess, is that such a good idea? Simon—"

"I'm a nurse, Mother, I am very good at what I do, as Dr. Gaines himself told me. I could be able to help. Can Father pull a few strings? I need an interim posting there while my situation is being considered. I can't walk in and ask to be allowed to help with a single surgical case."

"Yes, I'm sure he can see to that. If not, then I'm sure Dr. Gaines will be able to arrange it." She started toward the telephone closet, then stopped. "If it's any consolation, I think you're doing the right thing. Simon made me promise, you see. And I don't break promises to Simon Brandon lightly." She turned on her heel and left me standing there.

Several hours and countless telephone conversations later, I was told to report to the clinic on Wednesday morning at nine. That was two days away. I didn't know how I was to keep myself from pacing the floor into the night.

I found my mother in the kitchen, scrubbing the tabletop while our Cook stood there frowning at her, tight-lipped and clearly troubled.

I said, "We're going to find Sabrina Morton. I don't know how we'll manage it, but we will."

Her face brightened. "I believe your father left her direction on his desk. He hadn't decided to give it to you."

"Why not?"

"I think he was worried about this business with Major Carson. That you might discover something speaking to her that would take you back to France. Darling, Simon is fighting for his life, and that nice Captain Barclay has reinjured his leg. Your father is looking for some way to keep you safe. Until then, he wants you to stay in England."

I remembered that arm around my neck in the darkness as I was about to wash my face. And the way the wing of that motorcar brushed against me in Rouen. But I said resolutely, "I don't need protection. Dr. Hicks and his people were keeping an eye on me. They would again."

"You might not be posted there next time. And your father has learned that you weren't expected in Ypres at all. Once you left the security of Dr. Hicks's aid station, you were vulnerable. And you said yourself that he believed the message was completely genuine. He could be wrong another time as well."

Dr. Hicks had done his best for me, but he was overworked and exhausted like the rest of us. He couldn't be expected to ward off every danger.

"Then let's go speak to Sabrina. *She* can't do me any harm, and we just might learn something that would put an end to this frightful business."

And so it was that we found ourselves on the road to Cornwall. I'd thought that Sabrina lived in Oxfordshire, but my father didn't often make mistakes, and if he said Cornwall, then Cornwall it was. Because of the distance, we had planned to stay the night.

We drove through Devon, crossed the Tamar, and set out across Cornwall to the seaside village of Fowey, which actually sat above the river for which it was named. Taking a room at the Fowey Hotel, we had dinner there on the charming terrace overlooking the estuary where the river met the sea.

Afterward, as the evening was fine, we walked down toward the harbor. Unlike other harbor towns, Fowey had very little flat land along the riverbank for a settlement to grow, and so it was built upward, a maze of gardens and paths and houses and cottages cheek by jowl and leading ever downward until we reached St. Fimbarrus Church, and from there it was only a few steps to the water.

The clerk at the hotel had told us that The Mermaid Inn was along the water, and more accessible by boat than by foot. But we strolled along the river for a bit and watched the ferry plow toward Polruan across the way, and then saw the sign for The Mermaid. A narrow walkway bridged the gap from the small restaurant where we stood to the entrance to the inn, and led up steep stairs to the doorway. From there I could see just below where boats could tie up.

The inn had seen better days, thanks to the war and the fact that many of the men who brought their own boats or yachts to this place were now fighting in France.

There was a woman behind the desk who watched our approach without enthusiasm, as if she knew we weren't looking for lodgings. I moved slightly ahead of my mother and said pleasantly, "I believe Mrs. William Morton lives here?"

"And who would be wanting her?" the woman asked, her voice neither friendly nor unwelcoming.

My mother, just behind me, answered the query. "Mrs. Crawford and her daughter, Sister Crawford. We knew her brother and her parents. Since we were in Cornwall while my daughter is on leave from her duties in France, we felt we ought to pay our respects."

The woman regarded us for a moment, then said, "I'll see if she wishes to receive you."

I thought at first the woman was being rude. But she walked into the dimly lit interior of the inn where I could just see a staircase leading upward and to one side, a tiny dining room down two steps. A potted palm stood next to the entrance to the dining room, and a table with fresh flowers in a green vase added a spot of color by the side of the stairs. Nice touches, but even these couldn't eliminate the depressing air of the inn.

The woman returned shortly. "She's in room seven. Just knock at the door."

We thanked her and walked farther into Reception before taking ourselves up the stairs to the first floor. Number seven was at the end of the passage, and we knocked lightly, as we'd been told. My mother gave me a conspiratorial look, then faced the door as it opened.

Sabrina Morton had always been the prettier of the two Carson sisters, but in the late evening light she appeared to be the elder of the two rather than the younger.

"Come in," she said, inviting us into a room looking upriver and set out as a sitting room. A door into a second room was open just a little, and inside we could see a bed and a crib. "I can't think why you should wish to call on me. Did Valerie send you? Or was it Julia, having a sudden change of heart?"

"Neither, as it happens," my mother said. "You weren't at the memorial service for your brother, and we were sorry to have missed that opportunity to offer our condolences. You were fond of Vincent, as I remember."

"Once upon a time," she said.

"Yes," my mother replied, as if Sabrina had agreed with her, then turned to me. "I think you remember Elizabeth? She's a nursing sister, Vincent may have mentioned it. She's currently on leave from France, and as we had a few days before she goes back, we decided to visit Cornwall again. I remember coming to Fowey as a small child. It's hardly changed at all, has it?"

Sabrina greeted me coolly, then offered us chairs. "I can't offer you tea as well. I'm afraid the restaurant has closed."

"Thank you, but we dined at our hotel," I answered, resigning myself to a difficult conversation. "It's good to see you again, Sabrina."

"Is it? I don't recall a visit from you after my marriage."

"You hadn't invited us to the wedding," my mother reminded her with a smile. "We thought perhaps you'd excluded us when you excluded your brother."

"He was a hypocrite. Vincent. Brother or not. He could have made our lives a little easier after our father died by offering me my inheritance. He kept it instead, you know. My sister was given our mother's inheritance as well—as the elder daughter, that was fair enough. I didn't quarrel with it. But it was cruel to deny me *anything*. I can't forgive him for that, and I couldn't in good conscience go to his service when I felt as I do."

"He knew what his father thought about your marriage. Perhaps he found it difficult to go against *his* express wishes."

"He chose to do that. He didn't like Will any better than our father did. And what had Will ever done to my brother? Or even my father, for that matter? He married me because he loved me, and I loved him. My father married for love. Vincent as well. Where's the difference?"

The bitterness in her voice touched me. There was no polite way to point out that her choice of husband, however much she loved him, had not been quite the same as Vincent's marriage to Julia. Or Valerie's to her banker. They had come from the same circle, while William Morton had definitely not.

"I never met Will," I said. "Do you have a photograph of him? I should like to see it."

"We could never afford to have a family likeness taken," she told me bluntly. "Even when he was leaving for France."

"A pity. For your sake and your son's."

My mother said gently, "We came, Sabrina, because we remembered you as a child. What your father and your brother decided to do is not our fault."

I thought then that Sabrina was going to cry. But she lifted her head and said, "You'll go home and tell Valerie what I've come down to. Living with Will's cousin in this inn that struggles to keep itself afloat financially. On a private soldier's pay, I couldn't contribute much to my keep, but I do what I can to help Constance." She put out her hands, red and rough from a servant's work. "Tell them about these too."

"I have no intention of telling Julia or Valerie anything," my mother retorted. "If they wish to know where or how you live, then let them come and see for themselves."

There was a whimper from the bedroom. Sabrina said, "My son. I've just put him to bed. He's begun to crawl, and I live in dread that he'll fall into the river when I'm not looking. But I have nowhere else to go."

It was self-pity, but as the lower doors to the inn must lead directly to that tiny docking area where the usual house would have a porch, such a tragedy could happen.

"Nowhere else? But what of Will's family?" my mother asked.

"Will's father and brothers live in the Welsh Marches, near Hay-on-Wye. They offered me a home, but I couldn't accept. They were no happier than my own family when I married Will. If I must live on charity, I prefer to be here."

The whimper settled into a sleepy grumble, and then there was silence.

Thinking to change the subject, I said, "How long have you lived here in Fowey?"

"Since just after Boxing Day. Where we lived in Woodstock, the owner of the cottage refused to give us any more credit. She kept most of our belongings as well. Except for the cradle. I wouldn't let her take that. It was Will's when he was a baby."

"I'm sorry," I said. "I didn't mean to bring up a painful subject."

"You couldn't have known." She took a deep breath. "My father would tell you that I have made my bed and should lie on it without complaint. It would be easier if I didn't have a child. I could find work, with so many men gone to fight the Kaiser. I could support myself. But I don't want to leave him. He's all I have now, and I would rather accept charity than put him in the care of strangers. Or leave him with Constance, because she's too busy keeping the inn from going under to watch him."

I repeated, unwilling to believe my ears, "All you have?"

"An actor is paid to act, not to fight the Germans." She turned to look out the window. The port wasn't visible from here. It was up-river, where the ships that once carried clay and other goods docked. "Do you know, I'd been so afraid Will might contract influenza. I wasn't prepared, after all this time, for the telegram reporting he'd been killed. It seemed so terribly unfair, somehow. As if God had spared him the sickness because he was destined to die in battle." The unshed tears fell now, and she let them fall.

My mother took out a handkerchief and handed it to Sabrina. She murmured her gratitude as she took it.

"You're a widow?" I asked. "But—"

"He died two weeks before Vincent did. I'll always wonder if my brother killed my husband. They say this sometimes happens, that scores are settled on the battlefield. If this is true, then God avenged Will, and someone shot Vincent."

She broke down then, and there was no comfort we could offer. I was still shocked by what she'd told us. After a moment she said, "Please go. Please."

We took our leave, and my mother embraced Sabrina. She resisted at first, and then flung her arms around her.

We were back in the passage when I thought of something. It didn't really matter now. But still, I felt I should ask, if only to settle a point.

I stepped back into the room. "Sabrina. I'd like to know. What color were your husband's eyes?"

Her voice was almost inaudible. "Blue. Palest blue, like ice. Except when he smiled for me. Why? What does it matter?"

"I was hoping perhaps your son had inherited them. To keep Will's memory alive."

She smiled through her tears. "He has."

I thanked her and rejoined my mother.

We reached the stairs and went down them. Constance was no longer there in Reception.

My mother said, "See if you can find an envelope or something in the desk over there, Bess, dear. I'd like to leave a little gift for the child."

I did, searching through the stationery before finding a fresh one. But as I handed it to my mother, something fell on the floor, and I retrieved it to replace it amongst the other papers in an untidy stack.

And then I realized that the envelope on top was postmarked from France, and I opened it, telling myself that it was not snooping. But it was.

It was the letter from William Morton's commanding officer, telling Morton's widow how her husband had died—gallantly and without pain at the end, his mind on his wife and child, not his fate. That he had fought well for King and Country and inspired his fellow soldiers with his courage.

A standard letter, meant to make the grieving family feel that their sacrifice was not in vain, that their son or husband or brother had died as a man should, with courage and dignity.

No mention of the reality of dying in a filthy trench or alone somewhere in No Man's Land, the rotting corpse brought in during the next collection of the dead and wounded. No mention of his fellow soldiers stoically watching as he took his last breaths or the orderlies racing to find and stanch the bleeding, the nursing sister shaking her head, accepting that he had died on the way to the aid station. None of the panic, the screams, the blood, the despair. Only comfort.

I looked at the signature, expecting to see Colonel Prescott's name there. But a Colonel wouldn't write a letter for a dying soldier. His Captain would, and this was duly signed by a Captain Forester, who may have been kinder because he knew Morton by sight and could even speak with some familiarity about how he had served.

I set the letter back in its envelope and put it in among the papers, then realized that the other sheets I held in my hands were copies of correspondence to a dozen or more charitable organizations for widows and orphans, begging for assistance. Sitting here at Reception, Sabrina had filled the empty hours writing these, swallowing her pride for her son's sake. I could understand now how deep her feelings went against her brother for denying her what she felt was hers by right.

Her family had failed her, and it appeared that these organizations, overwhelmed by similar requests, were finding it hard to spread their funds thin enough to help everyone.

Sabrina had come a long way from the happy child racing through the orchard with her sister at her heels, the first week after we'd come home from India. Long curls flying out of their ribbons, no inkling of the future in store.

I put the papers back together as carefully as I could so that Sabrina wouldn't have the added shame of realizing that we had seen them. Better by far to accept my mother's gift for the child as it was meant, rather than wonder if it had been given out of pity rather than love.

The light still danced in the current as the river made its way to the sea, but the color had changed to gold as the sun cast long rays across the estuary. Upriver the shadows were already deep where the trees crowded down to the banks and shut off our view of the port. We stood there for a moment, looking down at the fortifications at the river's mouth. They too were gold flecked, and I thought how lovely this setting was. And how much sorrow it encompassed.

My mother said, as we started back the way we'd come, "Well."

I sighed. "It wasn't Will Morton, was it? That letter from Captain Forester looked all too official, and there was the telegram as well."

"No. It couldn't have been," she agreed.

"How awfully sad. Julia never mentioned that Sabrina's husband had been killed. Nor did Valerie."

"I expect she hasn't told them."

"We shouldn't have come. We've only upset her."

My mother said, "Yes, but we're talking about murder, aren't we? Better us than the police. Or the Army. They wouldn't have been as kind."

And that was cold comfort as we walked back to the gray stone church and then found our way in the gathering dusk up the twisting path back to the hotel. A small dog came out to a garden gate, barking ferociously, then jumping up to be greeted, his tail wagging madly. As I petted the furry head, scratching behind his ears, I thought about the child growing up on the river. Would he ever have a dog?

I couldn't understand how the young officer I'd known in India could have denied his widowed sister some financial help. But then he himself had died only a short time after his brother-in-law. There had been no chance to do anything. Still, he must surely have known about the child and guessed what Sabrina's circumstances must be. He could have written to Julia to make his wishes known. She would have carried them out, if he had. She would have done anything he'd asked. Even a small allowance would have made a huge difference in Oxfordshire and she could have kept the cottage.

For that matter, Valerie—with her inheritance from her mother as well as her father—who had visited Sabrina and must have seen the straits she was in with a new baby, could have done something to help.

I commented on this to my mother as we walked on.

"I expect everyone felt it was the Morton family who ought to step in, since Sabrina's family had cut her off. And they did offer Sabrina a home, didn't they? Perhaps Julia will have a change of heart, once the solicitors have finished and Vincent's estate is settled. I'll drop a word in her ear, without mentioning Cornwall. She has no child of her own, and she may be willing to consider the boy's needs."

But the boy was a Morton. Not a Carson. Would that make any difference?

As we reached the last few steps of the path up to our hotel, my mother took a deep breath and said, "Who killed Vincent? I'd have answered, Someone in his company who knew Morton and thought he and his family had been badly treated—if it weren't for the fact that Vincent wasn't shot and that his body was discovered some distance from the Front. Simple revenge isn't that personal or clever."

I had no answer for her.

"I'm very glad you're home and safe," she went on, putting an arm around my shoulders and drawing me to her in a brief embrace as we reached the tall white doors of the hotel.

Later I stood by the window of my room, watching the lights of boats plying the river. They couldn't go beyond the fortifications, for the sea was probably mined, or a submarine might be lurking in the black depths farther out.

As they bobbed about far below on their mysterious errands, fishing or simply longing for another time, I asked myself the questions I'd put off until I'd said good night to my mother.

If it hadn't been Will Morton who killed Vincent Carson and Private Wilson or had twice tried to kill me, then who was it?

If it wasn't revenge for his treatment of his sister that had brought about Major Carson's murder and all that had followed, what was driving this man?

There had to be a reason. But would any of us be able to find it?

CHAPTER TWELVE

WHEN I ARRIVED at the clinic, there were courtesies to observe before I could go and look for Simon Brandon.

First, the official visit with Matron to present my orders. She remembered me, and we talked about France for a few minutes, and then she passed me to Dr. Gaines. He welcomed me just as warmly and sent for tea.

"I've just made rounds. I could use a cup," he said, offering me the only other chair in his narrow office. "Tell me about France."

I tried to remember interesting surgeries or treatments I'd observed, because I knew that was what he wanted to hear, not how the war was progressing. The wounded in his care told their own tale of what was happening in the trenches.

And then Sister Masters was there to show me to my quarters and outline my duties. Once more with my experience I'd be serving in the surgical theater when needed.

It was after eleven o'clock by that time, and she suggested that I meet the rest of the staff at lunch. Some of them had been here when I first came to the clinic, and others were new. As before, the staff was handpicked by Dr. Gaines, and we enjoyed a lively discussion about the patients and what I'd been doing in France. Half my mind was elsewhere, but I managed to hold my own from long practice. We were just finishing our meal when mercifully Sister Masters suggested that I take the next half hour to settle in. I rose from the table, took my leave of the others as I thanked her, and went up the main stairs.

I'd done this so often that it took no more than five minutes to unpack and stow my belongings where I could reach them quickly when needed. My mother had seen to it that my uniforms were starched and ready to wear, and I was grateful.

And then I sat on the bed and stared at nothing for another several minutes. Finally I got to my feet and walked out of my room. Now that the time had come I was almost afraid of what I was going to find when I left this sanctuary and walked down to the wards.

But it had to be done. I went down the steps, counting them as I'd done so many times during my routine duties, the count always helping me put one patient out of my mind and prepare me to address the next.

As I passed the doorway to the room where convalescents sat to read, play cards, or talk, I glimpsed Captain Barclay at a table writing what appeared to be a letter. Fortunately he didn't look up. I had only a very little time in which to find Simon, and I didn't want to call attention to what I was about to do.

Simon, I'd been told, was in the surgical ward in the back of the house where the library used to be. Most of the books had been removed for safekeeping, although a few volumes were left amidst the medical kit filling the shelves now. As I entered, I could feel the warmth of the sun on my face from the long windows that overlooked one of the gardens. A slight breeze lifted the thin curtains and blew lightly against my cap.

The sister on duty smiled and nodded to me. She believed I was there to familiarize myself with all the patients, and I let her take a moment to describe the conditions of her charges. But at this present moment, I was concerned most about just one.

I tried to quell my impatience as we began to pace slowly down the row of cots, stopping to look at both sides. There were men in various stages of recovery, some of them asleep, others moaning in a drug-induced unconsciousness. One or two were barely awake, watching us as we stopped, their faces pain ridden and thin.

I was two beds from the end of the room when I heard a rapid-fire outburst of familiar words.

Sister Randolph was in the middle of a description about the man in front of us, and I lost track for a moment. She had to repeat her comment, and I nodded. Finally we had come to Simon's cot. He was still speaking rapidly, urgently, as if something mattered intensely in his drug-clouded mind.

"We can't understand him half the time," Sister Randolph was saying. "It's some foreign tongue, I'm told. One of our convalescents was in India for a number of years with his regiment. He didn't know enough of the language to translate, but he said he thought it was Hindu."

"Hindi," I said automatically. "Hindi is the language. Hinduism the religion. A Hindu is the man or the woman." But it wasn't Hindi that Simon was speaking just now, it was Urdu, the Muslim equivalent.

I went to his bedside. Someone had shaved him this morning, but his face was flushed with fever, his hair long and soaked with perspiration. But mercifully I could see both arms under the bedclothes. There had been no amputation.

"I was in India," I said. "Let me sit with him a bit, and see if I can decipher what he's saying."

"Please do!" Sister Randolph said gratefully. "It's very worrying not to know what's on his mind. I can tell that something is, and it may be hindering his recovery." She referred to her chart. "His name is Brandon. We don't know much else about him. Regiment, that sort of thing. Dr. Gaines admitted him as an emergency patient."

"What's his status?"

"If the fever breaks, Dr. Gaines expects he'll keep his arm. If it doesn't, well, there will have to be steps taken." She lifted the sheet, and I could see how swollen and inflamed Simon's shoulder and arm were. "We've kept the wound clean, we've fed him to keep up his strength, but it's a matter of time. I've grown rather fond of him, and I would hate to see him back in surgery. But I'm afraid . . ." She let her voice dwindle, as if not wishing to speak the words. "Such a strong, handsome man. A pity, isn't it? War and all this pain and suffering."

"Yes."

I brought a chair over and sat down. Simon was restless, and he still spoke in staccato sentences. I listened for a while, accustoming my ears to the sound of his voice and words I hadn't spoken except to my family for some years. But it came back to me surprisingly quickly.

Simon was on patrol. That much I gathered from the names he mentioned. They had been ambushed in the hills above the Khyber Pass, and he was trying to keep his men alive until a rescue column arrived. He'd sent a heliograph message to a watcher some distance away on the Indian side of the border and it was a matter of time before help got to them.

I heard Simon say, "Keep your head down, man!" And then he swore. "They've got a sniper up there somewhere. I saw the muzzle flash. He's damned good with that rifle. It must be British, not native, to be that accurate." And then someone must have said something to him, for he replied, "I told the Colonel Sahib that I suspected one of those damned traveling musicians might be a spy, but we couldn't prove it."

The switch to English was so unexpected that at first I couldn't follow it.

And then he was incoherent once more, encouraging his men, keeping them alive, and finally going out himself to hunt down the unknown rifleman. I remembered that engagement, long past, but when my father and a detachment of lancers went in search of the men who were pinned down, my mother had sat on the veranda all evening, waiting for news.

She had said nothing when the bloody remnants of the column came back, but I heard my father issue the order for the man who played the tambourine to be found and brought to him. I was never told what had happened to the spy. It had been regimental business only, and not for my ears or even my mother's.

Glancing at my watch after sitting beside Simon for several minutes, I saw that I had to report for duty, and I slipped away, brushing his face with my fingertips as I did, feeling the dry heat of high fever on his skin.

I told Sister Randolph as I left that the patient was reliving old engagements, a result of his fever, I thought, and nothing that would hamper his recovery. She smiled and thanked me again.

"It's such a relief to hear that. Perhaps since you understand what he's saying, you could visit him from time to time, in case anything changes."

I promised I would, grateful to her for giving me a reason to sit with him.

For the next two days I spent as much time with Simon as I could, but there seemed to be no change in his condition, and I found myself waking up in the night with a start, thinking that he had died. But he hadn't, he held on, as he so often did against impossible odds.

And on the third morning, when I hurriedly downed my breakfast and ran up the back steps to spend a moment with him, I found him awake.

Dark eyes under dark brows stared back at me, but I didn't think he knew me because he hadn't fully returned to awareness. I reached down and touch his face again. This time the skin was oily with the sweat of breaking fever, but cool. Blessedly cool. I was on the point of going to find Sister Randolph and asking her to bathe him—in fact, I had turned away to do just that—when his hand locked on my wrist and spun me around.

"Bess?" His voice was hoarse from fever and the constant barrage of words that had come bubbling up from the depths of illness. "Is that you, Bess?"

I looked down. He was staring at me, frowning, as if he couldn't quite believe the evidence of his eyes. Then he blinked and said, "Am I still in France?"

"No—I mean, it's been a while. You've been very ill. Your shoulder—you nearly lost your arm."

Frowning, he said, "Did I tell—did anyone tell the Colonel what happened there in France?"

"That you were wounded?" I sat on the edge of his cot. "Yes, of course. You even left the hospital, but then the fever overtook you and the Colonel Sahib brought you here."

"Dear God—"

He released my wrist and wiped a hand across his eyes. "Bess. Get word to your father. I've got to see him."

"Simon, it can wait."

His mouth was tight as he said, "Don't argue." His eyes closed and he grimaced. "Do it."

I'd been trained all my life to respond to that tone of voice. One obeyed instantly, doing as one was told, without question. In India, safe as we'd believed we were, danger was everywhere, and the memory of the bloody 1857 Mutiny, when the Indian Army turned on its English officers and their families, and massacred all they could lay hands on—soldiers, women, children—was always present. Hesitation or delay could mean the difference between living and dying.

Only this time I was ordered to reach my father at once—and only then could I see to it that Dr. Gaines was alerted about the change in his patient's condition.

I did as I was told, urgently begging use of the clinic's telephone, putting through a call to my mother and seeing to it that word was passed to my father. Then I went in search of the doctor. I found him watching Captain Barclay walk up and down the passage.

Captain Barclay smiled as he made his turn at the end of the passage and started back toward us.

"Look for yourselves. That knee is as good as ever it was." He saw me and his smile broadened. "Sister Crawford? What do you think?"

But Dr. Gaines was still watching the way he moved. "You've most certainly improved," he began.

"Then send me back to France. For God's sake, I'm needed there."

It was a familiar cry. But Dr. Gaines paid no heed. He was still staring at the knee. Aware of my presence, he said, "Sister?"

"The patient in the surgical ward is awake, sir. Brandon."

"Ah, yes. Tell Sister Randolph I'll be right there. All right, Captain, I'd like you to take the butcher's paper out from around that limb and then walk up and down again."

I turned away, but out of the corner of my eye I saw Captain Barclay's fair skin flame with embarrassment. It was an old trick, the butcher's stiff paper giving a little stability to a weak knee for a short distance. Only, if you listened closely, you could hear the layers rustle.

I went back to the library, where Sister Randolph was bathing Simon's face and making him more comfortable before an orderly arrived to shave him again.

"I've spoken to my mother," I said quickly in Hindi, and he nodded. I hurried back to my own duties.

I didn't know where my father was or how soon he could be reached. I had done as I was asked, and a little later I saw Dr. Gaines coming from the library ward, his face thoughtful.

As it happened my father arrived much sooner than he could possibly have in answer to my summons. I thought perhaps Dr. Gaines had sent for him as well. There were no doubt standing orders in regard to the patient Brandon that I knew nothing about.

It was not an hour before the evening meal when the Colonel

Sahib came striding into the clinic, tall, handsome, that air of command swirling in his wake.

I saw orderlies salute him and nurses smile at him. I was at the top of the stairs and heard him ask for Matron.

Five minutes later I was summoned to her office.

To my surprise, she wasn't there, but I thought perhaps my father was trying to downplay any military reason for his presence in a clinic. I said, "You've come to see Simon. I'll take you to him. He's been impossible to deal with, waiting for you to come."

His eyebrows rose. "Simon? I've been very worried about him. The reports from Dr. Gaines have not been good. Is he awake? I'll speak to him shortly. The fact is, I've come to see you."

That surprised me even more. "Indeed?"

"That nurse at the Base Hospital in Rouen. The one we were to distract with words of praise for doing her duty, after she'd given you so much trouble."

"Nurse Bailey? Was she difficult to appease?" My heart sank as I had visions of having to explain France to my superiors in the nursing service.

"I sent one of my men there to speak to her, and he reported that she had left the hospital to attend a funeral. That of Nurse Saunders. Didn't you tell me she'd seen and spoken to your erstwhile driver? She was found dead the morning after your departure."

Chapter Thirteen

I STOOD THERE with my mouth open, so completely taken aback that I couldn't think what to say.

The fact was, I'd nearly forgot about the nurse who had tried to stop me from leaving France. My father had told me he would deal with the matter, and in our household, that was that. I could put it out of my mind. I most certainly hadn't given a thought to Nurse Saunders, whom I hadn't met, but who had seen a killer face-to-face and never realized she was in any danger. It hadn't even occurred to me to warn her.

The note she had left for Nurse Bailey—and of course for me—had simply stated that my driver had come. But if questioned, she would have known what sort of uniform he was wearing, what rank he held, what he looked like. More to the point, she could corroborate any description that Matron—or I—could give.

"She's dead?" I repeated slowly. "What happened?"

"She was lying at the side of the street after a convoy of lorries had passed on their way to the Front. It was just after dusk. A horse had been startled, broke away from its owner, and charged madly down the hill toward the port as they were driving through. When she was found it appeared that the horse had knocked her down. She'd left the Base Hospital and walked to a nearby shop where they sold small gifts for newborns. Apparently her sister had just given birth to her first child. At any rate, her skull had the clear imprint of a horse's hoof around the ear. Her clothing was stained as if she'd rolled after being struck. No one saw the accident. It was too dark."

"Dear God," I said blankly. My father had had time to absorb the news. I could only think about that poor unsuspecting woman walking out of the Base Hospital on such a happy errand, and instead walking straight into a vicious killer. In the darkness, with the horse running amok, he could have struck her down with impunity, and who would see it happen? Every eye would have been on that horse. "I'm sorry—"

"My friend looked into the matter, Bess," my father said, interrupting me. "I don't think it was the accident it appeared to be. Of course there was the wound on her face, the imprint of a horse's shoe. And a horse had in fact run loose. But my friend was told by one of the orderlies at the Base Hospital that the surgeon who examined the body was surprised that the blow hadn't gone deeper. Deep enough to kill, yes, but there was also the weight of the animal behind it, you see, and her skull wasn't crushed. They decided it was a glancing blow, but the surgeon—from somewhere in Minnesota, I believe—wasn't buying it. Then a cast shoe was found just beyond where the body lay, and our friend from Minnesota was finally satisfied."

I thought about that. "There are hundreds of horses coming through Rouen. And dozens of horse-drawn carts. A shoe could easily have been come by in the town."

"Quite. However, the French police ruled the death an accident, and the Base Hospital didn't dispute it. They could think of no possible reason why Nurse Saunders should be murdered."

"Very likely she was," I agreed. "She'd seen his face clearly. Whoever it was, pretending to be my driver. She could have helped us show that my driver was the same man as the Colonel Prescott who spoke to Matron about Sister Burrows. I thought that once I was out of France it would be over. That there was no need to kill anyone else. Should someone speak to the French police? And what about Matron? Is she in any danger? Is there any way we can warn her?"

"No one in Rouen has connected Nurse Saunders to you in any way. And it's best for now to leave it like that. As for Matron, I think she's safe enough. For one thing, she's always surrounded by staff and patients. For another, you told me that she herself was rather suspicious of this Colonel, and if he sensed that at all, he'll stay clear of her for fear of making matters worse. Besides, it's entirely possible that he doesn't know you've spoken to her. On the other hand, if he saw Nurse Saunders on the street and discovered that you'd been sent home in disgrace, he could very well have considered that any investigation into your behavior in Rouen would lead to a counterfeit driver with counterfeit orders. And only Nurse Saunders had seen this man."

"I hadn't thought of it from that direction." I took a deep breath. "We only learned of Nurse Saunders's death because you took the trouble to allay any suspicions Nurse Bailey might have harbored. We wouldn't have known otherwise. It's rather frightening to think that a woman I've never met was killed because of me." I shivered at the thought. "But who is this man?" I asked. "He couldn't be William Morton. William Morton died two weeks before Captain Carson. Didn't he?"

"Yes, I've looked into that. There's no doubt of it. But he had brothers, and one could have taken it into his head to exact a little revenge. I don't want you to return to France for the time being. Not until we've located all six of them."

"Revenge is one thing. Indiscriminate killing is another. Vincent Carson is dead. Why isn't it finished?"

"That's why I've been as careful as may be about any inquiries. I don't want to start a witch hunt until we have a better idea of what's going on. The Army is like Scotland Yard in one sense—any investigation is by its very nature official. And we've too little information, much less proof, to take that step."

"I understand," I said reluctantly. Still, the sooner we could get to the bottom of this affair, the sooner I could return to France.

"One more thing. I've spoke to the Carsons' solicitors. There were no provisions in Vincent's will for his sister or her offspring. But then the will was drawn up just before he left for France in the autumn of 1914. He'd have had no reason to add such a bequest at that stage. Morton hadn't enlisted, the war was expected to end by Christmas, Sabrina was still in disgrace. There was a letter from Vincent to the solicitors after her child was born, indicating an intention on his part to provide for her straightaway. His solicitors drew up a proposal and sent it to France for his approval, but he never returned it. No one seems to know if the proposal was found with his personal effects. According to the solicitors, Julia was unaware of it, and so it was assumed that he must have changed his mind."

"How sad." I couldn't help but wish that Julia had been sent her husband's journal. There could be an entry in it that would make all the difference.

I've approved the proposal regarding Sabrina, but I haven't sent it to London. I want to tell Julia and Valerie first, but there's been no time to write . . .

But the entry could also have read, *I had every intention of helping Sabrina, but Morton was at me again yesterday, wanting a sizable settlement instead. It has shown me how right my father was to have nothing to do with that match . . .*

"Yes, very sad. All right, take me to Simon, if you will." He put a comforting hand on my shoulder. "It will be over shortly, my dear. Meanwhile, best to keep you safe."

I led him from Matron's office to the surgical ward and presented Sister Randolph, who was on duty. He asked about her patients, and she gave him a brief report on their conditions. He thanked her, walked slowly down the row of cots, nodding to the men who were awake and pausing finally where Simon lay waiting. I heard the Colonel Sahib clear his throat, then say, "Well, Brandon, you've decided to live, have you?"

The officer lying next to Simon was awake as well, and he shifted his head toward the two men, curious and unabashedly listening. Men of my father's rank were not often visitors here, nor did they know many of the patients by name.

I turned away as Simon lifted his left hand to take my father's.

And then behind me I heard Simon's voice begin speaking in Hindi, clearly, concisely, a soldier reporting to an officer. I couldn't help but overhear some of it, but Sister Randolph was saying at my side, "Oh, how nice, he's found someone who understands the same language."

"Yes, isn't it?" I replied, my ears pricked. What were they saying? For my father was answering, and then Simon's voice responded with additional intelligence.

But even as I was listening with only half my attention on Sister Randolph's chatter while trying to hear information I was not supposed to have, I felt guilty.

Behind me, my father swore feelingly in Urdu.

"Do you realize what you're saying? And damn the War Office for keeping it from my people. It would have made a difference if I'd known." He turned and glanced my way. I was already leading Sister Randolph away.

The conversation went on for another several minutes. Then my father said, "Heal. We need you."

He was striding up the room toward Sister Randolph and me, and as he thanked her, he reached for my arm and guided me toward the door.

"Come with me. Let's hope we don't encounter Matron along the way."

We didn't. The staff was busy handing out medications, and Dr. Gaines was closeted with one of his patients. We walked calmly toward the door and out into the evening sunlight. I blinked. The

Colonel Sahib led me down the short shallow steps and across the lawns to a bench set under a stand of trees.

"How much do you know about why Brandon was in France?"

I'd learned long since to tell my father the truth when it came to regimental business.

"Only a little," I told him, adding, "It was the Gurkhas who brought him in after he was wounded. I never saw them, but suddenly he was there. I could guess that he'd been behind the German lines."

I remembered too that I'd drugged him, to keep him quiet, when he'd asked specifically to get word to my father. A wash of guilt swept over me.

"What else?" My father turned his back on the clinic, his eyes on my face.

"There's a German spy behind our lines. Or so Simon believed."

"Go on."

"And he was trying to find him. That's why it was necessary to capture a German officer to question."

"Yes. All right. You shouldn't have overheard any of that, but no harm done. The question is now, who are we looking for? Who killed Carson and your Private Wilson, and Nurse Saunders? William Morton or one of his brothers? Or a German behind British lines looking for an identity."

There had been talk of spies from the start. Even before the war began. German waiters in popular restaurants or staff in hotels were accused of spying. Professors and clerics and students from Germany were suspected. Even men from the north of England, whose accents were unfamiliar, found themselves stopped and questioned by overzealous citizens and policemen. The English coastline, broken by a thousand river mouths and inlets and hidden beaches, was always rife with speculation about spies being landed from submarines or small boats that had escaped the notice of the Royal Navy. There were even tales of spies being lowered from Zeppelins on misty nights and disappearing into the countryside. But was any of it true? Seeing monsters under the bed was one thing, real spies quite another.

"I don't quite see what a spy has to gain," I answered. "But if he exists, he must have spent some time in England. No one who spoke to this man we're concerned with mentioned anything about him that would indicate that he was German. But there are his eyes, a very pale color. You'd think Berlin could find someone without any characteristic that would stand out."

"Yes, well, this spy hunt is of course a secret. I haven't been told anything about it officially. And apparently Simon was only given enough information to carry out his foray. In fact, he was ordered not to question his prisoner. But between us, I think we've begun to piece together enough to worry both of us."

"Did he bring someone in?" I asked, curious.

"He says he did, and that when he was wounded in a rearguard action, the Gurkhas split up, half the company getting Simon to an aid station against all orders, and the rest taking the prisoner in."

"They were to leave Simon?" I asked, shocked.

"They were to see that there were no wounded left behind who could be questioned by the Germans." My father's voice was grim.

Which meant that they were to kill any wounded who were in the way. It was a measure of their respect for the Sergeant-Major that they had disobeyed that order. It explained too why the Gurkhas left him at the nearest aid station and then vanished.

I bit my lip, trying to see where my father was going with this. "What are we to do?"

My father was studying the sky, watching a few scudding clouds that had appeared on the horizon, just visible now from under the leafy shelter of the trees.

The Colonel Sahib turned to me. "A single man, this spy. A single target? If he didn't come for information—troop movements and the like, where the next attack might come—then he came for *someone*."

"Who?" I asked. "Who in France is irreplaceable?"

"If he were in the American lines, I'd say one of their commanders. Surely they're the biggest threat to the Germans just now."

"But he isn't behind the American lines. And he passes himself off as a Colonel."

"Hmm," my father said.

And then I knew. Or thought I did. Just as my father said under his breath, "The Prince of Wales."

He wasn't allowed to fight. But he visited the Front often enough, and he was very popular with the men.

"What good would that do? How would it affect the war?" I went on. "And not to be unfeeling about it, the Prince does have other brothers."

"It would shock the country, hurt morale."

It was hard to believe, all the same. And yet I couldn't think of anyone else who was as popular as the Prince.

"I can't believe—he and the Kaiser are *cousins*!" I said, still arguing with myself.

"What the Army does and the Kaiser knows might not be the same. Of course it's possible that our problem and Simon's aren't connected—they seem to be because we know only a part of the story. Are you willing to beard a lion in its den?"

"A lion?" I asked warily.

"There are seven sons in the Morton family. Will was the actor, the others were miners and farmers. Respectable enough men, five of them. I shouldn't think they're a problem to themselves or others. And then there's Hugh. He was closest to Will, or so my sources tell me, and he was a union leader before the war, best known for hiring several rather disreputable men to enforce his will. At the moment, he's missing from his unit in France. He has been since his brother was reported dead. He could have killed Carson. He could be dead himself. But we need to know. And as quickly as may be."

"Could Hugh Morton impersonate an officer?" I asked doubt-fully. If he had been a union leader, he knew something about charming and haranguing his followers, but those were not the skills that would help him carry off such a charade.

"If there's one actor in the family, I don't see why another brother couldn't have a talent in that direction. For all we know, he might be even more talented and simply chose not to use it. Take young Barclay with you. The best approach is that you are concerned for young Sabrina. Find out, if you can, which sons can be accounted for. I don't think we're going to find that Hugh is our man. He's dead, very likely, just as William is. Still, if he's our killer, then we have nothing to do with this spy business and can safely leave it to those who *are* involved."

"What if Hugh is there? In Wales?" I asked.

"He isn't. I can almost guarantee that. How is he going to get out of France? What I want to know is if the family mourns him. Or if they consider him still alive."

"And Simon?"

"He's best where he is. I don't think Dr. Gaines will let him slip through his fingers." He looked toward the clinic again, and I read the emotions flitting across his face. Worry, doubt, and a stronger feeling, anger. He had never left one of his men behind. Of course Simon had known the risk. To my father, it made no difference.

He left soon after that, and later in the evening, I asked Dr. Gaines if I could borrow his motorcar and of course Captain Barclay on my next free afternoon.

I was given permission and went to ask Captain Barclay if he would accompany me. He'd been avoiding me. Not quite making it obvious, but he hadn't been seeking out my company the way he had before he'd become Barclay the orderly. One of the sisters had com-mented that I'd lost my beau to someone else.

He said, shaking his head as I told him I needed an escort, "I let you down in France."

"My father asked if I'd take you to Wales with me. He must not agree."

"Hardly the most dangerous place in the kingdom."

"It could well be. All right, I'll go alone if I must." I'd been a witness to his attempt to trick Dr. Gaines with the butcher's paper and it must have stung. I realized that this was not the best time to ask a favor.

Almost as if in response to what I'd just been thinking, he turned his head away and stared out the open door. "I'm useless. To the Army. To you. To myself. It's appalling to think of my men dying in France while I'm forced to pace the floor here in an effort to strengthen a leg that might as well have been amputated for all the good it is to me."

I read something in his face that I hadn't seen before. Despair. And that worried me.

"Useless?" I said sternly, in my best imitation of Matron's brisk tone. "That's self-pity, Captain, and I'll not have it. Buck up, young man, and fight for what you want. If it's so important to you."

In spite of his depressed spirits, he couldn't help but smile.

I smiled in return and added in my own voice, "I expect I simply wanted your company again."

After a moment, he shook his head, not in refusal this time but in surrender. "Yes, of course I'll go with you. Do you have another wonder to show me?"

With that he walked away, limping more lightly on his cane than he himself could see. With a pang, I recognized that he would have his wish and return to France in a matter of weeks. If he didn't give in to his despair before then and do something rash.

I waited until late in the evening, when I'd finished my duties, and then went to sit with Simon for a little. He was sleeping, his breathing quiet, his skin cool, without fever.

It was impossible to think of Simon Brandon being sent behind enemy lines, knowing that if he were severely wounded, he would be killed by his own men. It took incredible courage. Still, he had a strong sense of duty, as did my father. But even my father had been angry at the waste his death would have been.

I just didn't know whether the spy behind the lines or one of the Morton family was the person behind my own brushes with death. But if it was the spy, then his thoroughness in eliminating anyone who could identify him was his very survival.

And what would Simon Brandon say if he learned that I'd already encountered the very spy he himself had been sent behind the German lines to uncover?

I said nothing to Simon about the death of Nurse Saunders. I just watched his slow improvement and encouraged him to rest as much as he could. And since he'd spoken to my father, his mind seemed to be at peace, as if duty done, he could now think about his need to recover.

When Thursday arrived, Dr. Gaines remembered that he'd agreed to let me take his motorcar for the day. I hadn't said anything more to Captain Barclay, but after breakfast he reported to the doctor and was sent to join me as I came down the stairs to the foyer of the house.

It was a fine day, and we drove through the countryside of Somerset and into the Marches of Wales, the border country that had known its own struggles in the past but today was peaceful. Rolling hills and pastures, villages tucked in their lees, narrow streams and the occasional stand of trees marked the landscape. We stopped briefly to eat the picnic that the kitchen had provided, and I was reminded, painfully, of the picnic Simon had arranged as a backdrop for his encouraging me to stay in Britain and not return to France. I couldn't help but wonder what would have changed if I'd taken his advice and never gone back to the battlefields.

I must have sighed, for Captain Barclay, finishing his sandwich, looked across at me and asked, "There's more on your mind than a simple outing in pretty countryside."

And so I told him about the Morton family. He'd known some of the story, but not about Hugh or about the other brothers who had fought for King and Country.

"You feel the father will tell you where his son is?"

"I don't know whether he will or not. But you can judge, can't you, how people mourn? Perhaps the way he says the name. Or the way he looks when he speaks of Will and his relationship with Hugh. Whatever that was. Good or not."

"What possible excuse can you find for prying into a family's losses?"

"Actually, there's a little more to it than that." And so I told him also about Sabrina and the life she was living now in Fowey. "She told me Will Morton's family had asked her to come to them. Perhaps she should. But there's no way of knowing, is there, until I've seen them for myself."

"You can't make other people's decisions for them."

"Of course I can't. I won't. Still, if the family really cares about Will's son, perhaps they should go to Fowey themselves, rather than simply write a letter." I shook my head. "Look, if Hugh isn't a murderer, all well and good. If he is, I'm certainly not going to ask a young widow to go and stay with his family."

The Captain smiled grimly. "All right. God knows, if it's Hugh Morton we've been dodging all along, I'd just as soon know of it. I owe him for what he did to you and to me."

We repacked the remnants of the picnic and drove on to the small village of Helwynn, where I'd been told the Mortons lived.

It was picturesque in its own way, running up from a small stream to the crest of a hill, a smattering of houses and shops, a stone chapel with a short steeple, and several outlying farms that lay like patchwork across the stream.

We stopped the motorcar in front of a small baker's shop, and I went inside to begin my inquiries. The woman behind the counter stared at me in my uniform, and then her face seemed to freeze.

"Can I help you, then, Sister?" she asked, her voice that of Wales, as well as her dark hair and eyes, her fine skin, and her straight back.

"Hello," I said with a warm smile. "I was traveling through and I remembered a family that I'd known who lived here. The Mortons. Are they still here?"

"Those that're left," she said. "Seven sons Ross sent to war. It hasn't been easy for him."

"No, I expect not. It's Will I knew. Well, his wife. He was the actor, wasn't he?"

"He was."

"Could you tell me how to find his father? Ross Morton?"

"He lives on the farm you can see across the little stone bridge. Nobody to work it for him now. Most of the fields fallow or given to cattle. There's still money in milk and butter."

From the look of her wares, I found it easy to believe that.

We were all obligated to give to the war effort in some fashion. But sometimes in the smallest villages, the food they could produce barely sufficed to feed the people living there. Although it was sometimes hard to convince the men who procured hides for shoes and meat for rations, and other goods for the Army. They had quotas, and the needs of people compared to the needs of the Army were often unimportant.

I thanked her, bought two small buns for our tea, the Captain's and mine, and left the shop.

Several small boys had clustered around the motorcar, leaning in to look at it, asking questions about how it ran and where it had come from. The Captain, with that easy American way of his, was letting them persuade him to lift the bonnet and show them the motor when I came out the shop door.

The boys stood back to stare at me, and I said, "Go on, open the bonnet."

Captain Barclay got out to do just that, but when they saw his limp, their questions were about the war and his wound, the motor-car forgotten.

"My Da had his head blown off," one told the Captain ghoulishly. "They couldn't find it, however hard they searched. So he's buried without it."

"A pity," the Captain answered. "All right, off with you. See you mind your mothers. They have enough to worry about without your adding to it."

They nodded, but I doubted they'd remember the lesson half an hour on.

I saw the small school as we went back down the hill to search for the stone bridge. It was scarcely wide enough to pass over, but we managed, and the Captain whistled. "Oh, well done," he said, turning to me after making certain the wings were still part of the motorcar.

A sign on the far side of the bridge read in faded green letters, PEACE AND PLENTY FARM.

We came shortly into the muddy farmyard where half a dozen black-and-white milk cows with bursting udders had come in on their own, ready for the afternoon milking. They turned to stare at us with their large brown eyes, and then their attention was caught by the man who had just stepped out of the barn.

"Lost, are you?" he asked, wiping his hands on a bunch of straw.

I gave our names, then said, "I was hoping to find Ross Morton. Is this his farm?"

He was still, like the woman in the shop, wondering if I brought bad news with me.

I said quickly, "I'm a friend of Sabrina Morton's. Your daughter-in-law. I thought perhaps I should stop, for her sake."

"Sabrina, is it?" he asked, moving away from the barn. A big man, taller even than Captain Barclay, broad of chest and shoulders, he added, "Have you seen the boy?"

"He was asleep," I said. "But I was told he had his father's eyes."

The elder Morton digested that. "That would be my wife's," he said after a moment. "Pale as winter ice."

His own were hazel, his hair still fair but thickly interlaced with gray. There must have been some English blood in the Morton family, because the Welsh were as a rule dark.

"I never met your son," I said. "But I've known Sabrina since she was a child."

He ignored me. "Will's son ought to be brought up here, where he belongs. Not in England. I told his mother that. I offered her a home as well. My wife died in the Spanish flu, there's no one to do for us. It would be a kindness to come and take her place."

I could see what he meant, that there was no one to feed the chickens or cook the meals or do the family's washing, mending, or marketing. I couldn't imagine Sabrina fitting into this world. I could understand why she had chosen Fowey instead.

But I could also understand this man's needs. He had a farm to keep going without his sons, and the house needed a woman in it.

I said, "Are your other sons married?"

"My namesake, Ross, had a wife. She died of childbed fever, and the babe with her. A pretty little thing, but with no strength to live."

"Where is Ross now?"

"Drowned off the coast of Ireland when his ship went down. The Huns never tried to save the men. The surprise was, they didn't machine-gun them in the water. It's done, I'm told. Will's dead, but you know that, if you saw Sabrina. David's lost a leg and sits in his room, staring at nothing. The girl he was to marry didn't want a cripple. The twins are in France somewhere, and they write when they can. But I never know from day to day if they're alive or dead. Llewellyn's in hospital in Suffolk and not right in his head, nor ever will be, they're saying. Shell shock. Only Will has a son. And this farm once had seven."

I'd been counting with my fingers behind my back. Ross, the

CHARLES TODD

elder, the namesake. Will. David who lost his leg. The twins.
Llewellyn in Suffolk. That made six.

"You had seven sons?" I asked gently. "Is the last also among the
dead?"

Ross Morton shifted. "That's Hugh," he said. "Nine months
younger than Will and a hothead into the bargain. The image of
his mother's own Da. The one who went down the mines and lived
to tell about it. A fighter he was. Mary's father. I never quite got my
mind around that boy. I couldn't see how he could be so much like
his grandda, and so unlike me."

You could almost imagine him questioning the boy's paternity,
something he must have done a thousand times over the years. And
yet somehow I had a feeling he'd never doubted his wife.

"A changeling," he said, finally, as if in echo of my own thoughts.
"They used to talk about that. The old ones. I never put much stock
in it, until Hugh. And then I knew it could be true enough. I just
don't know how he got to be in the Morton cradle."

"But you said—Hugh's alive still? Along with David and the
twins and Llewellyn?"

Morton took a deep breath. "They tell me he's missing. There
was the telegram saying at first that he was dead. And then a letter
from his commanding officer to say he was among the missing after
a push that was repelled. I don't understand why they couldn't find
him. Do you?" He swung around to stare at Captain Barclay, as if he
were to blame for the confusion. "Hugh wouldn't be easy to kill. And
he wouldn't care to be penned up behind a fence in a prison camp.
It would drive him mad. He was always a roamer, Hugh was, and I
can't see the Army changing that. Why haven't they found my son?"

I could hear again the little boy telling us that his father had lost
his head and had been buried without it.

The Captain was saying, "It's not so easy. There's shelling before
an assault, and then there's the attack across No Man's Land. Men
die, they're shot, they're blown apart, they're wounded and fall into

a shell hole where the body may not be found for days. No certainty, you see. The sergeant calls the roll and no one answers. And no one saw him fall. If he hasn't already been taken behind the lines to be treated for wounds, they can only wait and see if he turns up. He could even be a prisoner. If he is, word comes back after a time, and his status is changed. I'm sorry. But that's how it is."

"A damned poor way to run a war, if you don't know where your own men are," Morton said contemptuously. "While families sit and wait for news, and none comes. At least not any good news."

He turned back to me. "Do you think Sabrina might want to come and bring up the boy here? For Will's sake?"

"I don't know," I said, wishing fervently that I hadn't raised false hopes with my invented reason for coming here. "Perhaps if you write to her again?"

"I wrote once. I'm not likely to write again." I could hear the stiff-necked pride in his voice. He'd offered his home and all he had to Will's widow. There was nothing more to say.

He couldn't understand as I could that Sabrina had been brought up in a very different world. She would break here, on this farm, cooking and cleaning and washing for the men of the house. With no hope of escape, no chance for a life of her own. And yet I could see that a boy could run wild here when not at his lessons or doing the everyday tasks assigned to him, and grow up as his uncles did. Compared to that narrow little hotel in Fowey where no one came on holiday now because of the war, with the danger of drowning not far from the door, it offered much.

I said, "I think perhaps your son's death is still a shock to her. To Sabrina."

"She has a son to care for," he said stubbornly. "My grandson. He may be too young to know or care now, but one day he'll want to see where his father came from, and it's likely there'll be none of us left to tell him. If this war goes on for much longer and they're all dead, I won't see any reason to stay."

He nodded toward his cows. "I have them to milk and feed. I don't have time to give over to wishful thinking. I'll bid you good day, Sister. Captain."

And he walked past us, calling to his cows. They formed a line as tidy as any drawn with a rule, and followed him into the barn.

Captain Barclay nodded to me and I turned the motorcar to drive away.

As I did so, I happened to see, in an upper window of the farmhouse, the thin, drawn face of the son who'd lost his leg.

I'd seen too many like him to have high hopes for his survival. If there was no gun in the house, there was always the shallow stream or any of a number of ways to end the pain.

I was torn between wishing Hugh Morton was not a murderer and would come home to his father, and thinking that if Hugh took after his mother, as Will did, then he too had those pale, pale eyes.

Captain Barclay said as we once more drove over the narrow little bridge, "Hugh's alive. His father doesn't want to hope. And there've been no letters. But he believes Hugh is too much like his grandfather to have been killed so easily by the Germans."

And I had, reluctantly, to agree with him.

CHAPTER FOURTEEN

THAT EVENING, AFTER the motorcar had been returned to its proper place and I'd thanked Dr. Gaines for the use of it, I went up to my room and began a letter home to my mother.

It was very simple, my letter.

I told her that Simon was steadily improving and that meanwhile I'd enjoyed a picnic with Captain Barclay.

I never mentioned going to Wales. I wrote that it was sad to hear that Will's brother was missing and that there was still no news of him all these weeks since it was reported.

It would suffice to inform my father of what I had discovered.

After I'd set my letter in the basket for the morning post, I went back to my room and sat by the window, looking out into the night. There were three people dead. All I could be certain of was that the same man had killed all three. He'd nearly succeeded in killing me as well.

What's more, I'd rashly promised Mrs. Wilson that I'd try to take away the stigma of her husband's suicide. I still felt strongly about that. It was cruel that a woman and her daughter had to live with a lie. But I'd made little enough progress.

Still, I'd learned how Major Carson must have been surprised and killed. And Private Wilson as well.

When I'd felt that arm around my throat, it was frightening, and

I'd fought desperately to live. I expect that, even caught by surprise, Major Carson and Private Wilson must have fought too. Both were tall men, but slender in build. And their attacker? Remembering the size of the elder Ross Morton, the width of his shoulders, and the power in his body even in middle age, I realized that if Hugh was anything like his father, I'd been unbelievably lucky to have survived. But then whoever it was had needed to kill me as silently as possible, and that bucket, rolling and clanging across the muddy ground, had put paid to that.

I shivered. If my booted foot hadn't found it and given it a hard kick, I could very well be dead now, not sitting in Somerset watching the moon rise.

Would Hugh come to England looking to finish what he'd begun?

I couldn't really answer that. But I realized with a sudden sinking feeling in my stomach that my arrival at the Morton farm might have changed the future. Assuming that Hugh was still alive and learned that I'd been there, asking questions.

Was Sabrina safe? I'd used her name.

On the whole, I thought she would be.

But he might well be goaded into searching for me because he suspected why I had been there.

If, of course, the killer was German, what happened in Wales would have no bearing on my life or anyone else's.

I'd have to go back to France. Simon couldn't accompany me, and Captain Barclay wasn't fit to be released for duty either.

Then I'd have to go alone. There must be some way to do it safely.

I'd need a reason to travel. I couldn't hope to search properly if I was sent to one station and one station only. What's more, I could be found all too easily.

With a sigh, I came to a conclusion and went quietly down the stairs to retrieve my letter.

Upstairs again, I opened it and added a second sheet, outlining the conclusions I'd drawn while sitting at my window.

I didn't think the Colonel Sahib would be happy with this addendum, but I had a feeling he'd see the reasoning behind it and agree, however reluctantly.

I tiptoed down to the foyer again to leave the resealed envelope in the basket, and I was just on the point of going back up the stairs when a movement in the dimly lit passage to my left caught my eye.

For the past half hour I'd been dealing with murder and murderers. I froze, waiting to see who was there, but no one came forward, not Matron, not the night duty orderly, not one of the sisters on evening watch.

As my eyes adjusted to the dimness, I could see a shadow at the end of the passage, where someone had halted and was waiting for me to go on about my own business.

I debated shouting for help. But I'd feel silly if it was only one of the officers who found it hard to sleep and who sometimes walked off whatever nightmares kept him awake. But that was generally in the small hours, two or three in the morning.

I moved forward as silently as I could, keeping to the wall as much as possible. I'd exchanged my boots for slippers, as I often did off duty, embroidered silk ones from Benares in India. Halfway to the arch where I'd seen the shadow, I listened and could actually hear someone breathing.

Flattening myself closer to the wall, I went on, cutting the distance in half again and finally, holding my own breath, I was there.

Movement again on the far side of the arch, someone turning and softly heading back the way he'd come. Even listening as hard as I was, I almost didn't catch it.

Softly—someone in bare feet. I was sure of it.

I was through the arch in a burst of speed, and just in time I saw whoever it was disappearing through a door into the room where ambulatory officers gathered to play cards or chess or read.

I was fast on his heels, opening the door he'd left ajar so as not to make a sound closing it.

The room was dark, but because the night was warm the windows at the far end stood open, giving onto one of the gardens. I saw the silhouette just ahead of me spin to face me as I said, "Who's there?" At the same time I drew matches out of my pocket and struck one. It flared and I found myself staring at Simon Brandon's pain-lined face.

"What in heaven's name are you doing?" I demanded, anger replacing the fear that had driven me to follow the shadow this far.

"Bess," he said in some relief. "I thought it might be Matron at the stairs."

"And so it should have been," I said. "You should be in your bed, recovering—"

"I can't," he said. "If I lie on that cot for another day, I shan't be able to walk at all."

"And whose fault is that?" I demanded.

"Yes, I know. Duty, and all that. The last two nights, I'd slip out and walk for a while. They won't allow me to try during the day, but it doesn't damage my shoulder, after all. It just brings back the strength in my limbs."

I knew he was right, but yet I couldn't get over my anger. It was a measure of my earlier fright.

He smiled. "Dodging you used up more energy than I realized. Will you give me a shoulder back to the ward?"

I took a deep breath. "Sit down, Simon. Please. We'll walk back in a few minutes. Rest."

He sank down in one of the chairs, and although he tried not to let me see what a relief it was, I could read him as well as he could read me.

After a while, he said, "Why were you following me?"

"I thought—I don't know what I thought. That someone was sleepwalking or had come in through the windows—" I stopped, not wanting to go down that road.

"Does France still worry you?"

"A little," I admitted. "But it will pass."

"True enough." He leaned his head back against the chair, then said, "Did I babble when I was unconscious? Did anyone comment on anything?"

"You were in the Northwest Frontier. Not in France. And so you were speaking Urdu most of the time. I don't think anyone else here understands one word in ten of the language."

"Thank you. I knew something I shouldn't like to have gossiped about here or anywhere else."

"The staff doesn't know how you came to be in this clinic. They don't even know your rank. It's just assumed that you're an officer like the rest of the patients. Dr. Gaines has listed you as a special case because of your shoulder. He sometimes takes on very difficult cases, that isn't a matter for comment. And he needed to keep you under his eye."

"Is Barclay here? Has he said anything to anyone?"

"You can trust him to be discreet. I expect one of the reasons you're kept isolated at the far end of the surgical ward is to prevent other patients from talking to you and asking more questions than you'd care to answer."

"I'm grateful," he said. These were questions he would never have asked my father. But he felt he could ask me, and I was glad I could put his mind at ease.

"You frightened us, Sergeant-Major," I said lightly. He understood.

"I'm sorry. It wasn't my intention. There are some matters more important than one's life."

I wanted to tell him that there was nothing I could think of more important than his. And I was still refusing to accept that he had been given orders that could well have meant his death. I had been born and brought up in an Army household, I understood duty and sacrifice as well as any man in the Army or any woman married to a soldier. Waste I could not endure. This wasn't something I could talk about even with my mother. Melinda Crawford, a distant cousin, would understand. She had seen a very different war in the Great Indian Mutiny. She had lost a beloved husband to war. I felt like putting through a telephone call to her and telling her the whole story. But I couldn't. The telephones were not safe for confessions of that sort.

I said, "Are you ready to return to your cot?"

"Yes, I think I am." He got unsteadily to his feet, and I gave him my arm. After the first several steps he'd regained his strength, and it was an uneventful return to the ward.

To our relief, the sister on night duty was about to collect the medicine tray, and we waited in a doorway until she had gone. Simon walked the last distance to his cot himself without my assistance, and I'd just seen him safely under the sheet when Sister Roberts returned to the ward.

Peering down the length of it, she said, "Sister Crawford?"

I replied, "Indeed. I was passing on my way to my quarters and I thought I heard someone ask for water."

"Who was it?"

I was already halfway up the ward. "I expect he was calling out in his sleep."

"Oh, yes, of course, that must be the surgical case from this afternoon," she answered, coming to look down on the sleeping man. "He's not allowed anything to drink yet. I'll just find a cloth and dip it in cool water. That should help."

I knew better than to offer to do it for her. I wished her good night and went on to my room.

It had been a long day, and to my surprise I slept well. It would be at least two days, possibly three, before I had an answer to my letter.

My father was difficult to convince.

He said, as we walked under the trees, "Have you mentioned this to Brandon?"

"I thought it best not to."

"Yes, quite right. Your mother is against it, of course, but she left the matter to my own good judgment. I'm not sure that I don't agree with her."

"We'll never know, will we, if we don't go looking for this man. And there are several points in favor of returning this way." I'd given the matter a good deal of thought while waiting for my father's opinion. "I'll be far less vulnerable than I was before. I'll be under orders that can't be meddled with. My schedule will be random, not rigid or predictable. And I'll be on special assignment where any attack on me would draw instant attention. He'd be foolish even to try—whatever he's up to, he's not likely to risk everything on one attempt to silence me. On the other hand, there are only so many places a deserter—or a spy—can hide. There are patrols in towns like Calais or Rouen. Captain Barclay ran into one. The main supply routes and roads for columns moving up are too busy. He must stay on the fringes of military movement."

"True enough, but there will be other ways of hunting him down."

"Are there? You can initiate a hunt by the Army, but I'm the only one who can identify the man."

"You saw him in the motorcar. Was he of a size to be this Hugh Morton?"

"He was hunched over the wheel. All I could see was the muffler around the lower part of his face. I was concentrating on trying to identify him."

And then I remembered the driver's heavy dark brows. Hugh Morton's father had been fair, and so had David in the upper window, what little I could see of his face and head in that one brief glance. I hadn't thought then to ask Hugh's coloring. Even if I had, how would I have put such a question?

"Yes, of course." He walked away from me, then paced back again. "It's a terrible risk, Bess."

"If we don't find him, then Major Carson, Private Wilson, and even Nurse Saunders will have died for nothing."

"I understand. But what you propose—in light of what happened to Edith Cavell—may not sit well with your superiors."

"I shan't be looking for spies. Or dealing with the German Army. Or watching for an English deserter. I shall simply be visiting aid stations with a view to improving care. It's done, isn't it? The Queen Alexandra's Imperial Military Nursing Service maintains high standards with an eye to its reputation and that of its staff. I'm young to be filling such a role, but I've had many hours of battlefield nursing. Dr. Gaines can vouch for that, and Dr. Hicks as well."

"And if my information is correct, the Prince will be returning to the Front shortly."

"A single man in Sarajevo began this war," I pointed out. "A single sniper would be difficult to stop."

"I shall have to find someone in my wide circle of friends who knows someone with high enough rank in the Service to make the suggestion," he pointed out. "It should not come from me."

"Melinda Crawford, perhaps?"

He smiled, the lines of worry smoothing out on his face.

"A brilliant stroke, even if you are my daughter."

For Melinda, while not on the Service's staff, had advised them in the initial stages of their development and organization of training. Not only did she know most of the important women in the Service's governing body, but her own experiences in India had made her an ideal resource in studying the conditions that the Service's nursing sisters would be called upon to face. She had had much to do as well in choosing the sort of young women who would bring honor rather than disrepute to the Service.

My parents hadn't consulted her when I chose nursing, because they hadn't wished to involve her in a family decision. They had firmly believed that I should survive or fail on my own merits, rather than Melinda Crawford's influence. And I had always been grateful for that.

My father had already spent some ten minutes with Simon on matters not for my ears, and as he prepared to take his leave now, he asked how I thought the Sergeant-Major was progressing.

"As well as can be expected," I answered, trying for middle ground and not betraying Simon to my father.

The Colonel Sahib nodded, leaned forward to kiss my cheek, and then was gone. As I crossed to the house, I listened to the sound of his motorcar disappearing in the distance.

I had got my way. Not completely, but far enough to feel a sense of satisfaction that my father had listened to me.

But in spite of everything I'd told him—and I believed all that I'd said, that this was the safest way to proceed—I would have to be very careful indeed. Or I could still fall victim to this killer.

CHAPTER FIFTEEN

FROM THE MOMENT my father had turned the bonnet of his motorcar toward Kent, things moved very rapidly. Whatever qualms she might have had for my sake, Melinda Crawford was quick to see the advantage of what my father proposed. What's more, he would have given her a full account of all that had happened. She had known Vincent Carson. She too would wish to see his killer brought to book.

Three days later I was summoned to London to discuss reassignment to France.

I stayed that night in London with Mrs. Hennessey at the flat.

She was overjoyed to see me and spent half an hour telling me all the news about my flatmates and about her own cronies. She insisted that I have dinner with her in her small dining room, asking after my parents and Simon.

She had once been involved in an attempt by a murderer to reach my rooms, and afterward she had sung the praises of the Sergeant-Major for saving both our lives. Since that time, he had ranked with my father in her opinion, and she admitted to being quite fond of him.

I didn't tell her about his wounds—there was no need to worry her—and I enjoyed my dinner immensely, for she had told her friend the butcher that she expected him to do her proud with a bit of beef that he held back sometimes for his special customers. It was not legal, but even butchers had to stay in business for the duration, and the small roast we ate wouldn't have made the tiniest dent in the needs of the nation.

The next morning I took the early train to Portsmouth, with my father to see me off, and slept a little while I could. In my pocket were the credentials I would need over the next few weeks, or for as long as it took to find a murderer.

The ship made good time against heavy seas, for the weather broke with a vengeance as an early summer storm moved in off the Atlantic. The skies turned gray, the rain pelted down, and the warmth I'd enjoyed at my bedroom window vanished in cold air that made standing on deck unpleasant in the extreme.

It was still raining when we reached Rouen, but the worst had passed. A driver was waiting for me, and I was glad to see as he came forward to take my valise that his eyes were a very Cornish brown, his name Trelawney. He was also a member of my father's old regiment, and he said as he escorted me to the motorcar, "Your father's daughter is safe with me, Sister."

I thanked him, and we slipped and slid out of Rouen on the mud-slick roads, and headed west.

It took a day and a half to reach the forward lines approaching Ypres, and I slept that night in a nearly roofless shed that smelled of horses. Trelawney brought me tea at first light, and then we were on our way once more.

The first aid station on the top of my list was small, hastily set up, and overrun with wounded from a breach in the line that had mercifully held. I dropped all pretense of being there to observe and was busy sorting the cases as they came in and then doing duty in the operating theater.

There had been a gas attack as well, and the scent of new-mown hay lingered on the air as men gasped for breath and we did our best to lavage the burned areas of skin and mouths. We all carried gas masks with us every hour of the day and night, but there had been no time for some men to react to the first conspicuous low cloud coming toward them.

We loaded the ambulances lined up behind the station and sent stretcher cases back for more extensive care, then turned our attention to the walking wounded. It was late in the evening before we could draw a breath, and the nursing sister in charge thanked me for my help.

I stayed for the rest of the night and spent most of the morning there as well, until the wounded were no more than a trickle. The guns were silent, and it seemed that both sides were trying to recoup their losses. A few more cases were brought in from a flag-of-truce collection from No Man's Land, and then those who were not on duty went to their cots and slept deeply.

I sat drinking tea with Sister Mason, who ran this station with such courage.

"There's not much choice," she said grimly. "Dr. Beddoes was taken back a week ago with a burst appendix. He never mentioned feeling ill or told us what he suspected. I've had to carry on, and I don't know when or if we'll have another doctor sent to us."

Somewhere nearby a soldier was playing a mouth organ, a haunting version of "Roses of Picardy." I thought how homesick he must be, letting the instrument put into words what he couldn't, that the war had lasted far too long and there was still no end in sight. He had lost heart, and I couldn't fault him for that.

I made a note of Sister Mason's concerns, and as she watched me, she said, "I thought when I first saw you that you were here to make trouble. But you worked as hard as any of us."

"It isn't trouble I'm after," I replied. "I'll report your need of a doctor, and it's the best I can do at the moment. But you can be assured I won't forget."

She shrugged. "They say the war may end soon. Another year at most. I don't know. We'll all be dead by then, there will be no one left to fight."

I asked if she had sufficient supplies. "We never have enough. But we manage. Every ambulance that goes back is under orders to bring forward what they can."

Such conditions were common. But that didn't make it any easier for those who had to work with first cases out of the trenches and knew supplies were running short. I had done it too often.

"The French hospitals are worse, they say," she added. "I've heard tales. How true, I don't know. But if I were dying, I'd rather come here and stand a chance than go to one of theirs."

I smiled. I'd heard the same tales. Of men crying for water, and one overworked sister trying to save the worst of the wounded while the rest hung on grimly in the hope their turn would come.

Setting down my cup, I said as casually as I could, "One of my flatmates worked with a Dr. Percy in a station near Ypres. She asked me to say hello if I saw him."

"Percy? I don't think I've met him."

Interesting. I said, "Perhaps he's been reassigned," and I left it at that.

An hour later, I set out for my next stop.

Trelawney—he'd never told me his rank—was always there, ready to drive me when I turned toward the motorcar. I don't know where he'd found this vehicle, held together by the rust that was trying to destroy it. But the motor was sound and the tires were reliable, the two most important factors in transport out here.

While I was working with the wounded, the resourceful Trelawney had done a little scouting in the area. The Germans had reached this far south at the start of the war—there had been bloody fighting in this sector at one time—and he had told everyone he was hunting for souvenirs. They'd laughed at him but left him to it.

"Any luck?" I asked when we were out of earshot of the aid station.

Trelawney shook his head. "You couldn't hide a wee mouse out there."

He didn't need to say anything more.

On our way to the next station, we quartered another area and were almost strafed by a German craft, which veered away at the last minute, having spotted something of greater interest down the line.

I could hear Trelawney swearing under his breath as he zigged and zagged across the ruts and dips, fearing for his tires and his suspension. We were conspicuous just here, where there were no convoys of ammunitions and supplies at the moment, no troops moving forward or ambulances rumbling back. What's more, motorcars were usually driven by officers, always a tempting target. But it was necessary to be thorough, and we nearly paid dearly for it.

The only structure was so pitifully small in this blasted landscape that it couldn't even provide shelter from a good rain. But we did discover two cellars, once part of a tiny village, their entrances partly blocked by rubble. Rat-infested—according to Trelawney, I didn't go down to see—and filled with more rubble and water, they were unfit for human habitation.

Putting away his torch and his revolver, he said with disgust, "I daresay there are bones down there as well. I didn't care to have a look."

It was dawn when we reached the next station on my list, and I worked until dusk with the sisters there, doing what I could, wondering who would step in to help when I had to leave. And then it was quiet, the last of the wounded dealt with, including a head injury, and they found a cot for me. I fell asleep almost at once, glad for a place to rest.

We continued to move slowly east along the Western Front. And so far no one had tried to attack me. Nor had we learned anything that was useful. Except that there was no Dr. Percy in this sector. In another cellar we had found two German dead, wounded men who must have crawled in there long ago, their uniforms barely recognizable, their bones already disturbed by the ever-present rats. Trelawney searched for identification all the same, saying, "They'll have families, and someone will want to know what happened to them." Afterward he marked the location for a burial detail.

Another dawn, and we were nearly caught by surprise when a gas attack came, the mist moving silently across the ground, almost invisible in a light ground fog. I caught the faintest whiff of new-mown hay and fumbled for my ever-present gas mask, got it on quickly, tucked my limbs under my skirts and my arms under my cape, leaving no skin exposed. It passed over us, dissipating as quietly as it had appeared. We waited until we could hear a distant all clear, and then moved on. But ahead of us in the next station were men caught unprepared, asleep or nodding at their posts. I had heard tales of how the gas could creep across the ground and sink into the trenches, a killer that seemed to care nothing for either side, for if the wind shifted, it blew back to the German lines. We used gas as well. The cough of burned lungs was unmistakable to the trained ear.

When we arrived at the next station, I found lines of gassed men waiting for their turn to be seen. Bandages across their eyes helped some of the pain and was a distinctive marker. They had a hand on the shoulder of the man in front of them, stumbling along, tripping if no one warned them of uneven ground, at the mercy of orderlies and sisters who guided them.

We bathed their skin and did what we could for their lungs. The worst cases would die painfully, the less damaged would linger in a misery that was frightful.

One night when the shelling was renewed, some of the shells falling well behind the lines, the two of us took refuge in one of those blighted edifices that stood like sentinels as the Front moved forward or fell back. Our own guns opened up in reply, and the din was horrific this close. It felt as if my brain rattled in my skull, and I had to clap my hands over my ears to ease the pain.

We soon retreated to one of those distinctive French farmhouses, built on a square, with the house, the outbuildings, and the barns a part of the encompassing wall. Usually there were two entrances: a wider one in the rear for drays and carts, a narrower one nearer the house where riders and carriages came and went.

Part of the wall had been reduced to rubble, the roof of the barn had collapsed, and the house was no more than a cellar and a single wall. We pulled into the lee of the outside of the wall while Trelawney did a brief reconnoiter.

He came back, got into the motorcar once more, and drove into the sheltering arms of the section of wall still standing. Trelawney turned to me and said, "Sister, we're out of range here. It's best if we wait until the worst is over." He pulled out the oiled map we'd been using, scanned it in the shielded light of his torch, and grunted. "Just here, I think we are." He pointed to a dot on the map that represented this farmhouse. "It seems there was an aid station here, earlier in the war. I found a twisted cot or two left behind. And then it was a command post before the lines changed again. Nobody but us now. I was careful." He always was. "There ought to be a dry patch in a cellar. Or under the roof that's fallen in. There was a ring around the moon last night. We'll have rain by midmorning."

I'd seen the ring too, and I didn't relish being wet to the skin.

"Which should we try first?" He waited.

"I think the barn. I don't particularly like the idea of being trapped in a cellar."

"The barn it is. I'll have another look, then."

He disappeared a second time, and I heard chickens squawking as he walked in among the fallen timbers. They had taken refuge here too, I thought, their lives changed just as much as that of their owners.

After fifteen minutes Trelawney returned, and we moved the motorcar a second time to where it was least likely to be seen from the air or by any parties passing through.

In one section the straw was clean enough, and we spread the rug from the motorcar over it. The chickens were roosting in the timbers above the cowshed, out of sight. Trelawney, nervous about leaving it unattended, told me he would stay with the motorcar. I fell asleep in spite of the guns.

It was well before dawn, the sky no longer lit by the shelling but by a tank burning somewhere, the smell of metal and petrol and oil barely masking the odor of burning flesh, when something brought me awake with a start. I couldn't have said what it was—some change in the silence. Sometimes we noticed the guns more when they fell silent than when they were firing. I could hear my own breathing.

More to the point, I could hear the breathing of someone else inside the barn with me.

It wasn't Trelawney; he'd have spoken to me or in some way let me know that he had come into where I was sleeping. Nor was it the chickens, for even the rooster, if there was one, hadn't begun to crow.

I lay there with my eyes closed, listening.

The breathing got louder as someone approached even closer.

Where was Trelawney?

The fingers of my right hand moved among the folds of my skirt, then closed over the small pistol that Simon had given me.

I waited.

It was possible that Trelawney had heard something too and had come to warn me. I had to be absolutely certain someone else was there before I dared to fire. And if there was—what had he done with my driver?

Several thoughts ran through my mind. A handful of the Chinese laborers who worked for the British Army, looking for the eggs the chickens laid or, for that matter, one of the chickens?

They'd be wary of Trelawney. And a company of British soldiers would have asked him his business long before they came here to approach me.

A deserter? It was entirely possible, but how had he avoided being seen by the ever-vigilant Trelawney?

Or a murderer who had already dispensed with my driver, and was intent on dealing next with me?

We'd been so very careful. Perhaps too careful, lulling ourselves with our own certainty that we could protect ourselves.

If Trelawney was dead or badly injured, I'd have to make my shot count. But I dared not open my eyes yet. I could tell by the sound of breathing that he wasn't near enough. I couldn't be sure which direction to fire. There were stalls on either side of where I had slept, and tracking sound was nearly impossible.

I lay there, keeping my own rate of breathing as close to steady as possible.

Another sound, a timber creaking under an unwary foot.

My throat was dry. I was still reluctant to risk a look. And I could feel my heart rate quickening as the moment of decision came.

He'd stopped. Waiting? Making certain I was asleep?

I remembered my valise, tucked into the straw close to my right foot.

Was that what he was after, whoever was here in the barn with me?

And just as I remembered it, I felt the straw stir, as if someone had reached for my case.

I said, opening my eyes, "I'm armed, and I won't hesitate to shoot. Stay where you are—"

I broke off.

In the distant glare of the burning tank, a monstrous figure loomed before me, one side of his face lit by the flames, the other sinister and dark. The one eye I could see appeared to be so pale that it seemed not to exist in reality, only in my racing imagination.

I froze.

And I lay there accepting the fact that the small-caliber pistol in my pocket could never stop my murderer. He could kill me as he must have already killed Trelawney, and there was absolutely nothing I could do about it.

CHAPTER SIXTEEN

WE STARED AT each other, neither moving for an instant.

I thought, *I must shoot him anyway. While I can. It won't stop him, but it will mark him. It might even do enough damage that he'll eventually die of the wound.*

My finger tightened on the trigger, slowly, as Simon had always taught me, a steady pressure that wouldn't spoil my aim.

And then the man in front of me spoke.

There was the rich Welsh lilt to his voice as he said, "I'm bad wounded. Do you have anything in that valise will help?"

I thought at first it was a trick, but when my eyes swept down his frame, I saw the darkish patch at his hip. Blood, and not fresh.

It dawned on me that I might have shot this man out of fear, and I felt cold with the realization that I'd have had his death on my hands.

"What's your name, rank, and regiment?" I demanded.

"No, I won't tell you that. I'm not going back into the line. I've got this far, and with any luck at all, I'll make it back to England before I die."

He wouldn't budge from that. I thought, *If he sees the pistol, he'll know what it can do. And if he's a deserter, he could still be a danger to me.*

And so I kept my hand in my pocket.

"What have you done with my driver?"

"The Cornishman with a tongue on him like a hair shirt? He's bound and sitting by the motorcar. That's my ticket home, that motorcar. I won't be stopped. Not now. I won't do you a harm, Sister, but I've rope enough for you as well."

"They won't let you aboard any ship in a torn, filthy uniform and without proper papers. They'll take you up and sort you out later."

"I'll find another uniform. The dead won't care," he said, an edge of desperation in his voice.

And I understood then why Major Carson had had to die. His officer's uniform was someone's ticket home. But for what reason? Simple desertion or something far worse?

He started for me. I ordered him to stop, then waited until he was near enough before I fired.

My aim was excellent, despite the awkwardness of firing through my apron pocket with only the flickering light of the flames, now dying down, to help me.

He threw himself to one side as the shot went whizzing past his ear, and the face he showed me when he'd raised his head up out of the hay would have made me laugh, it was so ludicrous. He smothered an oath.

"Sisters don't go armed," he said in an aggrieved tone of voice.

"I did warn you," I told him sharply.

"You damn—you nearly took my ear off!"

"The next shot will be between your eyes. I was taught by an expert marksman, and I won't miss." I let that sink in, then I added in the no-nonsense voice of Matron, "Now sit down over there. No, too close. On that bucket over there, if you please."

He turned over the bucket and winced in pain as he lowered himself onto it. "Not for long, please, Sister, I can't handle it," he pleaded.

"Then speak up. Name, rank, regiment. And don't lie to me, I will know it, believe me."

He gave his name as Jones, private, Welsh Sappers.

"You're too large to dig tunnels under the German lines," I retorted. "Try again."

He grimaced. "You'll only send me back to be shot. I'd rather you do it now and be done with it."

"Tell me why you deserted."

"There's no one to do the farming if I'm gone."

I had been watching him throughout. And I was nearly certain he wasn't the man who had tried to run me down in the motorcar. His eyebrows were dark, yes, but although he was indeed a big man, he wasn't large enough to be Ross Morton's son. Still, he was tall enough and strong enough to have throttled me with one arm around my throat, but so were dozens of soldiers in the British Army.

I rose from the hay rather awkwardly, my hand still in my pocket. "We'll find my driver now. If you've harmed him, you're a dead man yourself. If he's all right, I'll dress that wound."

He got up nearly as awkwardly as I had, his face twisted in pain until he was on his feet.

I marched him before me out to where the motorcar had been left. And there, by the wing, sat Trelawney, bound, his head on his chest.

I thought for an awful moment that he was dead, his face was so battered. He'd put up a fierce battle in my defense. I turned on the Welshman. His own face showed the marks Trelawney had left there.

"Untie him," I ordered, and my prisoner had to kneel to accomplish that. His face was white as he rose, and for a moment I thought he'd faint. I felt no sympathy.

I was beginning to wonder if I'd found Hugh Morton after all. Or someone very like him, a deserter too hurt to fend for himself and too inexperienced to find a way back to England. It was naïve to think a dead officer's uniform and a motorcar would see him safe. And a killer would have taken his chances, charged me in the expectation of throwing off my aim, and been done with it. Certainly if this man had had six brothers, like Hugh Morton, even the former champion pugilist of the British Army would be no match for such rough-and-tumble training. What interested me was why Trelawney hadn't shot him outright, if he'd had the opportunity.

No longer held erect by the rope, my driver slid down to lie on the ground, and I felt for his pulse. It was regular, but it was impossible to tell whether he was pale or his color was normal. I looked in the motorcar, found his revolver, and turned it on my captive in place of my own little weapon.

"Back into the barn," I ordered the Welshman. "Find a clean patch of hay and lie down. That wound needs attention, and while you don't deserve it, I'll see to it."

He argued with me until I had to threaten once more to shoot him.

It was not a pretty sight, that wound. He had been shot in the hip, creasing the bone, tearing up the flesh around it, and possibly doing internal damage. The one encouraging fact was that the bullet had passed through, although it must have left God alone knew how many fragments of cloth and bone and skin behind. He must have the constitution of an ox, to have survived this long, much less battled Trelawney. But he had seen salvation in that motorcar, and it had given him the strength he needed.

I got what I required from the boot where I'd kept a scant supply and proceeded to clean the wound, sprinkle it with disinfectant powder, and then bind it up. Halfway through, I saw that my prisoner had fainted. Kneeling there beside him, I could only think he'd been sent back for urgent care and had slipped away in the dark before reaching the aid station.

While he was unconscious, I had no compunction about going through his pockets, but I found nothing of importance—a few cigarettes, a lighter, a crumpled photograph of a girl, a packet of sweets, and, oddly enough, a St. Christopher medal. I wondered if she had given that to him. Next I looked at the inside of his tunic and saw what I was after. Someone had sewn his name behind his breast pocket. The same girl? His mother?

At that moment, I heard Trelawney bellowing my name.

"I'm all right," I answered. "In here."

He came charging through the barn door, stopping short at the sight of his attacker lying at my feet.

"Good God, Sister. Have you killed him?" he exclaimed, his gaze rising to my face.

"I just cleaned that wound. The question is, what ought we to do with him?"

"Tie him to something and leave him for the patrols to find." He put his hand to his head, gingerly touching what must have been a painful lump. "I'd searched the premises, Sister, there was no one here. I'd have sworn to that. The motorcar was secured as well. And I'm a light sleeper, mind you. I heard him creeping up and went after him. I'm ashamed to say he got the better of me."

And that would rankle with Trelawney for the rest of his life.

"I expect he saw us coming and went away. It was the motorcar he wanted. I don't believe he intended to kill either of us." I didn't add that Trelawney would have been dead, if he had.

"That's not what my head is telling me," Trelawney said tersely.

My patient groaned, coughed a little, and opened his eyes, rearing up as he saw Trelawney's enraged face. It cost him dearly, and while he was sitting there with a cold sweat breaking out from the effort, I said, "That's enough, Hugh Morton. Or I'll have your father take you out behind the woodshed."

He wiped his face with one hand and said plaintively, "You looked inside my tunic."

"Yes, of course I did. You're a large man, but no match for your father, wounded or well."

"You never met my Da," he said, angry now. "Besides, I take after my mother's side of the family."

"Oh, haven't I? I've been to Peace and Plenty, and I've spoken to

your father. What's more, I saw your brother David's face in an upstairs window."

"You have never." But I thought he believed me.

"Did you kill Major Carson? I want a straight answer."

His surprise was genuine. "I've been hunting him. Are you telling me the Hun killed him?"

"I don't know."

"He's a cold bas—man, is Carson. He could have helped Will.
He'd promised he would, but Will died in my arms, and when I
spoke to the Major afterward, he said it would have to wait, there
was something he had to attend to first. I ask you, what's more
urgent than looking after a widowed sister and her boy?" He was
properly incensed.

"Something? What something did he have to attend to first?" A
letter home to his solicitor, or his wife?

"He didn't say. But he wasn't there next morning, and the Lieutenant told us he'd been sent for at HQ."

The summons that had taken Carson to his death?

"What did you intend to do, if you caught up with him?"

"Knock some sense into him. Officer or not. Will deserved
better. There's no shame in being an actor. He was good to Sabrina."

"What to do with you, Hugh Morton," I said with a sigh. "If I
leave you here, you'll be shot for desertion. I can take you to the
nearest aid station and tell them I'd found you wounded and out of
your mind with fever. The wonder is that you aren't."

"I want to go home," he said, weariness and despair in his eyes.
The first light of dawn was touching the horizon, and I could see
how very pale his eyes were. But they were blue, not gray. Very definitely blue. "I've no will to fight anyone now. William and Ross are
dead. There's David with only one leg, and Llewellyn not right in his
head. There's only me and the twins left, and I've had no news of
them for weeks, now. We've done our bit, this family has, and my Da
needs help on the farm."

I remembered the fallow fields, untended because there was only one man to work them and he could only do so much. How many times had this same predicament happened across the length and breadth of England? Women had been sent out to help till fallow land, to turn Commons and Greens and even estate parks into cropland. But no one had come to Peace and Plenty to remedy the lack of labor.

I was my father's daughter, and this was a deserter. In wartime. I looked at Trelawney for support.

His face was hard. A soldier all his life, he had no sympathy for a farmer in Wales or anywhere else. Take the oath to serve the King, and you were his as long as you were required. Nothing else mattered.

In the distance the shelling had recommenced, this time the German guns. Range finding, they were laying down a blanket of fire in the hope of taking out ours.

Trelawney, casting a worried glance over his shoulder, said, "We ought to be going. This farm has been hit before."

He was right. I said to Hugh Morton, "You'll come with us for now. Into the front of the motorcar. I'll be just behind you, and I don't need to remind you that I'm armed."

"I'll stay here. Take my chances."

"You're lucky a patrol hasn't found you before this. And if that hip isn't seen to by a doctor, David won't be the only Morton son with only one leg."

He refused. And as I listened to the shells dropping closer and closer, I said, "I'll shoot you myself. You won't be going home either way."

Hugh Morton studied my face. What he read there must have been determination, although he couldn't know I was bluffing.

"I won't give my parole," he said. "You can't force me to do that."

"And I won't promise not to shoot to kill when you run. Quickly, now!"

But it was too late. A shell threw up black earth not fifty feet
. from the side wall of the farm. Between us Trelawney and I dragged
Morton to the motorcar. His wound, after my probing and cleaning, had left his leg too weak to hold him up, and it must have hurt
ferociously. He kept swearing under his breath in Welsh, for I didn't
understand a word, but I heard *Sister* once, as he blamed me for
crippling him, however temporarily. Even if he'd tried to run, he
wouldn't have got twenty paces.

Just then the next shell splintered the barn, sending shards of
wood and debris all over us. Chickens flew out of the milking shed,
squawking in terror, and even an owl, blind in the morning light,
went swooping up from somewhere, trying to escape.

We'd just shoved Hugh Morton into the motorcar. Trelawney
shielded me as best he could, then all but lifted me into the rear seat
before dashing around to get behind the wheel. Thank God, he'd already turned the crank, and he spun the wheel, racing for a break in
the farm wall, but it was already in flames, the shed next to it burning like a torch.

He began to turn away, looking for another exit, but there was
no place left, fire spreading so rapidly we were all but encircled by
smoke. It seared the lungs and made all of us choke and cough.

"Hang on," Trelawney shouted, and pointed the bonnet directly
toward the shed, so engulfed that the opening in the wall was invisible. He had searched the farmyard carefully, and even without being
able to see the break, he would know how to judge it.

But I felt myself tense, and Hugh Morton yelled at Trelawney,
telling him he was going to miss the opening. For he too would
know this farmyard well.

Braced for hitting the wall at speed, I kept my eyes on Trelawney.
He would be the first to know if he was wrong. Behind us another
shell burst, showering earth and wall and fragments of farm equip-
ment over us, rattling against the motorcar.

I could only think what a target we would have been in the night,
Trelawney and I, if the shelling had begun while we were asleep.

Metal shrieked like banshees as the near wing brushed stone wall, and then we were through, still blind, when suddenly dawn broke ahead of us, and the sun breached the horizon in a bloodred ball.

I lifted a hand to shield my eyes, Trelawney swore, and Morton was clutching the dash with white-knuckled hands.

Angling away from the line of shells, we saw what they were searching for, massed troops making their way forward into the line. I shuddered, thinking of the wounded who would be streaming back to the nearest aid station. I reached out and touched Trelawney's shoulder.

"We're needed there," I shouted over the din, but Morton caught his sleeve.

"For the love of God, no," he pleaded.

"Your father believes you're missing. That's cruel."

He was digging deep into his trouser pocket and pulled out a set of identity disks, dangling them where I could see them. "Here's proof I'm Tommy Morris, and I'm not right in my head."

He fell into a posture of vapid uncertainty, his mouth down at one corner, his eyes squinting and sometimes rolling as if he couldn't control them.

"I saw a man once who looked like this. They took him away. Bad influence on the rest of us," he said as he relaxed his face muscles.

And his brother was an actor. Hugh had enough of that talent to master his condition. I'd have believed it myself.

"Then why are you hiding in the ruins? Why haven't you tried your trick on someone in an aid station?"

"The truth, Sister, is that I've lived in the cellar of that farmhouse for weeks now. Someone caught me foraging and took a shot at me. I didn't know the password, see? That's the wound you dressed. I wasn't wounded in the line, I simply disappeared in the dark, taking another man back to the aid station. He died before I could get him there, his blood all over my hands. And I thought, 'Here's Providence providing.' So I took my chance. I couldn't outrun another patrol, not with this hip. But the motorcar was Providence all over again. I blessed my luck, and I'd have had it too."

He'd come into the barn for my kit, to find something to help his wound and give him a chance. He couldn't have held out much longer in the ruined farmhouse, but there were chickens, and surely eggs, and he must have found something to keep body and soul together before he was shot.

It was an interesting dilemma.

I found it increasingly difficult to believe he had killed the Major or Private Wilson. He wasn't cunning enough to waylay me or set up an accidental death for Nurse Saunders. But what to do with him?

And what if I was wrong?

CHAPTER SEVENTEEN

WE HADN'T GONE two miles when a shout went up, followed by the appearance seemingly out of nowhere of a patrol. I heard Hugh Morton groan, and Trelawney spoke swiftly, hardly moving his lips, "What do we do? Sister?"

"Stop the motorcar. Have your papers ready. Private Morris, I hope your disks save you now. There's nothing more I can do."

We waited, listening to the shelling, to the sound of a motorcycle runner heading forward to the Front, to barked commands by officers steadying their men in the line.

The company quick marched toward us, and by the time they reached the motorcar, I had taken out my papers from the Queen Alexandra's Imperial Military Nursing Service and had them ready. Trelawney had produced his own, and Hugh Morton, his face pale but set, held his false identity disks in one hand.

The Sergeant in charge of the patrol went over our papers carefully, then looked at the disks that Hugh Morton presented.

Turning to me, he asked, "He's wounded?"

"Yes. As you can see. I was taking him back to be looked at. An ambulance couldn't be spared for one patient."

He insisted on seeing the bandaged wound, then frowned, as if something about Hugh Morton registered in his memory. I prayed his hadn't been the patrol that had fired on the Welshman when he was foraging. Deserters and looters got short shrift from the Army.

After what seemed like an interminable wait, the Sergeant nodded and told us where to find our next destination.

Trelawney thanked him and moved off under the Sergeant's eye. And he continued to watch us out of sight, as if worried about our presence here in the midst of troop movements. Our own guns were replying to the German artillery, the noise deafening.

We reached the aid station and I presented my credentials to the young, harassed sister in charge.

Supplies were being stowed, and the few patients with trench foot, gassed lungs, and minor wounds were being sent back by ambulance to clear the station for the major wounds to come.

I could see Hugh Morton—Private Morris—being sent to join the queue, and I asked Trelawney to keep an eye on him until I'd thought of a way to prevent it.

But I needn't have worried. Sister Wharton was anxious about the pending attack and how prepared she was to deal with it. In the end I decided to leave her to handle the influx of wounded on her own, with her staff to help her, rather than become the Senior Nursing Sister in her place. I'd learned my own strengths in her shoes, and I knew from the brief conversation I had with her that she would cope very well and be the stronger for it, knowing she had.

We were all so young, I thought as we drove away, the men who came to us and the sisters who treated them. I had seen and done things that my grandmother would have wondered at, but I had also discovered that courage was the ability to face what had to be faced, when it was impossible to run away.

At a rear hospital, I asked one of the doctors to have a look at Private Morris's wound.

He examined it, nodded, and said, "Well done, Sister. I've given him something for the pain. Let him rest for an hour or two, and we'll send him on to Rouen."

I thanked him, dealt with my patient, asked Trelawney to sit with him—receiving a thunderous frown for my trouble—then started toward the wards. At that moment a courier came through, on his way to HQ. Stopping by the sister in charge of sorting patients, he showed her his wrist. She examined it briefly and pointed to a bench where others were waiting for attention. He argued with her, but she shook her head and moved on to the next man in her line.

The courier looked around, spotted me, and walked toward me. Where his goggles had been were two pale circles around hazel eyes. The rest of his face appeared to have black measles, it was so splotched from hunching over his machine as he sped cross-country.

"Sister? I spun out in the mud and I think I've sprained my wrist. Will you have a look at it? I'm overdue as it is—I can't wait with that lot."

I glanced across at Sister Henry. She was busy with the line. "Come this way," I said, and took him a little apart, where I examined his wrist—it was painful but not broken—and taped it so that he could be gone. "But you must promise to see to it as soon as you can," I admonished him.

"I promise, Sister. Thank you."

He was about to turn away when I seized the opportunity. "Could I add a message to your pouch?"

"Hurry! I can't wait."

There was paper and pen in my valise. I wrote my father's name and rank on the outside of the envelope, and inside simply scribbled a single word: *Nothing.*

It would reassure and disappoint him at the same time.

The messenger gingerly drew his gauntlets on over the tape, adjusted his goggles, and walked away to where he'd left his machine.

On the spur of the moment, I went after him, calling, "You said HQ. Have you encountered a Colonel Prescott there?"

"No. Should I have?"

I shook my head. "I was just curious. I appear to have missed him at every turn."

He nodded, started his machine with a roar, then cut back on the throttle. "Prescott, you say?"

"Yes, that's right. A big man with startlingly pale eyes."

"That sounds more like Major Carson."

I tried to keep the excitement out of my voice. "Then perhaps my information was wrong. Where did you see him?"

He resettled his goggles. "Rouen. He's returning to England. He stopped me to ask if I'd been given his orders."

There was no time to rewrite the message for my father.

"Do you usually carry such orders?"

"These were especially cut. From Colonel Crawford, he said."

I felt cold.

"Did you—were you asked if there were orders in your satchel for other officers?"

"Yes, as a matter of fact he did ask if there were any others. He was worried that his had been mislaid. But there weren't. Not that time." He gunned the motor, eager to be off now.

"I can't explain," I began, "but don't look for Major Carson the next time you're in Rouen. He's—" I couldn't think of a good reason to disparage the Major, except of course for the fact that he was dead and someone had assumed his identity. "He's not in good odor at HQ. That could be the reason why his orders are not yet cut. Colonel Crawford could well wish him to cool his heels for a time."

"How do you know this?" he asked, suddenly suspicious.

"I'm Colonel Crawford's daughter. If you look in your pouch, you'll see his direction on the letter I gave you." I offered him my best smile. "Just—be careful, will you?"

He regarded me for a long moment, nodded, and then was gone in a roar.

I went to find Trelawney as quickly as I could.

"The man I'm looking for. He's in Rouen. We must leave as soon as we can."

But there were already wounded coming in, strafing injuries

from a low-flying aircraft as well as shrapnel from exploding shells. The guns were busy, and it was baptism by fire for the raw recruits facing death for the first time. I held one boy of seventeen while the doctor dug shrapnel out of his legs, and I pretended not to see when he wept with the pain.

I worked late into the night, and I rose early in the morning, before sunrise, as the long lines of ambulances and an overburdened lorry brought us more and more wounded. A hardened veteran, watching the long lines being sorted by one of the sisters, said, "There'll be no one left in England over the age of sixteen."

I worked long into the night again, and when I came off duty, Trelawney said, "Morton is gone. He slipped into one of the ambulances heading for Rouen."

"Hardly unexpected." I sighed, remembering my own predicament over proper passes. "If they don't pick him up at the port, he'll be very lucky."

"Aye, that's so."

On the third day as the flood of wounded slowed to a trickle, I found time to tell the sister in charge that I would be leaving for Rouen, to complete my report. She thanked me for my assistance, and then said, "I've met one of your flatmates. Mary. She was with us for a few weeks, earlier on, then was sent home after falling ill with the influenza. They tell me it will return with a vengeance in the autumn. I pray every night that it can't be true."

I'd heard the same, but I said bracingly, "We've seen the worst of it, I'm sure. I can't think of anyone who hasn't had it."

But even as I said the words, I remembered Mrs. Hennessey, Simon, and my parents.

We set out for Rouen an hour after lunch, working our way back through the quagmires that were roads, and then encountering a rainstorm that turned the mud into a morass. We took shelter for a time beneath a lone chimney standing by the road, at least breaking a little of the wind if not the rain.

Rouen was busy as we drove in late that night, and I had the credentials now to ask for a bed at the Base Hospital, one for me and one for my driver.

I sent Trelawney to search the port for the man calling himself Major Carson, and he was away for three hours before returning to report.

"If he's here, I can't find him. But that messenger, the one who told you about him—he was killed and his motorcycle taken. Just last night. The French police are conducting a house-by-house search for it. But I'll lay you odds it's already in Paris or points south."

I didn't think so. The killer's destination wasn't Paris; it was London. The motorcycle was most likely in the river, where it wouldn't be found straightaway, allowing the hunt to go on. I felt a surge of anger mixed with sadness. I'd warned the courier. Either he hadn't taken it seriously, or he'd come upon this man sooner than he'd expected.

Someone's orders had been in his pouch. I could guess at that. Orders worth killing for.

But in whose name?

It wasn't until much later that I realized that my letter might still be in the courier's pouch, depending on his route. With my father's direction scrawled hastily across the envelope.

If nothing else, it would surely tell the killer that I was once more in France.

I went down to the port, looking for any ship whose officers I recognized. There was no way of knowing if Major Carson, or whoever he claimed to be now, had already left for England sometime last night. Or if he had had to wait, as I did, for the next available transport.

Finally, in late afternoon, I spotted Captain Grayson. He saw me as well, throwing up a hand in silent greeting as he finished his business with the port master, and then coming forward to meet me.

"Hallo, Sister Crawford. I didn't know you were back in France. On leave, are you?"

"Yes, I am," I replied, smiling. "Any chance of space aboard the *Merlin*?"

"I should think that's possible."

"I have my driver with me. And a motorcar. Do you think there could be room for that as well?"

"I'll tow it behind us if I must. Do you have time for a cup of tea? I'm dry as the desert. It was a stormy crossing, couldn't search properly for periscopes or torpedo tracks because of the high seas. I never left the bridge."

I went with him to a small café near the cathedral, and he drank his tea with gusto. We talked about France and the war, and then he told me that his brother had been killed in the North Atlantic. I remembered Joseph Grayson as a man with a kind smile and a quick wit, and said as much.

"Thank you," the Captain replied, his voice husky. "I'm not accustomed to the fact that he's gone. We were close."

To change the subject, I asked if there were other passengers on board this crossing.

He shrugged. "God knows. They give me the count after we've been searched. There are quite a few wounded coming back with us. At least that's the rumor. Not surprising. I could hear the guns as we came upriver."

He paid for our tea and escorted me back to the Base Hospital before rejoining his ship. It would sail just after dark, and I promised to be on board before that time.

I had just walked through the gates of the hospital when someone called my name, and I turned quickly, unable to identify the voice.

It was Hugh Morton, drenched by the earlier rain, despair in his eyes.

"I don't have the proper papers," he told me. "Beside which, they're determined to keep me here as well, not send me home.

Wound's not serious enough, they claim. I don't know what to do. Rouen is bigger than I knew. I'd come over through Calais, not here. And I can't speak the language."

"What about your head injury performance?"

He smiled wryly. "I tried. They couldn't find any wound on my head. That's when they concluded I was feverish and would be admitted here."

I said, "I'm leaving Rouen tonight. There's nothing I can do."

"You got me this far," he reminded me.

"No. You left with the ambulances. As a hip wound."

"I thought it best. How was I to know?"

I looked him over. "When did you eat last?"

"Two days ago."

"Come along then."

I walked back out the gates and took him to a restaurant where the food was not the best but was of enough provenance to trust it.

He ate cabbages and potatoes and what appeared to be minced chicken cooked in a sauce. There was a pudding, and he ate that as well. I refused to let him have wine, and he drank tea almost as thirstily as the Captain had done.

When he was finished, I took pity on him. He was a man who only wanted to go back to his father's farm.

I said, "Look, even if I could get you to England, what then? As soon as you reach Wales—that's to say, if you manage it without getting caught—the entire village will see that you've returned home. The next thing you know the Army will be there to take you up. They don't turn the other way, Hugh Morton. They'll search for you and in the end come for you. I don't think you've considered that."

"I have thought about it. I look enough like Llewellyn to pass as him. I could pretend to be one of the others, but Will and Llewellyn and I were alike as peas in a pod. Someone was always blaming the wrong one of us. And if anyone comes, I'll just do my little mad bit, and they'll turn away. They always do."

"But he's in hospital. And it isn't much of a life for you."

"Who has traveled across England to see him? Nobody. Which of my father's neighbors will call me a liar?"

It was madness. The madness of desperation.

"Go back to your company, Private Morton. I'll tell the Base Hospital how I found you wandering and confused. There won't be charges to face."

"Sister, I left my company to avenge my brother. It's all I wanted—revenge for how Will was treated. But Will's dead, the Major is dead. I've no more stomach for fighting. And I can do more good at home, helping my Da in the fields, than I ever could here."

"I won't be responsible if you're caught. Do you understand that?"

"I do, Sister. I won't even tell my father how I got home. What's more, he won't ask."

"He may think you a coward for leaving France. None of your other brothers ran."

"I doubt they would have stayed, given the choice. I doubt Will preferred to die in France, never seeing his son. Or Ross, drowning in the cold sea. Or David, when he looked down to find his leg gone."

"All right. Go sit in the cathedral until dark. Meet me at the port gates. They're taking wounded on board, and whatever I say to you at that time, you'll do your part."

"On my honor, Sister."

But did a deserter have any honor to swear on?

I took him as far as the church, saw him safely ensconced by the organ loft stairs, and then walked away.

I wondered what my ancestress whose husband fought at Waterloo would have to say about what I was going to do.

I turned around and went back to the cathedral and found Hugh Morton where I'd left him.

"You will make me a promise," I said.

"Anything, Sister."

"If you survive this war, you will go to Cornwall and speak to your brother's wife and see his son. Do you swear?"

"On my honor," he said again. And this time I nodded.

I had left the cathedral and was making my way back to the Base Hospital when I happened to glance in a café window. Music was spilling out of the doorway, someone playing a plaintive tune on the piano, something about lost love and heartbreak.

And my own heart seemed to leap into my throat as the man sitting at a small table in the shadows of the doorway looked up at the very same moment.

He was wearing a British officer's uniform, wearing it as if it were his, although it was a little tight across the shoulders, but his eyes were as cold as the winter sea. By comparison, Hugh Morton's were as blue as a spring sky. And I'd last seen them shadowed by a muffler in the driver's seat of a motorcar trying to kill me.

I couldn't help my own response. This encounter had been too sudden, too unexpected, and we both knew, he and I, that I'd recognized him in the same instant he'd recognized me.

He had killed four people that I knew of. How many more I couldn't say.

But those four were enough.

I walked on, half expecting him to stand up, walk out of the café, and follow me. But at the corner of the next street, when I looked back, there was no one behind me except for two elderly women in black, struggling to carry a tub of washed clothes between them.

Either I was no longer a danger to him or he was too close to whatever objective drove him to take the risk of killing me now. But why sail for England if the Prince of Wales was scheduled to come to France?

At the Base Hospital, I looked for Trelawney, but I was told he'd taken the motorcar down to the quay. The Chief Engineering Officer had sent word that it could be stowed aboard now.

I hurried after him, but he was nowhere to be seen. One of *Merlin*'s officers was coming through the gate, and I went to speak to him, asking if he'd seen my driver and my motorcar.

"The Chief is haggling with him now," he told me, grinning. "He wants the tires for his own motor, at home in Chichester."

I had to laugh. Good luck to him, getting the best of a Cornishman.

Thanking the officer, I moved off a little to wait for Trelawney to disembark, but he and the Chief Engineer must have moved past haggling and were swapping stories now.

Looking at the collection of people hanging about the port, I saw no sign of the Major from the café. It was possible he wasn't on *Merlin*, but if he was here in Rouen, he would have to land in Portsmouth sometime. I had only to get there first and wait.

I was tired of standing, waiting, but I dared not leave until I'd found Trelawney. Finally, after I'd nearly given up twice, he came off the ship and saw me as he passed through the gates.

"She's as snug as can be," he told me, pleased with himself. "I saw her tied down myself. There was just room for her aft."

"I'm glad. Trelawney, I found the man we've been looking for. He was in a café halfway between the cathedral and the Base Hospital. I doubt he's there now. He saw me as clearly as I saw him, but he didn't follow me. And that reminds me, Hugh Morton is in the cathedral. I'm going to try to get him aboard."

"A deserter?" he demanded, aghast. "Sister—you can't mean it!"

I said, "I won't be the one to hand him over to be shot."

"I have no such qualms," he told me.

"But you will do as I tell you. It's more important to find this Major than it is to see Morton in irons."

"Bloody coward," he muttered, then realizing that I'd heard, he begged pardon.

"Nevertheless," I said. "This you will do for me. My reasons are sound."

He said nothing for a moment, then changed the subject. "What do we do, if he's on this ship? This man you're after?"

"The Captain is a friend. I'll ask that he be held until my father can come to meet the ship."

"He'll do that?"

"Yes," I said with far more assurance than I felt.

Trelawney nodded. "And if he's not on board?"

"I think he'll come to Portsmouth within a day or two. He has the orders he needed. It's only a matter of time. What's more, we'll have a chance to prepare. He won't get away in England. He mustn't."

"I was told he might be looking to kill the Prince of Wales."

"I don't know," I said, uncertainty loud in my voice. "There's something he intends to do. Or else he would stay in France."

"Makes sense, doesn't it?" Trelawney agreed. "He doesn't know me. Why don't you go aboard alone, and I'll watch until the last minute?"

"Yes, all right. But be very careful. He's killed four people that I know of. He won't be taken by surprise. If he even suspects you've recognized him, he has a choice. Kill again or wait for another ship. And waiting would be far more dangerous."

He said, "I'll leave you then. What about Morton?"

"If he reaches the ship, I'll put him with the wounded on board. Ah—here comes the first of the ambulances."

And indeed it was making its slow approach to the port.

Trelawney disappeared, there one minute and invisible the next. I scanned the dozen or so onlookers, and I saw no one I recognized.

I had to collect my valise, and I hurried back to the Base Hospital for it. I was just leaving with it, thanking the duty nurse for the hospitality shown me, when I saw ahead of me a man in the uniform of a British officer, his back to me, but there was something familiar about his shoulders and the way he walked.

And then I realized where I'd seen him before.

He wasn't the man with the bandaged shoulder who'd gone into the makeshift canteen just a few yards from the shed where the dead were taken. He had been the orderly carrying a mop and pail. The orderly Sister Burrows must have stopped and asked to bring fresh sheets to the ward. I'd been trained to observe—and so had she. I didn't think I was mistaken.

I followed at a distance, making certain that I wasn't where he might glimpse me in a shop window. Soldiers saluted him as they passed, and I tried to judge whether he was actually an officer—or a private soldier masquerading as one. I came to the conclusion he was a sergeant, for his back was ramrod straight, and his officer's cap didn't have that jaunty angle I saw so often. Rather, it sat squarely.

As if he felt my scrutiny, he turned and looked back the way he'd come, but a party of sappers had just cut across my path, and I was shielded by them. When they had passed, he was walking on again.

I tried to judge if he was British or German, but it was impossible to be sure. And someone sent to spy or act as an assassin would have been carefully chosen for his ability to fit in. Even his voice would be suitable, his English more than acceptable.

He'd reached the ship. I stopped to gaze at a window of cheeses, my back to him, and let him board. Apparently his papers passed inspection, and when I looked again, he was nowhere in sight.

Someone took my arm, and I nearly leapt out of my skin.

I turned quickly, prepared to scream if need be.

It was Hugh Morton.

"Would you have waited for me?" he asked. "Or left me in the organ loft?"

"I had other worries. But yes, I would have come. Trelawney is aboard with the motorcar, and there's someone I didn't want to encounter just ahead of me. He'll be on the same vessel."

"The officer you were following?"

"Yes."

"I'll keep an eye out for him. He won't know me."

"That would be helpful," I said. "But he's not a fool. You must be very careful."

He gave me that one-sided grin, his eyes all but crossed, his mouth drooping. "I told you. People don't see the afflicted," he said. "They're too uncomfortable to look at." It was a perceptive remark.

Just then more ambulances turned in toward the port, and I took Hugh Morton with me to add to the queue, explaining to the sister in charge, God forgive me, that he had been left off the list.

He was ordered on board with the others, and at the end of the long line, I myself handed over my own papers. I didn't see the man I'd been following, but I thought perhaps he was taking care not to be in plain sight, just in case someone could identify him—or inform the port authorities that he wasn't who he claimed to be. The only other possibility was that he wasn't on *Merlin* at all, that he was scheduled to depart on the ship just tying up behind her, and he'd come early to keep out of sight.

In due course, *Merlin* was given leave to sail, the lines were hauled in, dripping wet, and coiled neatly on the fore and aft decks. I stayed by the rail, looking out over the city, watching the flashes of the guns in the distance. My father remembered France from well before the war, and I wondered if it would ever look again as it had then.

The ship eased into the current, then turned to steam slowly down toward the sea. The night was dark, the running lights masked, and as I looked up to the bridge, I could see Captain Grayson's profile, tense and focused on what lay ahead.

He had given me his cabin for the voyage, as he wouldn't be using it as long as *Merlin* went in harm's way.

Indeed, as soon as we reached the sea, word was passed that we were being shadowed by a submarine, and the watch was doubled. The rating who came to my door was young but steady, assuring me that we were safe. But of course I knew otherwise, having sailed on *Britannic*. It was a long journey, seemingly longer than the usual, nerves stretched almost to the breaking point as we waited for the shout of "Torpedo!" My life vest was too warm but I kept it on, in case.

We reached the shelter of the Isle of Wight without being attacked, and Portsmouth Harbor lay ahead. I slipped out on deck to watch us come in, standing in the shadows, where I wouldn't be in the way or noticed.

But someone had seen me.

Out of nowhere, someone put hands on me, thrust a canvas bag over my head before I could scream or struggle, and then I was being dragged toward the railing.

It had happened so fast—a matter of seconds—and then I was being lifted over the railing, my muffled cries covered by the racket of the heavy anchor cable paying out as we came into the roads to await a berth.

I could feel myself dangling now, no foothold or handhold, and unable to see, I couldn't tell where to reach out and save myself.

And just as suddenly I was being pulled up so roughly that I struck my head on the teak railing, seeing stars in the blackness of the bag. I landed on deck with such force I was winded, and then as I reached shakily for the bag, someone stepped on my skirts. I realized that just above me, two men were locked in a fierce struggle. Only their feet were visible, and I quickly rolled out of the way.

As the heavy bag fell away, I could see their shapes. One in an officer's uniform, the other in the distinctive blue worn by Base Hospital patients. They were surprisingly well matched in size and reach. But Morton's hip wound put him at a disadvantage, unable to keep his balance on the moving deck. He was quickly losing the battle, pushed until his own back was hard against the rail, and as I watched, the other man rammed his knee into Morton's groin and hip.

The crew, busy with docking, had no time for us, but two orderlies had just come on deck from below. If they saw him fighting with an officer, he would be taken up for the offense. I could do nothing then.

He had saved me.

I still had my little pistol in my pocket. Scrambling to my feet, dizzy at first, and then quite determined, I brought it out, aimed, and fired.

The shot seemed so loud in our ears that we froze where we were. Morton turned his head to look at me, stunned, and in his grip I could see his attacker's eyes incandescent. I wondered how anyone could have described them as cold.

A trickle of blood began to run down the side of the man's face where my bullet had grazed his skull. With an oath he let go of Morton, turned, and stumbled away, disappearing down the nearest companionway as three ratings converged on Morton and me, alerted by the shot.

They caught his arms, pinning him, and I realized that they thought he'd been attacking me. I shoved the pistol into my pocket, and pointed over the railing.

"There!" I shouted. "Someone just tried to climb aboard. Look!"

They held on to Morton but ran for the railing, staring down into the dark, swirling waters. I joined them, pointing down the side of the ship now. "Over there. Stop him!"

Leaving Morton where he was, they raced along the railing, still searching for the intruder, shouting to the watch to ask if anyone could be seen.

I took Morton's arm. "Quickly. Get back to the wards. What were you thinking, coming on deck like this?" Trelawney had warned me Morton might try to escape.

"I told you I'd keep an eye out for him. He was searching the ship, and I watched him. I didn't see you there in the shadows, and then he had you pinned and was tossing you over the side." He leaned against the companion doorway wearily, hurting. "I don't want to be sent to hospital. I want to go home."

It was blackmail.

Hugh Morton had saved my life.

"I'll see to it. Go find Trelawney and tell him what happened. He'll be readying the motorcar. Don't leave him."

"But the Major's somewhere still. He'll find you again and I won't be there."

"Not now. There are too many men on deck. Go, before they come back to question you."

Reluctantly he did as he was told.

I went back to Captain Grayson's cabin, and a moment later, the Second Officer knocked, asking around the door, "You saw someone trying to come aboard? Is it true?"

"He was wearing an officer's uniform. He fired at me."

"Gentle God," he said, and disappeared again.

A false rumor, but there was nothing else to be done. Otherwise I'd have had to explain why I'd shot a British Major with a pistol I was not supposed to possess. I'd be detained while the Major disappeared.

I poured water from the Captain's carafe onto my handkerchief and held it to my aching head, where it had come in contact with the railing. I didn't think I was concussed, but it had been a hard blow all the same and I could feel the swelling under my hair.

I could hear racing feet and shouting for a while longer, and then the same officer returned to tell me that they'd found no one, and whoever it was had presumably either drowned or swum back to the port. The authorities there had been alerted to watch for him.

I was asked if I could identify the intruder, but I shook my head. "It all happened so quickly—by the time I'd realized what he was doing, he'd disappeared over the side again."

It was tempting to catch the Major in this net of lies. But his uniform was dry, they would never believe he'd come out from shore.

"You're a brave woman, Sister Crawford. Who was the patient who came to your aid?"

"I didn't stay to ask, I came directly back to my cabin."

He nodded. "Very wise."

As the door shut behind him, I found myself wondering what on earth my father would say, when he learned I'd thwarted a would-be boarder who didn't exist, rescued an unreported deserter who did, and shot a purported British officer in the head.

Soon afterward the anchor came up again, we tied up to the dock, and Trelawney was at my door, reporting that the motorcar had been offloaded.

"What have you done with Private Morton?"

"He's in the motorcar. The sister in charge was glad to be rid of him. It seems he'd wandered the ship all night, alarming the other patients and mumbling unintelligible drivel."

After I'd thanked Captain Grayson and accepted his apology for the fright I'd had, I prepared to leave *Merlin*.

I'd asked earlier if he would signal Portsmouth as soon as possible to ask if my father could be summoned. He told me now that my father was in London and couldn't be reached.

I was on my own, then.

Trelawney escorted me off the ship and to the waiting motorcar, and with my papers in hand, we left the harbor behind. Just outside gates, in the street where once my father and I had considered what to do about the charges against me, Trelawney and I conferred.

"I saw him leave *Merlin* just ahead of us," Trelawney told me. "I marked where he was heading. Did you give him that bloody crease? Every time he wears his cap, that's going to hurt." There was no pity in his tone.

"We've got to find him," I said, knowing how impossible that would be. "We can't let him disappear into the countryside."

"There's the train," Trelawney said doubtfully. "Crowded and slow. In his shoes I'd look for a motorcar."

And where better to find one unattended than the ship officers' billet.

Leaves were short, and a motorcar could make the difference between reaching London or one's family in time to spend a few hours with them or wasting it in Portsmouth.

Trelawney, at my direction, quickly found the nearest billets.

As we got there, several motorcars were heading out of the nearby mews, and Trelawney counted rapidly, "Naval uniform. Naval uniform. Naval again. *Army.* That one. *And I saw his bloody eyes.*"

There was no way to conceal Hugh Morton's bulk, but I had made myself as small as I could, taking off my cap so that I couldn't be seen as easily. And so I trusted Trelawney's assessment, and as our motorcar turned at the end of the mews to follow, I said, "I wish I'd had the chance to telephone someone."

"Too late now, Sister," Trelawney answered. "All right, you can sit up again. He can't see you, he's too far ahead."

We kept a discreet distance, which was fairly easy as the sun rose and we wove in and out of convoys heading down to the port. The green hilly landscape of Hampshire rose beyond the town, and the road to London was just ahead.

But our quarry didn't take it.

Instead he turned west, toward Dorset.

Here it was more difficult to stay within sight of the other vehicle. The roads now followed the curve of the land rather than a Roman rule, and there were villages stretched out along it like tiny jewels on a necklace. The problem was, we couldn't always be sure our quarry hadn't stopped at one of them or turned off. It wasn't until we were on the far side of each that we could pick out the glint of the sun on his boot in the distance or actually glimpse his motorcar rounding a bend far ahead.

My head was thundering and we were all three tired and thirsty and on edge for fear of losing the Major.

And then, as we were coming down a long sloping hill, we saw in the distance that he'd turned into a lane lined with hawthorn trees, leafy now, their white blooms long since faded.

At the far end of the lane we could just pick out the chimneys of a house.

It made no sense. Was this where the Major was intending to go? Or had he spotted us and tried to throw us off?

CHAPTER EIGHTEEN

TRELAWNEY PULLED TO the side of the road, the motor idling.

"I could use a company of Sepoys," he murmured under his breath. Then aloud to me, "What now, Sister?"

"I must find a telephone," I said. "My father needs to know where we are. There isn't much he can do, if he's in London. But someone must be told that man is in England now."

"I can't leave you here—"

"But you can," I said quickly, taking the decision out of his hands. "Go to the next village—ask for a telephone. I'll tell you how to reach three people. Leave a message with anyone who answers. Describe how to find us."

I began to dig in my valise for pen and paper, fumbling in my haste.

"I don't like leaving you, Miss," he said, his failure to use Sister a measure of his anxiety. "He almost got to you on *Merlin*. What was I to tell the Colonel then?"

"I asked you to guard the motorcar."

"It wouldn't suffice, Sister, if you were at the bottom of Portsmouth Harbor and the motorcar safe as houses. The Colonel— never mind what he'd want to do. But you know him as well as I do, and how he'd take such news."

I said as I wrote down three names and three telephone numbers, "I've reloaded my pistol—"

"It wouldn't stop a fly, Miss, begging your pardon. Nor someone as determined to see you dead as this bast—as this one is."

"I'll be all right. I'll take Private Morton with me, if he can manage to walk that far."

He swore he could, and while I didn't believe him, his was a comforting bulk to have beside me.

I handed over the sheet of paper. We got out, Hugh Morton and I, while Trelawney, with a last reluctant glance over his shoulder, drove away, leaving us by the side of the road.

Private Morton foraged for a moment in the hedgerow to the far side and came away with a stick he could use. The two of us started toward the distant farmhouse in a roundabout way, trying to keep out of sight. The hawthorns and the lay of the land contrived to help us. I didn't think that even from the upper floor of the farmhouse we could be seen unless someone was looking for us.

"What if it's a trick, and he leaves before the Sergeant comes back?"

I shook my head. It was a risk we had to take. I wanted to find out who lived in the farmhouse.

Gripping the stick with a tight fist, Private Morton managed to keep up across the pasture, but began to fall behind as the ground beyond the stile changed to a field with humped rows of marrows. He called to me, keeping his voice low.

"I'll wait for you," I said, "closer by the house."

On the far side of the field I came to small yard and a derelict shed, one that had been used for shearing sheep from the smell of it. I stepped into its shadow just as the sun went behind a cloud and looked back for Hugh Morton, but he had turned toward the trees along the drive, where it was easier to walk. I watched him, fearful that he would be in trouble if the man suddenly reappeared.

Just then, from the direction of the farmhouse, across the back garden from where I was standing, I heard two distinct shots.

I started to run, Private Morton forgotten. It was faster to go around the house than try to find my way through it. I had barely reached the first of the trees that lined the drive when I heard a door slam and then the motorcar was racing toward me at reckless speed. The driver's face, bent forward over the wheel, was a twisted mask of hatred.

I didn't hesitate. I spun around so that I was half protected by the nearest tree, letting him pass. But I don't think he'd have noticed a line of cavalry if it had stood in his way.

I didn't look to see where he was heading. I went straight toward the farmhouse door.

It was a lovely old house, three stories and built of local stone. There was a bow window to one side of the door, which stood ajar, and somewhere through the open panes I could hear a woman crying. I stopped on the threshold and called out.

"I've come to help," I said. "Please don't be frightened."

There was no answer. I went inside.

The wide hall was empty.

There were stairs just to my right, and beyond the newel post was an open door to my left.

I moved to it and stepped into the room, stopping almost at once as I tried to take in the scene before me.

An older woman, a maid judging by the way she was dressed, her arm bleeding badly, dripping down her hand to the floor, was struggling to help the young woman who lay in the middle of the floor on a patterned carpet.

There seemed to be a great deal of blood, more than could be explained by the arm wound. I said, bending over the younger woman, "Let me see." But I had to push the maid to one side even to tell if the other victim was still alive.

For a wonder she was breathing, although it was labored, and the cloth that the maid had pressed against her side was already making its own pool across the carpet.

My kit was in the motorcar with Trelawney, but I said, "Scissors, quickly, and more clean cloths."

The maid, still quite dazed, scrambled to her feet with an effort, and disappeared. Meanwhile, I was trying to find where the shot had actually gone in—and if it had come out.

The woman moaned as I moved her, and I said gently, "You're with friends. I'm going to stop the bleeding and make you more comfortable."

I wasn't certain she could hear me, but I kept making soothing noises as I worked and finally determined that she had been shot in the side. It appeared to me that the bullet had dug furrow along the ribs. I didn't think it had reached the lung—there was no froth of blood on her lips.

The scissors came, and I cut away the once-pretty white and green fabric of her summer gown for a better look. The problem was, I couldn't find where the bullet had stopped. Although it was very possibly lodged in her shoulder somewhere, without instruments I couldn't be sure, and internal bleeding was still a danger if it had penetrated the rib cage under her arm.

She was so much slimmer than the wounded soldiers I'd dealt with, not much muscle or flesh there to shield the ribs, and as I tried gently to probe the site, then stanch the bleeding, she cried out. I had nothing to give her.

It took time, more time than I cared to think about, to stop the bleeding and bind up the wound as best I could with the simple bandages the maid brought me.

And as I worked I spoke to the maid hovering over my shoulder.

"What is your name?"

"Maggie," she said, her voice shaking from shock compounded by her own pain. "Will she live?"

"Yes, I think she has a good chance. What happened here? Why were the two of you shot? Did you know the man who did this?"

"He came through the door, shouting her name. Over and over, in such a voice that I ran out from the kitchen and came to see what was happening. And then she came down the stairs, staring as if she'd seen a ghost. And it was. Dear God, it was."

"Her husband?" I asked, ripping lengths of cloth to bind the woman's arm to her side.

"No, oh, no. He's in France. This was the man she was once engaged to, and then broke it off. And he'd come for revenge."

"Her name?"

"Julia Palmer."

"His? Do you know his name?"

"Ralph Mitchell."

"Go on." I sat back on my heels, looking down at my handiwork, satisfied that for the moment Julia Palmer was out of danger. "She was on the stairs, you said?"

Getting to my feet, I took the scissors to Maggie's bloody sleeve, and I began to clean and bind up her wound as well. It went deep, and it must have been painful for her to endure my touch, but she went stoically on.

"He told her he'd come to ask her again to marry him. Then she said, cool as you please, 'Come into the parlor, Ralph. We'll talk about it, shall we?' And she walked ahead of him into this room and turned to face him. I'd come with her, not knowing what to expect. Before she could say anything more, he told her that he was a Major now, and as she was a widow, he had come to ask a last time if she'd marry him. She told him he was mistaken, she was still a wife, and he said, 'I'm an officer now, I outrank Palmer. What's more, he's dead. You should have heard by this time. There was a letter from Colonel Prescott. I saw it myself.'"

"Was Colonel Prescott his commanding officer?"

"Miss, I don't have any idea."

"Go on."

Fighting back tears, she said, "Miss Julia told him, 'But I haven't.' He was very angry, he told her she was lying. On purpose, to put him off. Then—then, Miss, he told her he'd killed the Lieutenant himself. Miss Julia cried out at that, and he went on shouting, 'Do you love me? Tell me you still love me.' But she couldn't, could she?"

I led Maggie to a chair, and she sat down suddenly, her face very pale. "He just stood there, waiting for an answer. I didn't know where to look. It was as if I could hear the ticking of the clock on the table behind me. But maybe it wasn't that, only my heart in my throat."

"How did Mrs. Palmer answer?"

"She told him then that she had never loved anyone but her husband."

I could imagine what must have followed. But as it happened, I was wrong.

"And then?"

"He said he couldn't live without her, and that's when he took out his revolver, and I thought he was about to kill himself right in front of us. But it wasn't that, was it? He pointed that revolver straight at her, and he told her that if he couldn't have her, no one else would. She answered that if he truly loved her, he would want her happiness above his own."

Maggie broke down as she relived the shooting in her mind. I knelt beside her, trying to comfort her.

"I don't know what possessed me. When he fired, I pushed her to one side, and the bullet struck my arm instead. He stepped forward, shoved me away so hard I fell against the wall, and then he shot her. Standing over her, he cried out, 'Damn you, Crawford,' as if someone else had pulled the trigger. Then without even waiting to see if I was alive or not to tell the tale, he was gone, out the door, driving away like a whirlwind."

I'd finished binding up Maggie's arm. Suddenly aware that Hugh Morton had been on my heels but had never appeared, I hurried to the door to look for him. He was nowhere to be seen. I called his name, and there was no answer. There wasn't time to worry.

I came back to the parlor and asked, "Is there a doctor close by? Do you have a motorcar—some way we can get Mrs. Palmer to him? She needs more care than I can give her. What's more, so do you."

"There's the dogcart," Maggie said, standing up. "Out back. And the old horse is in the pasture. I don't know if I can find the strength to harness him up. There's no one else here today. The cook's daughter got word her husband had been killed, and so the cook and the boy who does the handiwork went over to sit with her."

It was up to me, then.

"Stay here with your mistress," I said. "I'll fetch the cart."

I found my way through to the kitchen and then out into the yard. The small dogcart was in a good state of repair, and the horse in the field came at once to my call. It took no more than ten minutes to hitch him to the cart and then drive round to the house door.

It took much longer to bring Mrs. Palmer as far as the cart. Slender as she was, she had fainted again and couldn't help us. I sent Maggie to bring as many pillows and blankets as she could find, piled them into the cart, and then began the arduous task of settling my patient among them. It was impossible to bring Mrs. Palmer around sufficiently to help us help her. And all the while I thought about Hugh Morton, who would have been such a support through all this.

Finally, her face nearly as pale as the linens she lay on, Mrs. Palmer was ensconced among the pillows and I had shut the house door behind us before taking up the reins to drive to the nearest village. Trelawney hadn't returned either, but it could well have taken much longer to find a telephone than I'd hoped. If that was the case, then I would surely meet him somewhere between here and the doctor's surgery.

I drove as carefully as I could along the drive and out into the dusty road beyond, trying not to jostle Mrs. Palmer and start the wound to bleeding again. The sky was threatening, and although the distance to the nearest village was only three miles, it seemed much farther. All that mattered was whether or not it had a doctor.

"Shelpot," Maggie said and pointed. "The village. The surgery's down there. Just past the church. Dr. Glover."

It was a long, rambling house with a thatched roof and a pretty garden.

His nurse answered my knock, saw the cart with two blood-stained women in it, and with a shocked "Oh my dear Lord," she went to fetch the doctor.

He was a man of perhaps sixty years of age, straight as an arrow and strong enough to lift Mrs. Palmer himself and carry her into his surgery. I ushered Maggie in after him.

The nurse was sent for tea while the doctor examined my two patients. Looking at my uniform at one point, he asked, "On leave, are you? Well, it's a good thing you were, or Mrs. Palmer might not have made it. She's lost a good deal of blood, and her breathing is not as comfortable as I'd like to see it. There's the bullet, of course, but at the moment the bleeding worries me most. I'll have to keep her here. Maggie as well, I should think. I'm not happy with either of these women returning to the house." He finished rebinding Maggie's wound with proper bandaging and reached for the teacup his nurse had set on his desk. "Gunshot wounds are rare hereabouts. Who did this? Any idea?"

"Ralph Mitchell. So I was told."

"Good God. I thought he was in France."

"So, apparently, did Mrs. Palmer."

"His father owned a farm some miles from here. Young Mitchell took it into his head that he was going to marry Julia Baldwin. Made a right nuisance of himself instead, and then when he failed to qualify as an officer, he blamed everyone but himself and swore he'd win the VC before the war ended."

"Baldwin," I repeated. "What was her father's name?"

"Tobias. An Army man himself, although he'd been invalided out. Recalled to do something or other in London. Died there in a Zeppelin raid."

I knew who Tobias Baldwin was. And he hadn't died in a Zeppelin raid. That was the official reason, but he'd been killed during one, and his murderer had never been caught. He'd worked for my father, and the fear early on was that his death had to do with his work. As time went by, that seemed more and more unlikely.

Was Ralph Mitchell in London when Captain Baldwin died? My father would have to look into that.

I remembered what Maggie had told me. That Mitchell had stood over Julia and cried, "Damn you, Crawford!" And he had had more than an hour's head start—

"I must find a telephone," I said quickly.

"Actually, there's one at the house. Baldwin had it put in when he began reporting to London and Mrs. Palmer chose to live here after her father died in the bombing rather than stay in her husband's London house. She believed it was safer, poor woman."

If that was the case, where were Trelawney and Private Morton?

There was no time to consider that. I had only a dogcart at my disposal, and that wouldn't carry me any great distance in pursuit of a motorcar. I needed to make the calls that Trelawney hadn't. And as far as that went, where on earth was he? What had become of Private Morton? I was beginning to worry that they had run afoul of Mitchell somehow.

After asking Dr. Glover to send someone to the house of the Palmers' cook's daughter, to let her know what had become of her mistress, I set out alone in the dogcart, against all advice.

"If Mrs. Palmer is in danger, you will be as well, Sister," Dr. Glover warned me. "He could come back. The man's not stable if he'd do something like this to Julia Palmer. If he can't find her, he'll turn on you. Let me summon the constable; he'll need your statement anyway."

"There isn't time. I'll be all right. I must get to that telephone. I promise I'll speak to the constable as soon as possible."

"Then promise me as well that once your telephone calls are made, you'll return to the surgery."

Dr. Glover followed me to the door, quietly asking out of earshot of the others what was so urgent, but I wasn't prepared to tell him that I thought Mitchell's next victim was very likely going to be my father.

There was still no sign of Trelawney or of Private Morton on my return to the house. The door was shut, as I'd left it, but I took the horse around to the back where he couldn't be seen by anyone approaching down the drive, and with the little pistol in my hand, I went from the kitchen through to the wide hall, searching for a telephone. I found it in the room that Captain Baldwin must have used for his study. I locked myself inside and sat down at the burled desk.

I called London first, but I was told by a voice I didn't recognize that Colonel Crawford was not available.

The next call I put in went to Somerset and my mother. Iris, pleased to hear from me, was full of questions and finally told me that my mother was not to home.

"Where is she?" I asked, praying that she'd gone to market or was calling on friends.

"She went to the clinic, Miss Elizabeth. The one where you were. She should be coming home before very long."

Debating what to say, I settled on, "Tell my mother, and Sergeant-Major Brandon if he's with her, to close the house at once and go back to the clinic. They must wait there until I come. And you must go with them, taking Cook as well. Do you hear?"

"Yes, Miss, but Cook is in the midst of preparing dinner—"

"I'm sure she must be. But you must convince her to go with you. As quickly as you can, you must leave the house. There's something wrong, Iris, and I don't know what's about to happen. It's best if there isn't anyone in the house at all."

It took all of my persuasive powers to convince her to heed my warning. Iris, accustomed to the safety of the Crawford household, found it hard to believe that any threat could touch her there.

And my final call was put through to Longleigh House. Matron answered the telephone, and I asked if my mother was there, or, failing her, Simon Brandon.

She hesitated for a moment. "Sister, I shall be happy to take a message for them."

I sighed. Had Simon gone missing again? Was that why my mother had been summoned to the clinic, in lieu of my father?

I said, "If I could speak to Captain Barclay—"

She was happy to tell me that he was available, if I could wait.

In short order, I heard his familiar voice on the line.

"I haven't much time," I began, "and so you must listen closely and not ask questions. I'm in Dorset, I'm calling from the home of the late Captain Baldwin. My parents or Simon will know the name. There's been trouble here, and it's my old adversary from France. He's in England and bent on revenge. I don't quite understand—but he's shot the woman he wanted to marry, he's posing as a Major, and it may be that he's coming after my father. There's quite a bit more, but it isn't important right now. My father is in danger, and everyone else in the household could be as well. Where is Simon Brandon? Do you know?"

"There was a telephone message from London. A Captain Grayson in Portsmouth was trying to reach the Colonel. Your mother called here and is on her way to pick up Brandon. They're going on to Portsmouth."

Captain Grayson had probably told someone that I was attacked on board *Merlin,* and that someone had either tried to come aboard the ship or had gone ashore from it without proper authorization. All of it true, but it would sound to Simon as if the German spy he'd been hunting was in Portsmouth. And he'd be leaving the clinic to deal with it, with my mother to drive.

"Tell them to stay at the clinic until I come there. Portsmouth can wait, it's mostly a distraction and there's nothing for Simon there. I don't have a motorcar, Captain, but as soon as I can manage to find transportation I'm going to look for my father. He could be in grave danger," I said again. "Please, you must tell Simon that, and to wait for me. I think the man we're after is on his way to Somerset."

There was a pounding at the main door of the house, and I ignored it. If it was Mitchell returning, so much the better, I could deal with him. Or at least try. I began opening drawers of the desk, looking for a revolver. Or had Captain Baldwin taken it to London with him? Surely he'd have other weapons, souvenirs.

Captain Barclay was saying, "I'll take the doctor's motorcar and come for you. Stay there, and tell me how to find you."

"There isn't time. I must go, there's someone at the door."

"Bess—"

But I was already putting up the receiver, trying to think what best to do. I hadn't really expected Mitchell to come back again. Or to have second thoughts about witnesses when he had other quarry in mind.

But he had been very thorough, covering his tracks in France . . .

The main door crashed open. I could hear someone shouting from the passage, and I turned, opened one of the windows in the study, and went over the sill into the lilacs just beyond. The locked study door would keep him occupied while I went round to the front of the farmhouse and stole his motorcar.

I slipped toward the back of the house, where I couldn't be seen through the windows, and then went the other direction toward the front.

Peering around the corner of the house I stopped stock-still and stared.

The motorcar was Trelawney's.

Just then through the open parlor window I heard Private Morton call out, "There's blood all over the floor in here."

Trelawney shouted something, and I strode toward the voice.

"Where in heaven's name have you been?" I demanded, walking into the house through the broken front door.

It was Trelawney's turn to stare, and Hugh Morton, limping out of the parlor, said, his eyes on my uniform, "Is any of that blood yours?"

"There's a horse harnessed to a dogcart around back," I said quickly. "Put him out to pasture, if you please, Trelawney. And Private Morton, there's a window open in the study. Close it. I'll be waiting in the motorcar." I handed him the key and walked out before they could waste time asking questions. All I could think of was my father, and the man who was going to hunt him down.

In five minutes Hugh Morton was back. Minutes later, Trelawney returned, got behind the wheel, and looked over his shoulder to me to say, "I discovered the telephone was here and turned around. When I got back, that other motorcar was coming up the drive like a bat from Hades. Nearly ran down Morton. I stopped long enough to take him up, and we went after it. Miss, he's headed for Somerset. We followed him far enough to find out if he was returning to Portsmouth. But he's not."

Somerset.

It was all I needed to hear.

"He's going to kill my father," I answered, and told them what I'd found in the Baldwin house.

I knew I should have turned back and called Captain Barclay once more, but if my mother was on her way to Longleigh House, then Iris and our Cook were at home alone. And God knew where my father was. Time was not on my side.

I could only hope that everyone had taken my warning seriously. That Captain Barclay had given my message to my mother and Simon. It was more important to reach my home as quickly as I could, and trust to Captain Barclay's powers of persuasion at Longleigh. Unless he had rashly set out to find me.

The cloud that had moved over the sun was thicker now, joined by blacker ones moving onto the coast. When I looked back, there was a long stretch of intense gray, and I thought I saw a flash of lightning.

The journey ahead was a long one, and Trelawney had lost time coming back for me. But I was glad he had.

Every mile seemed to drag on forever, leaving me in an agony of impatience. Except for the cup of tea at Dr. Glover's surgery, I had had nothing to eat all day, and neither had my companions. We were well into Somerset before we had to stop for petrol. I dashed into the nearest shop for sandwiches and a Thermos of tea while Trelawney was seeing to the motorcar. Surely at some point, Ralph Mitchell would be doing the same, delaying him as we were delayed.

The storm was still behind us, skirting the coast. Ahead was bright sunshine, turning the Somerset hills to a rich green as the road looped and ran straight, then looped again, following the contours of the land. We were silent for the most part, uneasy, wondering if somewhere ahead of us Ralph Mitchell had found his target or had turned toward London when he had failed.

At a crossroads I saw Captain Barclay barreling down on us in Dr. Gaines's motorcar. Trelawney blew the horn, and both vehicles drew up by the verge. The Captain got out and came limping toward us, a frown on his face.

"I thought you had no means of transport," he said at once. "Who the devil are these men? And are you all right?"

"I was fortunate," I said, not taking the time to present my companions. "Where is Simon? Is he with my mother?"

"The Sergeant-Major is on his way to London, in search of your father. I passed on your message, but he has been ordered to follow up on what Captain Grayson reported."

"Alone? He shouldn't be driving."

"He persuaded your mother to drive him."

At least that meant she was out of harm's way as well. I could still see Mrs. Palmer lying in the middle of her carpet, bleeding heavily. I shivered.

"Where are you going? I'll follow you."

"No one has heard from my father?"

"No one had by the time I left," he said. "He could be in London, Dover, Portsmouth—Scotland, for that matter."

"Then we should go directly to my parents' house. Sergeant Mitchell will be there ahead of us, but with luck he'll wait for my father, just as we will. And we can stop him from walking into a trap."

"Bess, are you sure about this?"

"I'm sure. I don't know why he hates my father, but if he shot Julia Palmer, then he'll certainly kill the Colonel Sahib if he can."

Captain Barclay cast an eye over Private Morton, who stared back without a word. The Captain finally said, "I know you from somewhere."

"I doubt it," I intervened quickly.

But I could see that he was skeptical as he turned back toward his motorcar.

The sun was casting long shadows, summer shadows, across the landscape when I finally saw the chimneys of my home just ahead. I asked Trelawney to stop, and shortly afterward Captain Barclay came up to the motorcar to ask how to proceed.

"I'm not quite sure," I said. "If you will lend me Dr. Gaines's motorcar, I'll drive up to the house. Meanwhile, Trelawney should stay here in the event we've got ahead of Sergeant Mitchell."

Trelawney balked at that, but I shook my head. "You're armed, you can stop him. Meanwhile," I went on, "Captain, if you and Private Morris will please go around to the rear of the house, following that lane just there, by the signpost. It will take you only a few minutes of walking, but if you come in that way, he won't expect it."

It was reluctantly agreed upon, and I got behind the wheel of the doctor's motorcar and began to drive openly up to the house.

I found I was holding my breath as I rounded the last bend in the drive and could see the door directly ahead in the straightaway. It stood open.

And two motorcars sat there before it, both of them empty.

One was the vehicle that I'd last seen hurtling down the long line of hawthorn trees from the Baldwin house, and the other was the familiar motorcar my father drove.

My heart sank.

I was too late to prevent the encounter that I'd dreaded for the past seven hours.

CHAPTER NINETEEN

I BRAKED, THEN pulled Dr. Gaines's motorcar into the shelter of a stand of rhododendron, which more or less hid it from view. If anyone was watching for it, I'd already been seen, but I didn't care. All I could think of was my father.

I reached the door without being challenged. And I stood there, listening for voices, something to guide me to him.

There was only silence inside.

I'd already stepped into the hall when I heard my father's voice from somewhere inside. He was alive. The relief was overwhelming.

"I assure you, I have no influence over Sandhurst. If you failed to pass the standards set by the staff, I can neither change nor appeal their ruling in any way."

"You were there," another voice replied. "On the day I washed out. I saw you. Captain Baldwin didn't want me to marry his daughter, and the best way to go about that was to see that I was not allowed to finish the course."

"You give me far too much credit," my father said drily. "But that's neither here nor there. Why did you try to kill my daughter? Because she discovered the body of Major Carson?"

"Did she, by God" was the answer. "No, I saw to it that the man who did was removed. I wanted her for the same reason I killed Carson. To diminish you as you'd diminished me. Besides, he'd married a woman named Julia, and every time I looked at him, promising officer, darling of the regiment, I hated him."

"Indeed," my father said, in a tone of voice I knew all too well. He was deeply, furiously angry. "Carson. Private Wilson. Nurse Saunders. That's quite a list."

"You've forgot Palmer. I killed him as well."

"Did you? Odd that I've never been told he was dead."

My father's voice had come from his study. If I called to him, would Mitchell shoot? Or wait for me to walk into the room?

I could feel the weight of the little pistol in my pocket. If I used it, I would very likely not kill Mitchell, but if I fired first, I could very likely incapacitate him.

Where was Captain Barclay? Was he inside the house yet? Or still trying to find his way up from the kitchen? I began to walk as silently as I could down toward the study door. I knew the spots where the floors creaked, and my father was speaking, covering any slight sound I might make.

And then I was by the door. It was open. I wished I knew where Sergeant Mitchell was standing.

He spoke and his voice was loud now. I realized he must be very close.

"If you have any prayers to say, now is the time. You might wish to pray for your wife and daughter. I will find them, you know."

I looked around the edge of the door. My father was seated at his desk. The Sergeant's back was to me, but I could tell he held a revolver in his right hand, the barrel just visible from where I stood.

My father, long used to danger, never registered my presence.

I brought out the small pistol, lifted it, and took aim.

I was almost too late.

My shot was fired a matter of seconds before the Sergeant's and it went into the shoulder of the arm holding the revolver. He jerked but pulled the trigger anyway, and I heard my father bite off a cry as the heavier bullet struck home.

I was already taking aim again, this time with every intention of killing the man before me. But before the Sergeant could turn to face me, there was another shot from behind me, this time the report of a service revolver. It spun Sergeant Mitchell around, and the expression on his face was anger mixed with surprise.

And then he dropped like a stone.

I was already crossing the room to reach the Colonel Sahib. I couldn't see where he'd been shot, there was no blood yet, but he was looking down at his chest. I thought he must be dying. I wouldn't allow it, I refused to accept it.

Behind me Captain Barclay said, "He's all right, Bess."

In the same instant my father looked up. He smiled at me and said, "That was too damned close for comfort."

I stared as he put a finger into a tidy little hole in his uniform just to the side of his chest. Sergeant Mitchell's shot had gone wide and to the left.

And then he was getting to his feet, holding out his arms to me, and without a word, I went to him.

"I'm all right, my love, truly I am," he said, holding me close.

But Sergeant Mitchell was not.

Captain Barclay was already bending over him, and I left my father to kneel beside the wounded man.

Morton came in just then, hobbling toward the desk, and Trelawney was on his heels.

Without looking up, my hands busy with the Sergeant's tunic, I said, "There's a doctor in the village. Near the inn called The Four Doves. Quickly!"

Trelawney said tersely, "I'll go."

It was my duty to do for this man whatever I could, to save his life if it was within my power. I'd worked over German prisoners and felt no rancor. But as I touched his flesh, I had to shut my mind to what he had done to me and to my father, to a kindly man like Private Wilson, and even Nurse Saunders, who had tried to be helpful and leave a message for his passenger, or that tired courier who carried orders and dispatches behind the lines. If he wanted the world to believe that his love for Julia Baldwin had driven him to murder, then he was a liar. Mrs. Campbell, who had committed adultery and been divorced by her husband, knew more about love than Ralph Mitchell. But I very badly wanted him to survive and be tried for what he had done. Nothing less would take away the stigma of suicide from Private Wilson's death or the charge of desertion from Major Carson's good name. And so my mind and not my heart guided my hands.

The wound I had inflicted—in the shoulder—was bleeding but not serious. The chest wound—Captain Barclay's shot—was far more dangerous and I was hard-pressed to stop the hemorrhaging. By the time I had succeeded, Trelawney had brought Dr. Everett from the village, and we worked side by side for nearly half an hour and still the Sergeant wasn't stable.

I was aware, once, of my father leaning over my shoulder to see what was being done. I heard a quiet "Hmmpf," which gave no indication of what he was thinking. After a moment he touched my arm gently, and then ushered everyone out of the study but the doctor and me.

I spared an anxious thought for Hugh Morton. It was very likely that my father was now hearing an account from Trelawney of that long journey from Dorset, and even if he suspected who Private Morton was, he would say nothing in front of the others. But Trelawney knew. And I was afraid that Captain Barclay might see some resemblance to Ross Morton in the son's face and jump to the right conclusion. He was already suspicious. But there was nothing I could do. I worked in concert with Dr. Everett, following his lead. It was touch-and-go. I thought twice that we'd lost the Sergeant, but then he struggled to breathe again and his pulse steadied.

It wasn't until the doctor got to his feet and said, "I expect that will have to do," that I was even certain the patient was going to live.

Dr. Everett looked around, as if suddenly aware that we were in the Colonel Sahib's study, and he added, "Let him rest for a little while, and then we'll shift him to my surgery until it's safe to take him farther afield. Your father seems to prefer Dr. Gaines's clinic at Longleigh for difficult cases. I can't say that I blame him."

"Perhaps London would be best, when he's ready to be moved," I said diplomatically. "My father will have sent for Constable Medford, but I believe he considers this an Army matter."

"Indeed? That explains why your man Trelawney was asking for Medford. All right, London it is." He looked down at my uniform. "Go and change, my dear. I'll stay with him. Medford can spell me."

Grateful to escape from the study, I thanked him.

In the passage outside, I listened for the sound of voices, and heard them coming from my mother's sitting room. I tapped at the door, then opened it. As I stepped in, four pairs of eyes—Captain Barclay's, my father's, Trelawney's, and Constable Medford's—turned my way. My father rose and brought forward a chair for me.

"There you are, my dear. Come in. Will he live?"

"We believe he will."

"Good," Captain Barclay said grimly.

Trelawney said, "If you'll excuse me, sir, I'd just as soon not let the Sergeant out of my sight until he's in custody. Wounded or no."

Constable Medford said, "I'll go with you." He thanked my father, nodded to me, and accompanied Trelawney into the passage.

I shut the door behind them and smiled at the Colonel Sahib. He looked tired. For that matter it had been a long and trying day for all of us. But he was safe, and that made up for everything else.

He'd been studying my face as well. He said now, "I believe the Sergeant-Major will be very pleased to learn that you are as fine a shot as even he could have hoped."

Captain Barclay frowned, uncertain how to take the remark.

But I understood it. High praise from the Colonel to his daughter. I couldn't ask for better.

I was about to say something on the order of "It appears that we've been very fortunate," when I remembered that in all the excitement neither Iris nor our Cook had appeared. Julia Palmer's maid had been shot. Had Sergeant Mitchell got to them before he found my father?

"Dear God!" I ran out of the room and began to call, but there was no answer. I hurried down the back stairs to the kitchen, my anxiety mounting. And in nearly the last place I looked, I found them.

They had locked themselves into the butler's pantry, where my mother kept her tea service and table silver and other valuables. I had called through the door, heard nothing, and was about to head for the attics when the heavy key turned and they came out, faces pale and eyes wide.

"What's happened, Miss? Did we hear gunshots? Is everyone all right?"

"How did you know to lock yourselves in?" I asked. "Did my father warn you?"

"Oh, no, Miss, we talked about your telephone call, then your mother telephoned from the clinic and told us not to go to the door if anyone came. When I heard a motorcar coming up the drive, we decided to come down here and stay until help arrived."

From the way the two motorcars had been left in the drive, my father had arrived first, and he must have gone into the study without any warning that Sergeant Mitchell was on his way.

I felt ill, thinking about it.

Surely he'd seen the color of the man's eyes when he came through the study door. Surely *that* had alerted him to his danger.

Private Morton was waiting when I came back up the stairs.

I thought, after so much exertion, he must be in great pain, and I said, "It's best if you stay out of sight. Let the doctor look at your wound, and then I'll find a way to get you to Wales as soon as it's safe. No one will think to look for you in the footman's old rooms. They've been empty since the war began."

"I want to go back to France," he said. "I don't know why I thought my father would want a coward creeping home, even to work the farm. Can you find a way to get me there? And a satisfactory explanation for my disappearance? I don't want to be shot for deserting, much as I deserve it. I'd be grateful. I've let everyone down. I can't live with that."

I wondered what had made him change his mind. And he answered that without my asking.

"I must have run mad."

But I thought he had felt like so many men had, that the only end to their suffering would be death, and home seemed so very far away and unreachable.

Chapter Twenty

It wasn't until much later that my father and I could talk quietly. Sergeant Mitchell had been removed from this house, and Iris was already on her hands and knees, scrubbing his blood out of the carpet. She'd taken an instant dislike to him as he was being carried out the door on a makeshift stretcher, with Trelawney, Constable Medford, and Dr. Everett hovering in the background.

"Vicious, that's what he is. I could see it in his face."

I wasn't certain that she could, for his eyes were for a mercy closed again. I'd seen the look of absolute hatred in them when I had stepped into the study to tell Dr. Everett that the ambulance had arrived. He hadn't got what he wanted, after all, Sergeant Mitchell. And I was quite happy to be the person who had thwarted him.

We were sitting together in my mother's morning room. The Colonel had personally searched the motorcar the Sergeant had been driving, and he had found the name of the true owner as well as an officer's kit that Sergeant Mitchell had brought to England with him as part of his disguise.

He opened it now, and I saw that beneath the extra clothing it contained personal items—toothbrush and powder, shaving brush and straight razor, a cake of soap, the small box of thread and needles that most soldiers carried with them, several boiled sweets, and a silver frame with a photograph of the girl left behind in England. A very young Julia Baldwin. Digging deeper, my father found an oiled packet. He pulled it out and opened it. There was a worn Testament on top and, under it, a book bound in Moroccan leather. Even that wasn't unusual, for many soldiers as well as officers carried a favorite volume with them. Shakespeare, a treasury of English verse, the works of a favorite poet—it varied with each man's taste. Something to read during the crushing boredom waiting for the next attack or to steady the nerves in the long hours before an assault.

The Colonel Sahib took out the volume, opened it at random, and then seemed to be riveted by what he could see written on the page. Opposite him, I sat and waited.

"It's a journal," he said slowly. "And if I'm right about the handwriting, it belonged to Vincent." He leafed through a few more pages and then passed it to me.

I also chose a page at random, and read, next to the date, *Attack came just before dawn.*

There followed every scrap of information he could remember: the length of the attack, the number of Germans in each wave, ground won or lost, which German regiment had been involved, number of casualties on both sides, weather conditions, whether or not gas was used, how many men were sent to the aid station, whether there had been air or artillery support, and, finally, strength in numbers remaining after the attack. It was an impressive accounting, and I could see why my father had believed that Vincent Carson would one day be the Colonel.

Turning a few more pages, I discovered a copy of a letter written to Julia. I didn't read it. Instead I went to the beginning of the journal to see what name was inscribed on the board. But there was none, only a scribble that seemed to make no sense—unless one had been in India and recognized it.

It was the date when Vincent Carson received his commission, written in Hindi, and below that a copy of the inscription on a sword that hung in the Officers' Mess wherever the regiment was stationed. No evening ended without a toast repeating it.

I die at the pleasure of my God. I serve at the pleasure of my King.

It was as personal as a signature. Sergeant Mitchell, a farmer's son from Dorset, had never served in India. But Vincent Carson had. With this journal in the Sergeant's possession, we could show positively that he had killed the Major.

After a moment, I said, "Julia will be pleased to have it. But what of the other Julia—Julia Palmer? Did her father know she was being courted by Sergeant Mitchell before she met Lieutenant Palmer?"

"I doubt it. It was my doing that young Palmer went to Dorset in the first place. And he was most persuasive. Captain Baldwin agreed to come out of retirement. Sadly, it cost him his life. We were fairly certain Captain Baldwin was murdered in 1916. But we could never discover who his killer was. Until now."

"That's why the cause of death was listed as a Zeppelin raid."

"Yes. We didn't want it to be generally known."

"And Simon's spy? What's become of him?"

"I'm afraid you'll have to ask MI6 about that. Which if you did, would see you shot at dawn in the Tower. They've been damned quiet on the subject. I expect nothing came of it."

"Well, at least the Prince of Wales is safe."

"He's on his way to the Front now, as a matter of fact. You can see why it was worrying."

"And Mother? How do we explain the damp spot on the study carpet where Iris has been scrubbing away at a bloodstain?"

"We'd better tell her the truth. She'll find it out anyway."

I smiled. "Now, about Portsmouth, and the man I reportedly saw trying to climb aboard *Merlin,* presumably from a small boat in the harbor . . ."

It was some weeks later when I drove back to Cheddar Gorge during a few brief days of leave. Mrs. Wilson was busy in her garden, and I saw her tense as she looked around to see who it was in the motorcar stopping before her gates. She recognized me at once and made me welcome, but I could see new lines in her face, and I thought she had lost weight. It gave me great pleasure to tell her that the man who had killed her husband was almost well enough to stand trial for his murder.

It wouldn't bring Private Wilson home again. But I had kept my promise to her. And her daughter would no longer have to grow up as the child of a suicide. There would also be a pension, to help with the farming.

She made tea for me while I petted Toby, the cat, cried into the handkerchief I handed her, and, as I left, gave me a round of aged Cheddar to take home to my mother.

I thought about Captain Barclay as I drove back to Somerset. He was in France, finally. I didn't think his leg would ever heal fully, but it had mended well enough to return to duty. He wrote often, and, in his latest letter, told me a little of what he felt about rejoining his men.

There are so many new faces, Bess. Replacements for the dead and the wounded. But my old Sergeant is still here, and Lieutenant Britton. They've survived against all odds, and I'm very happy to be back where I belong. God bless Dr. Gaines, he worked something of a miracle.

But I thought perhaps it was not trying quite so hard that had helped his leg heal.

I'd also had a message from Private Morton. He was alive and well, back with his regiment, and had not forgot his promise to visit Sabrina one day. I hoped he survived the war.

I found Simon waiting for me in Somerset. He was still in London when I returned to France shortly after I'd given my statements to the Dorset police and to Scotland Yard, and finally to the Army. According to my mother's letters, he was nearly recovered, back in his cottage, and impatient to return to duty.

Greeting me on his doorstep, he said, "It's been some time."

He looked well, and I'd seen no twinge of pain as he'd opened the door to me. The shoulder must have healed completely.

"It has indeed," I said lightly.

"I put the kettle on when I saw you walking down the lane. Tea?"

"Please."

I came in and sat down by the window overlooking the back garden. It was a pretty place to sit, the sunlight coming through the panes and spilling across my lap.

We were silent for a time, waiting for the kettle to boil and then the teapot to brew.

Simon handed me my cup. "I haven't thanked you properly for saving my life."

"It was Dr. Hicks and Dr. Gaines who did that. Their skill."

"Nevertheless."

He brought his cup and leaned his shoulder against the mantelpiece as he drank.

"You were right about not going back to France," I said finally. "But for the wrong reasons."

"I know."

"Mother has told me that it was arranged for Lieutenant Palmer to have compassionate leave. My father saw to that, I'm sure. Trelawney wrote to say that Mrs. Palmer is much better."

"Yes, that's good news. We thought at first that Mitchell had killed the Lieutenant as well."

"And Julia has agreed to settle a sum on Sabrina. She and her son will be able to live comfortably wherever they choose. That's to say, if Sabrina will accept the gift. But I think she will. My mother's hand there."

He nodded.

I set my cup aside. We'd come to the real reason I'd wanted to speak to Simon today. He already knew what I was about to say. But I needed to talk about it.

"Sergeant Mitchell will certainly be found guilty on all charges. Still, I'm told he claims that Julia Palmer had so turned his mind with her promises that he went mad and didn't know what he had done."

"It had nothing whatsoever to do with madness, Bess. He's the sort of man who wanted his own way, and when he didn't get it, he blamed everyone around him. Your father had nothing to do with the decision to ask Mitchell to leave Sandhurst. But he looked up Mitchell's record, and it was dismal. The man had trouble following orders and taking responsibility for what he did—or failed to do."

"He killed so many people."

"They got in his way."

It was a rather sobering evaluation, but Simon was right. No one set Sergeant Mitchell on the road to murder. Cold comfort, all the same, to his victims. And I'd nearly been one of them.

Simon collected the cups and took them through to the kitchen, setting them in the sink. When he came back, he said with a grimness unusual to him, "If you want my view, he will pay too easily for all he has done." He'd known Captain Baldwin and Major Carson. He'd seen how close I'd come to dying, and my father as well. This man had not only struck at the regiment, but he had struck at the Crawfords personally. And Simon hadn't been there. There would be no forgiveness on offer that could ever change his feelings about that.

He held out his hand, changing the subject. "It's too fair a day to sit here. Let's walk for a while, shall we?"